## Praise for the Detecti



***Hollywood Ending***

"Day is funny and determined, the sort of woman who really WOULD make a wisecrack when faced with danger. She's the perfect guide to the lifestyles of the rich, famous, and homicidally inclined."—Donna Andrews, Agatha and Lefty Award–winning author of the Meg Langslow series

"Kellye Garrett's *Hollywood Ending* glitters with stardust. A fun, fast-paced mystery, it's definitely an A-lister."—Elaine Viets, author of the Dead-End Job mysteries

"Nobody puts Dayna Anderson in a corner. She'll be gone with the wind if she can't solve the high crimes in the wild, wild west of La La Land. She's in hot pursuit of bad boys and girls who wanna have fun. It's star wars in Hollywood, and the happy ending is up to Dayna. Fasten your seat belts. A star is born!"—Nancy Martin, author of the Blackbird Sisters mysteries

"Kellye Garrett's *Hollywood Ending* is an entertaining whodunit that provides readers a peek behind Hollywood's star-studded curtain."—Diane Kelly, award-winning author of the Paw Enforcement, Tara Holloway, and House-Flipper mystery series

***Hollywood Homicide***

Winner of the 2018 Lefty Award for Best Debut

Winner of the 2018 Agatha Award for Best First Novel

Winner of the 2018 IPPY Gold Medal for Best First Book

⋆ "[A] winning first novel and series launch … Garrett writes with humor and insight about the Hollywood scene. Readers will look forward to Day's further adventures."—*Publishers Weekly* (starred review)

⋆ "A smart, sassy debut, introducing an appealing protagonist with amusing friends."—*Library Journal* (starred review and debut of the month)

"Veteran TV writer Garrett uses her *Cold Case* experience to inform her debut, which sets up more than one charming character and isn't afraid to go cynical on all things LA."—*Kirkus Reviews*

"Fun, smart, endearingly flawed, and impressively determined, Dayna Anderson is a heroine readers will fall in love with."—Kyra Davis, *New York Times* bestselling author

"Garrett has written a novel with great voice, characters, hilarious moments, and a lot of Hollywood, which is a perfect start to a series." —*BookRiot*

"Funny, lively characters populate this new Detective by Day series . . . this will be an entertaining entry into the amateur sleuth genre."—*RT Book Reviews*

"*Hollywood Homicide* is a non-stop, fun read with humor sharp as a stiletto heel."—Ellen Byron, *USA Today* bestselling author of The Cajun Country Mysteries

"Toss in a hit-and-run, a steep reward, and more one-liners than a Marx Brothers marathon and you've got *Hollywood Homicide*."—Catriona McPherson, Agatha Award–winning author of *The Reek of Red Herrings*

"There's a spunky new sleuth in town: Dayna Anderson takes readers on a madcap ride through the underbelly of La La Land, laced with high fashion, Twitter feeds, celebrities—and murder!"—Lucy Burdette, author of the bestselling Key West Food Critic Mysteries

"*Hollywood Homicide* has a heart as big as Los Angeles, a plot as twisty as the 110 Freeway, and a heroine just as complex as the burger battle between In-N-Out and Fatburger . . . Can't wait for the next adventure with Garrett and Dayna Anderson!"—Rachel Howzell Hall, author of the critically acclaimed LAPD Detective Elouise Norton series

"Buckle up for a fun, fast-paced joyride through the streets of Los Angeles. *Hollywood Homicide* is packed with action and suspense, but it's Garrett's fresh voice and sharp dialogue that really sets this book apart. A delight from start to finish!"—Marla Cooper, author of the Destination Wedding Mystery series

# Hollywood Ending

Kellye Garrett

First Edition
First Printing, 2018

Book format by Bob Gaul
Cover design by Shira Atakpu
Cover illustration by Richard Méril

Midnight Ink, an imprint of Llewellyn Worldwide Ltd.



**Library of Congress Cataloging-in-Publication Data**
Names: Garrett, Kellye, author.
Title: Hollywood ending / Kellye Garrett.
Description: First edition. | Woodbury, Minnesota: Midnight Ink, [2018] | Series: A detective by day mystery; #2
Identifiers: LCCN 2018010484 (print) | LCCN 2018018351 (ebook) | ISBN 9780738755434 (ebook) | ISBN 9780738752976 (alk. paper)
Subjects: LCSH: Women private investigators—Fiction. | Murder—Investigation—Fiction. | GSAFD: Mystery fiction.
Classification: LCC PS3607.A7725 (ebook) | LCC PS3607.A7725 H63 2018 (print) | DDC 813/.6—dc23
LC record available at https://lccn.loc.gov/2018010484

Midnight Ink
Llewellyn Worldwide Ltd.
2143 Wooddale Drive
Woodbury, MN 55125-2989
www.midnightinkbooks.com

Printed in the United States of America

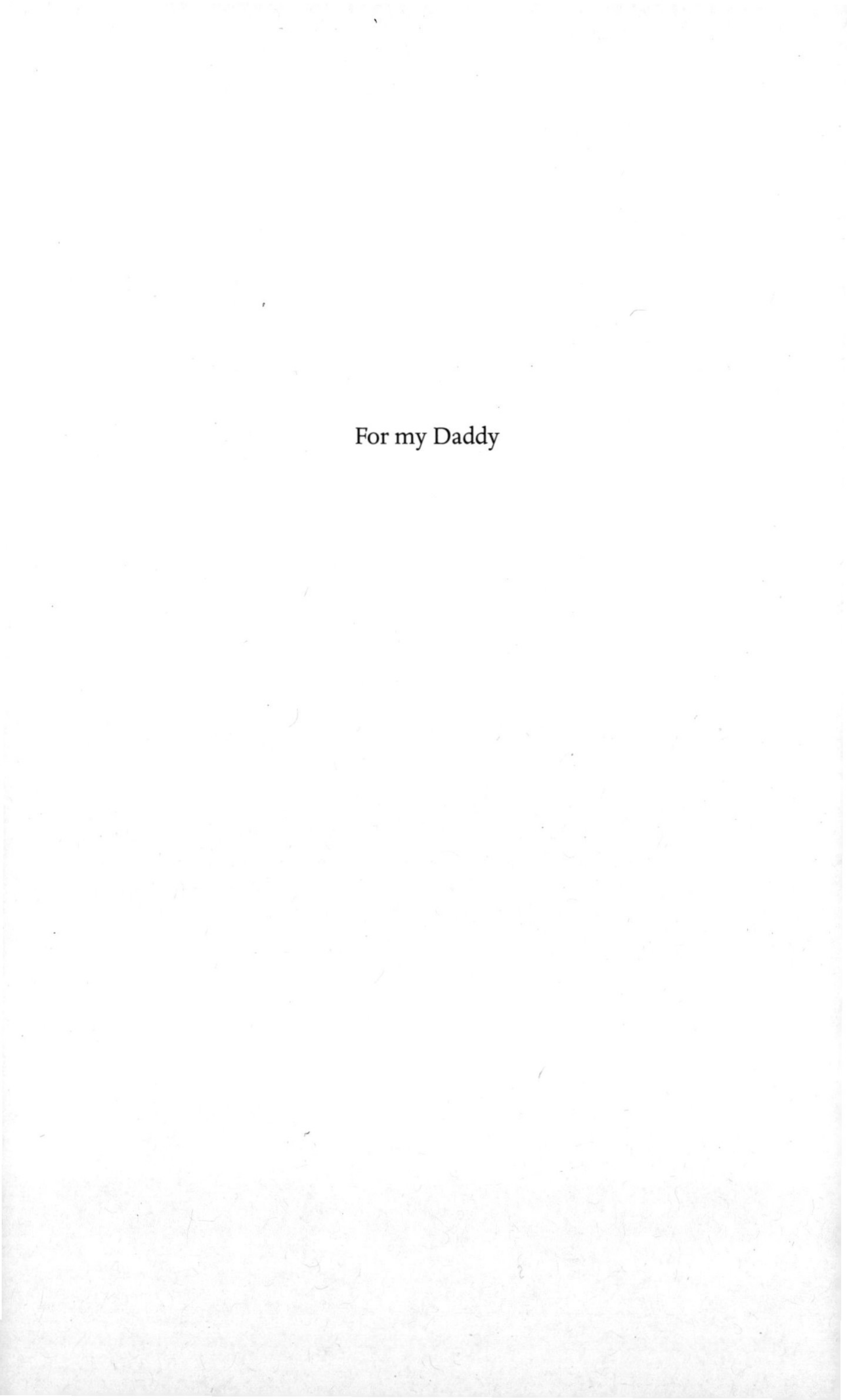

For my Daddy

# One

The instructions had been pretty clear. At least I thought they had. Show up at Bix Financial Check Cashing Services in Hollywood at exactly 11:30 a.m. Go inside. Talk to the guy standing behind the counter and tell him the code. Not my name. Not my date of birth. Definitely not my social.

Just the code.

Like I said. Easy-peasy. So why was I so nervous? I'd mentally played out the moment more times than a viral video. Yet the butterflies had taken over my stomach like a studio exec charging to set when their movie's first-time director was $50 million over budget and getting a little too close with the leading lady.

When the cashier motioned me over with a wave and a "yeah?" I walked up. "Yes, hi, ten. Eighteen." It came out just as I'd practiced in the car. So far, so good.

Having done my part, it was time for him to do his. I'd had months and months' worth of dreams about this moment. And in each and every single one, he reached down, extracted a bag from the counter's nether regions, and handed it to me with a smile. In reality, I got nothing more than a blank look. So I tried again. "Ten. Eighteen."

I even remembered to smile, but still got nothing. He seemed even more confused the second go-round. Blurg. At five foot eight and greasy-looking, he looked eerily like the skeevy cashiers you always see in movies. The ones who get shaken down by the main character for information. Obviously not one for eye contact, the cashier instead opted to stare at some spot behind my shoulder. At least it wasn't my boobs.

Not sure what to do, I looked at him kind of looking at me. I'd always been the kid who followed instructions in school. I lined up for lunch when I was supposed to. Held tight to my classmates' hands as they desperately tried to squirm away. Didn't so much as think of moving from "that couch" when my mother told me not to. It hadn't made me popular as a kid. It clearly wasn't doing much for me as an adult either.

I forced myself not to panic. Instead, I thought it over. The instructions hadn't covered how to say the number. The paper just listed 1018. Maybe I'd mispronounced it. Just like I could never remember how to say *barista* or *homage*, for that matter. I went for it again. "One. Zero. One. Eight."

I nodded encouragingly while the cashier continued to look like I was trying to bring back Latin as an everyday language. The guy behind me sighed. Very loudly. I ignored that one to still focus on the task at hand. I went for another variation. "One thousand and eighteen." Another case of the nothings. I'd reached my limit. "Look, I'm pretty sure you have something for me. Right?"

A voice answered. Unfortunately, it came from behind me. "My dude. Just give her the drugs so that we both can get out of here. I only got fifteen minutes left on my break."

Wait, what? Thank God we were the only people in the store because Old Boy was accusing me of using drugs way too loudly. I whipped around and gave him my full attention. He was close. Too close. Like "you should be professionally cleaning my teeth and assuring me I don't have any cavities" close.

In all my fantasies about this moment, there had never been a Trevor.

At least that's what I think Old Boy's name was. It was the one stitched on his uniform, next to a splotch of grease that oddly resembled a bowl of apples. Don't ask. I figured him for a mechanic. Or maybe just a really messy eater. If I were casting a movie, he'd get a callback for the jock love-interest's bonehead best friend. He was as stout as a keg of Guinness and just as hard for me to swallow. I wasn't a beer girl. At all.

"Do I look like a crackhead to you?" I asked. "In *these* shoes?"

They were Giuseppe Zanotti.

Trevor looked me up and down. "Nah. Crackheads are normally skinny."

"Hey!" I said, but my protest was halfhearted. I'd been mistaken for a lot of things in life. Someone who worked at Target when I made the mistake of shopping there in a red shirt. Someone who cared about Facebook statuses about what people had for lunch. Someone who had the slightest clue how to adult. But I'd never once been mistaken for someone who did crack, even when I *was* skinny.

Still, I attempted a death glare anyway as Trevor turned back to the cashier. "She has a point, though. My dude, you're clearly the one on something up in here. So how about you give *her* the money so she can give *you* the drugs?" I threw him another look. He smiled. "You gotta pay for those fancy shoes somehow, right?"

"This has nothing to do with drugs!" I was practically screeching. I hated myself for it. Trevor looked at me. I, in turn, looked at the cashier. They were both extremely lucky I practiced self-censorship when it came to curse words. At least the really, really bad ones. "Reward money," I said. "I'm here for the freaking reward money from the LAPD."

The cashier came to life, like someone must have changed his batteries. "Oh, right. That envelope of cash with the four numbers scribbled on it. My boss has the worst handwriting. Be right back!"

And with that, he disappeared into the back. Thank. Goodness. The last time I'd tried to collect a reward, I'd messed up big time by not calling the tip line as instructed. I was determined to get my money this time.

"Why not start off with that and save us all a bunch of heartache?" Poor Trevor sounded exasperated.

I shrugged defensively, mainly because I was wondering the same thing myself. "It's my first time actually picking up a reward, okay? Sue me for not knowing the instructions are actually more like suggestions. Besides, it's supposed to be anonymous."

"You're that chick on TV shucking and jiving for fried chicken. That ain't anonymous, sweetheart."

Yet another one of Trevor's many valid points.

"Perhaps, but I'm retired." Not exactly my choice, since Chubby's Chicken canceled my spokesperson gig almost two years ago to go in a "different direction." At the time, I still had a year left on my contract, but they cited a small clause that I couldn't be seen eating anything other than their two-piece combo deals. A photographer caught me during brunch and *Us Weekly* ran the pic in their "Stars Are Just Like Us!" section. I would have mentioned all of this to Trevor, but I doubted he cared that my agent really should have removed the clause from the contract.

"So you went from shucking and jiving to snitching for money?" Trevor asked.

Not only was he offensive, but he was getting on my already-frayed nerves. "I'm not a snitch and I'm not an actress. I'm a private investigator." An investigator's apprentice, but still. Trevor looked me up and down, then laughed. "I solved that big hit-and-run a few months ago," I continued. "The one all over the news. The story garnered millions of Twitter impressions."

I had no clue what that actually meant, but my friend Emme did. And she sounded ridiculously impressed when she told me. Trevor, however? Not so much.

The cashier saved me from further conversation when he came back holding a sealed white envelope. The LAPD's tip line was anonymous, which meant that they couldn't just send you a check for your reward money.

When he handed it to me, I resisted the urge to rip it open and make sure every penny of the $1,000 was accounted for. Instead, I managed to play it cool. I could always celebrate in the car. Maybe even become one of those obnoxious people who pretend to fan themselves whenever they get their hands on a significant amount of money. It *was* hot out, after all.

I waved goodbye to good old Trevor, got in my hot pink Infiniti, checked to make sure the money was all there, and drove off.

At least that was the plan, if Sienna had been in the front seat where I'd left her. She wasn't. Looking around, I didn't see her outside the liquor store. Or the *other* liquor store. Or the brand-spanking-new but seriously out of place Kendall Davis Gym—current Los Angeles workout spot-du-jour. I heard it was nice in there. Emphasis on *heard*. No way could I even afford bottled water in a place like that.

The mere thought of exporting all those calories only made me want to *import* calories. I definitely was hitting Tommy's Original Hamburgers. One was a few blocks east on Hollywood Boulevard. I could practically taste the oodles of chili they plastered on their cheeseburgers. I just needed to find my best friend first.

I was just starting to get worried when Sienna came out of liquor store number two holding a travel-sized bottle of vodka. Luckily, it was unopened. She slid into the front passenger seat as I glanced at the time on my iPhone. "Remember when you told me I should stab you in the clavicle if you ever started drinking before noon? You plan to wait eight minutes or should I start looking for a sharp object?"

Sienna didn't exactly cower in fear. "The vodka's not for me, silly. It's for the glycerin."

"Oh, okay," I said, since there was really nothing else I could add to the conversation.

She reached into the back to grab a spray bottle also filled with a clear liquid. I assumed it was the aforementioned glycerin but honestly was afraid to ask. She opened it and poured the vodka in, then noticed me staring. "I'm supposed to use water but the liquor store didn't have any."

"Cool," I said, because again, what could one really say to that. "Can we go now?"

"Not yet. Razzle's running a bit late."

Razzle. Ugh. He was a paparazzi—pap for short—which meant he made money chasing down celebrities so he could take pics of their "everyday lives." I'm talking mundane things like walking into clubs, walking out of clubs, walking into gyms, walking out of gyms, and—on a good day—covertly making out with their very married costars.

I wasn't his biggest fan. Frankly, he gave me the heebie-jeebies. "I didn't realize we were meeting Razzle."

"Me neither, but I figured since we were out anyway—oh look, he's here!"

Sienna jumped out of the car to greet him. You would have thought she'd spotted Santa Claus. Or at least a free Celine purse. She had taken to occasionally enlisting Razzle's services in her pursuit of a world record for only wearing red. Dubbing herself Ms. Lady of the Red Vine, Sienna had developed quite the fan base. Someone—my money was on Razzle—had her believing that paying him to take paparazzi pics to sell to major news outlets would help with her eternal quest for fame. So far, the shots had only made it onto low-level gossip blogs and a Ms. Lady of the Red Vine Instagram appreciation account run by her biggest fan—me. Posting pics is actually a great way to pass the time when on surveillance.

By the time I got out of the car, they were mid-conversation. "Gotta make this quick," Razzle said as I walked up. "Oscar Blue drops off his recycling in twenty minutes."

Sienna handed him a wad of cash. "There's an extra fifty bucks in there. You better get me at least on *Us Weekly*'s site or I'm calling Jesus next time. He has an in over there, sleeping with one of the assistants or something. He says he also has an in with Anani Miss."

I rolled my eyes at the name. Anani Miss was my former all-time favorite anonymous gossip blogger, but we'd had a one-sided falling out after she started a false rumor about my now-boyfriend. I hadn't visited her site since.

Razzle didn't respond, too preoccupied counting the money Sienna had just given him, his lips slowly moving as he struggled mightily to do the math. It must have all been there, because he stuffed the lot of it in his back pocket and reached down to grab his fancy photographer camera. "Ready?"

Sienna shook her spray bottle, then sprayed her boobs and torso, careful not to get any on her face. It instantly looked like she'd spent sixty minutes in a boxing ring. The fake sweat glistened like she'd had a run-in with a glitter bath bomb. She did one final spritz before finally speaking. "I'm always ready."

And with that, she walked over to the gym. It suddenly made sense why she'd been so eager to accompany me to Bix.

Razzle and I stood in awkward silence for a few more minutes before Sienna walked back toward us. In grade school, we'd always seen composite pictures of the world's races and ethnic groups mashed together. Well, that picture looked just like Sienna. Light brown eyes. Long dark hair. She was the color of desert sand and probably weighed just as much. She'd definitely be cast as the femme fatale. Razzle ran up and took her picture as she pointedly ignored him. She looked great, minus one thing.

"Fix your strap," I yelled.

She did without missing a beat. Perfect. Our 24,871 Instagram followers would love it. She stopped in front of the driver's side of a Bentley that none of us owned and put her hand on the door like she was about to get in. Guess my hot-pink twelve-year-old Infiniti wasn't quite *Us Weekly*-worthy. Just when I thought Sienna was actually going to attempt a carjacking, she stepped away. "Scene," she said.

Razzle put his camera down. She came over as he and I looked at the photos on his digital screen. "How'd I look?"

Razzle grunted as he turned the camera off. "Left is definitely your better side."

He ignored my evil side-eye as she and I both got into my car. Sienna did not have a bad side, thank you very much.

"*Us Weekly!* Or I'm calling Jesus," she called out.

"You need to call Jesus anyway," I said. Razzle overheard me, which had been the plan.

"You're going to need me one day, sweetheart," he said to me.

"We'll have a blizzard in Los Angeles first." I stuck the key in the ignition. Nothing happened. My car didn't make as much as a whimper. Fudge.

Guess I needed to buy a snow jacket.

# Two

Razzle gave me a jump *after* I gave him $20. Car properly started, I dropped Sienna off at La Perla, and then I headed to Tommy's for that much-needed chili-cheeseburger. They didn't have a drive-thru—unfortunate, because no way was I turning my car off. Instead I just left it on and ran into the restaurant. Faced with the choice of having a chili-cheeseburger or having a car, food won each and every time.

If I had a superpower, it'd be the ability to eat all the French fries in the world without gaining a single pound. So far I'd mastered half of it: the eating. Despite being a fast food chain, Chubby's had included contract stipulations about my weight. I wasn't a naturally skinny girl so I'd spent two years in an eternal state of hunger. Once they dropped me, I stopped dropping weight. I was a black girl from the South, so I always felt I looked better being what they call thick, anyway.

If you were to draw me, you'd probably pick a medium brown called Antique Brass from the Crayola box. I have naturally kinky hair that I wore in a silk press and size D boobs I bought with my first Chubby's check. I'd been contemplating going back to wearing my God-given corkscrew curls, but I had no plans to go back to my God-given chest. The implants were here to stay. You'd probably cast me in a group of black friends getting together for a fun vacation movie. I'd play the cute, annoyingly sweet girl currently dating the object of the main character's affections.

Once I got my food, I needed to figure out where to eat it. There was no way I'd last until I got home and I didn't want to leave my car running unattended for too long. For a brief moment, I was tempted to use the hood as a makeshift table. The weather was definitely nice enough for an impromptu picnic. It was in the low 70 degree range, which put it on par for an average LA day in January. Despite the weather being nice, the condition of my car's hood wasn't. I was overdue for a wash.

I ate in my car, passing the time checking the LAPD Crime Stoppers tip line page for new cases. The ATF and something called the National Sports Shooting Foundation were offering $10,000 "for information leading to the arrest and conviction of those responsible for the burglary and theft of firearms from a federal firearms licensee." Though I'd gotten a tad more confident in my investigation skills over the past couple months, I definitely wasn't ready to locate someone I *knew* had multiple firearms.

During my first attempt at an investigation last fall, I'd encountered former-cop-turned-investigator-extraordinaire Aubrey S. Adams-Parker. After we'd worked together to solve a hit-and-run, I'd begged him to take me on as his apprentice. In the ensuing two months, we hadn't looked into anything remotely as exciting as that first case. We'd started investigating an assault outside Dodger Stadium, but the police caught the guy before we could really begin asking questions.

Since then we'd mostly dealt with smaller cases, some we'd gotten from the Crime Stoppers site, including the missing grandpa that had brought Trevor, Bix Financial, and $1,000 into my life. But we'd wrapped up our last case weeks ago and there was nothing on the horizon.

Given that we'd found Mr. Scott, the grandpa, safe and sound, I was hoping for a similar type of case. Unfortunately, the rest of the Crime Stoppers page read like November sweeps episodes of *Law & Order*. Gangbangers. Serial killers. Child molesters. Uh-uh. Nope. And definitely not. None of them were my area of expertise. I wasn't sure I wanted them to be. Part of me knew that if I was serious about becoming an investigator, I shouldn't be scared to actually investigate. But still. I figured I could slowly work my way up. Until then, we needed something to look into. Short of stopping random people on the street to ask if they needed someone to follow their cheating husband around, I was out of ideas.

And Aubrey wasn't much help. He ran a rather informal business. No business cards. No office. Not even a company name. The cases he did accept weren't dangerous. They also weren't for money. Thank you, inheritance! I had no such trust fund. I also had no problem doing pro bono—it not only gave me great experience, but it was nice to help people who needed it. But I also knew we'd eventually need to get a steady flow of income.

My half of our just-received reward money was designated for a credit card bill that refused to fall below $1,000 no matter how many times I told myself it was "only" for emergencies. I'd already paid my parents' mortgage for six months, so I was good there, thanks to some money A-list actress Toni Abrams had given me for returning her grandma's necklace after her house was burglarized. Of course, there was the recent development of my car not wanting to start. My

Infiniti was twelve years old with a cracked windshield and more miles on it than an eighty-five-year-old hooker. Still, I hoped it was a one-time occurrence. And even if it wasn't, that was a problem for Future Day anyway.

Aubrey didn't seem to particularly care for his portion, so I told him I would use it for business expenses for our new firm, which I'd cleverly named ASAP Investigations. Among other things, like purchasing a website domain and buying these really freaking cool binoculars, I'd already gotten business cards. Because nothing says legit like a stack of business cards you get online for $5.99 plus free shipping. I was also getting a whiteboard. Not because we needed it. More because I'd always wanted one but never had a good excuse to actually get it.

I X'd out of the Crime Stoppers site to do some comparison dry-erase board shopping online. Forty-seven minutes and seventy-one Amazon reviews later, I'd made my decision on which one to buy. And it was available for in-store pickup at Staples. Score.

By the time I stopped at the bank, picked up the whiteboard, made two-and-a-half random bathroom stops—one was a false alarm—and arrived at Omari's super-swank loft, it was dark. Omari Grant had been a Harlem boy before moving to Augusta, Georgia, his junior year in high school (and meeting *moi!*), so when he got his CBS show last summer and was looking for a new place, he wanted to pretend he was back in New York. This meant his options were either downtown or squatting in the Warner Bros New York backlot. LA isn't brimming with the sky-high buildings you normally equate with big cities, and about the only place you can find anything consistently over twelve floors is downtown.

Personally, I would have preferred the backlot—it would have been easier to park. If someone put a gun to my head and said "Parallel park or I'll kill this sweet little kitten," the kitten wouldn't die. But only because I would accidentally hit its killer-to-be while trying to back into the spot. Omari had taken to letting me park in his space in the building's underground lot while paying to park his own car at a hotel across the street.

We ordered pizza for dinner. I paid. I'm all for equal opportunity in our relationship. As long as the bill isn't more than forty bucks—including tip. With Omari's growing profile, we'd become quite familiar with all the local delivery guys. It was less of a hassle than eating out. I'd experienced it myself in my Chubby's days. People staring at you, wondering if you were who they thought you were, or taking pics to send to their friends when they thought you weren't paying attention. You were.

Even the ones who *did* have the courtesy to ask for the photo presented a quandary: let your food get cold or be rude to someone who meant well? It was easier to just eat in.

Omari's publicist, Nina Flynn, had convinced him to splurge on an interior decorator because she hoped to pitch a feature in *People* magazine's Home section. The results were nothing short of amazing—a mix of different shades of gray interspersed with a few deep dark purples that were most definitely worthy of a pictorial. The first time either of us spilled something, we both gasped and expected Nina to jump out of his walk-in closet to yell. We were still getting used to the idea that Omari lived in a grownup apartment with matching curtains and random vases only there for show, not actual flowers.

We were sitting on his giant purple velour couch, my favorite thing in the apartment. At least, next to him. Probably because it made me feel as comfortable as he did. The giant television was on but it watched us rather than vice versa. I snuggled into the crook of his arm and stared up at him. He looked like an older version of the archetypal jock in a high school film, except one who was black. He had muscles, but also dimples, and used both to his advantage. Not that I minded. "You got three toppings," I said.

"True."

"That tells me you were planning on putting out today."

He considered this. "So, three toppings is like the equivalent of ordering lobster on a first date. I'm basically telling you I'm easy. What if I ordered plain? What would that tell you?"

"That you knew I didn't shave my legs tonight."

I was about to say more when someone banged on the door. Omari threw me a look and went to answer it. He returned a few seconds later with my favorite fifth wheel. Nina was already going a mile a minute. "Why aren't you ready? The Nominee Cocktail Reception starts in a half hour."

"Because I wasn't planning on going," Omari said.

Omari played Jamal Fine on *LAPD 90036*. He was one of five actors nominated for "Best Actor in Television" at the 18th Annual Silver Sphere Awards, a TV and movie awards show put on by a select group of respected entertainment journalists. It had recently surpassed the Golden Globes when it came to prestige and was nipping at the Oscars for the most coveted honor in Hollywood. Unlike the Academy Awards, it had a more relaxed vibe. Dubbing itself the "Biggest Party of the Year," the show plied its guests with alcohol and had a DJ instead of an orchestra. Milking the nomination like a perpetually pregnant cow, Nina had had Omari on a nonstop blitz of TV shows, magazines, blogs, and of course parties. He hated every single one.

"Did you not tell me that you wanted to win?" she asked.

"Of course I do," he said. And he did. I'd been there when he'd gotten the nomination. He didn't stop smiling for two straight days. "I told you'd I'd go to the press conference," he continued. "That's not enough?"

Nina shook her head. "Not if you want to go from nominee to winner. I worked for Silver Sphere for five years before leaving to start my firm. I know what a big deal this is, especially for a star of a freshman drama that's a procedural at that. You have to show face and network."

He looked at me and whispered, "Save me."

As much as it pained me to even think it, Nina was right. It would mean a lot for Omari's career to win, plus I knew how much he wanted it. When we were in high school, we'd talk about one of us becoming an "award-winning actor." Since I clearly wasn't getting even a Razzie anytime soon, that left it up to him. "You should go," I told him. "And it's not just because I've always fantasized about being with an award winner."

"You don't want to share the rest of the pizza," he said.

I nodded and we smiled at each other long enough for Nina to clear her throat. "Fine, Nina," Omari said, though he looked at me. He jokingly rolled his eyes and shook his head like an eternally put-upon 1950s sitcom mom.

Satisfied, Nina practically pushed him toward the stairs to his bedroom. "Please go jump in the shower. You reek of pizza and knockoff Chanel No. 5."

It was my turn to roll my eyes. My perfume wasn't a knockoff. It was just really, really, really old. I tried to figure out the best way to work that into a conversation as Omari disappeared up the stairs. I came up blank.

Only when she heard the shower running did Nina deem to acknowledge my presence. Blonde, late thirties, skinny with a booty she *didn't* get from her mama, and glasses I seriously doubted she actually needed, Nina looked like a grownup version of "last girl standing in horror film." I had a feeling she randomly stripped down to her bra and panties for no good reason as soon as she stepped inside her house. I also had a feeling she would slash someone with a knife without a moment's thought. Good or bad guy. She operated a "boutique" agency, which in publicist-speak roughly translates to "I can't afford any other employees." Omari was her biggest client, so he got a lot of her attention. Too much.

I can't say she was happy about me being in his apartment. But then, I wasn't happy about her being there either.

And it was because of Tomari.

Tomari wasn't a person. It was a rumor. One that had Omari dating A-list actress Toni Abrams. All the gossip blogs had run with it, but it was Anani Miss who'd given them the nickname Tomari. It was just wrong. The name. The rumor. Everything.

Omari preferred not to give it much attention. Whenever a reporter asked who he was dating, he'd give a curt "I prefer to keep my private life private." It was fine by me. I didn't date Omari because he was a TV star. I actually would have kind of preferred if he wasn't. I'd gotten quite comfortable outside the glare of the spotlight since my Chubby's contract was canceled.

It helped our relationship that we had two unspoken rules. I wouldn't complain about the Tomari stuff. He wouldn't complain about the investigation stuff. It had worked out well. However, I was 99.999999 percent sure Nina was the sole reason the Tomari "relationship" would not die a slow, painful death. I couldn't avoid her, so I'd settled for boycotting Anani. Call it a silent protest.

"Nina. What's up? What's going on with you?" I gave her my best girl talk voice, mainly because I knew how much it annoyed her to have to speak to me.

"What's supposed to be going on with me, in less than an hour, is the Silver Sphere Award Nominee Cocktail Reception. And instead of being ready, like he told me he would be, he's sitting here eating pizza. With you." Her tone made it clear this was my fault.

"He didn't mention any party to me," I said. "How was I supposed to know?"

"It's awards season. There's always a party!"

Touché. Awards season is all about getting dressed, getting drunk, and getting tiny gold statues that usually mean an extra zero in your paycheck and an extra line in your obituary. The three-month stretch kicks off with the Independent Spirit Award nominations in November and culminates with the grand dame of them all, the Oscars, in February. In between, everyone and their mama gives out awards like candy on Halloween. I went with the positive. "So he'll make a fashionably late entrance."

"I need to get him on that red carpet before the movie nominees show up. Once Todd Arrington steps foot out that car, no one's going to care about Omari. Arrington's people are getting him there early this year. He needs to be back on a plane to Dubai for a six a.m. call."

Well, when she put it like that. "Let me check on him."

I woke up the next morning tired enough to seriously contemplate hibernation. Based on the amount of leftover pizza I'd eaten the night before, I figured I was good until April. At least.

The plan had been to wait for Omari to get home. I'd lasted until 2:00 a.m., which is when all the clubs close in LA. If New York is the city that never sleeps, LA is the city that makes sure to get its beauty rest.

When Omari wasn't home by 2:30, I called it a night and took my butt home. We'd been together for two months, but I still didn't feel comfortable sleeping over without him.

Home was Sienna's two-bedroom penthouse off Burton Way in Beverly Hills. Before anyone gets too excited about moving on up, this was LA. It wasn't quite a deluxe apartment in the sky. More like deluxe fifth floor condo in the smog. Still, it was gorgeous. There were worse places a technically homeless person could wind up.

Six months ago, with my savings at an all-time low and my bills at an all-time high, Sienna had let me move into her spare bedroom-turned-shoe-closet-turned-back-to-spare-bedroom. The remnants of the room's past life housing Sienna's shoes still took up three walls. She'd gifted me most of her stiletto collection in the early days of her all-red world record attempt—we wore the same shoe size—and they were still beautifully displayed on individual shelves. I'd nicknamed my room the "bloset." It was the only room in the house that wasn't red.

When I did finally will myself out of bed, it was to use the bathroom. I had a bladder the size of a tick. As I padded my way back to bed, I could hear Sienna in the living room watching TV. A newscaster reported on a late-night shooting at a bank off La Brea. Two people were shot, one fatally. I didn't think much of it.

It was only after I got back in bed that I checked my cell.

Three missed calls. All from Omari. He wasn't the type to blow my phone up, especially in the middle of the night. I checked my texts. He'd messaged. It was quick and to the point.

*Don't worry. I'm alive.*

What. The. Fudge?

# Three

Between running red lights and trying to call Omari on my cell, I broke about a kajillion laws getting to his place. I even called Nina. When she didn't pick up, I turned on the radio. KFI was broadcasting a press conference.

"My name is Nina Flynn and I've been called to serve as a spokesperson for the Silver Sphere Organization in the wake of this terrible tragedy. Normally I'd be thrilled to be working with such an esteemed organization again. It's a shame it's under such unfortunate circumstances."

That explained why she wasn't answering the phone. Sienna had mentioned that something happened after the Silver Sphere event but I hadn't stopped to find out any details. I was too concerned with running out the door to find Omari.

"Last night at approximately 2:30 a.m., after leaving the Silver Sphere Awards Nominee Cocktail Reception, the organization's in-house publicist Lyla Davis was shot and killed at an ATM on La Brea

Boulevard during what appears to be a botched robbery attempt. The assailant fled with Lyla's bag and personal cell phone. Her driver was also shot when he attempted to stop the robbery. His injuries are not considered life threatening, and he is currently being held for observation at a local hospital, where he is expected to make a full and complete recovery. We will not be releasing his name at this time, and we ask that you respect his privacy during his recovery process."

The slowpoke in front of me stopped at a yellow and I was finally forced to hit my brakes.

"I'm going to turn things over to our president, Gus 'the Gossip' Ortiz, but I wanted to say one thing," Nina continued. "Lyla wasn't just a great publicist. She was also a great friend. I had the pleasure of having her assist me during the last two years of my time with SSO. And when it was finally time to resign, to fulfill my lifelong dream of starting my own boutique publicity firm, I knew that only one person could replace me: Lyla Davis. I can't tell you how much it saddens me she wasn't able to use everything I've taught her for this year's awards show."

Only Nina would use an informal eulogy to talk about herself. I tried calling Omari again.

"Lyla touched everyone's lives, journalist and actor alike," Nina continued. "That's why the Silver Sphere Organization, as well as this year's best actor and best actress motion picture nominees, are asking for the public's help in identifying her killer. We are offering a reward—"

Omari picked up just as the light finally turned green. I hit the gas and immediately shut off the radio. "I told you I was fine." His voice sounded sleepy.

"I know, but why wouldn't you be fine?"

"You heard the news? About the woman getting shot? I was there."

I almost hit the car in front of me.

"Well, right before," he said. "I was getting cash after the party. I actually let her into the lobby of the ATM. Didn't see anything, though."

"But you're fine."

"Yeah. I was already at the corner of Melrose when she was shot. I didn't even hear about it until Nina called to let me know. It's scary, though. If I'd gotten there a few minutes later ..."

I didn't even want to think about that. "You sound tired. Go back to sleep. I'll check on you in a bit."

We hung up and I made a left at the next street. I needed to see Aubrey. Pronto.

As I drove, I thought about Lyla Davis. Being dead was horrible, no matter the circumstances. But a case of "wrong place, wrong time" especially freaked me out. Just the idea that you'd done your best in life to avoid marrying any sociopaths, accidentally dropping a radio in the tub, or crossing the street without looking in both directions, and then you happen to head to an ATM at the exact same time as a money-hungry psycho with a gun. It could have been Omari. It could have been my parents. It could have been any of us. But it wasn't. It was Lyla Davis. Poor thing.

I used the red lights to google more info on her. Her headshot accompanied every article about the shooting. She was classic ingénue—dark brown hair, brown eyes, and a wide light-brown face that looked like it was created strictly to smile. She even had freckles. At the next red light, I learned that the police had already released video and stills from the incident. I couldn't look at the video on my phone—there was no time at the red lights—but I did check out the photos of the shooter. The bank hadn't exactly splurged on surveillance equipment, so the picture was as blurry as my vision before I got Lasik.

About the only thing I could make out was that he was tall and skinny. His face was covered in every pic, first by his hand and later by a ski mask. Not sure where he'd even got that in LA. Despite the mask, you could still clearly see something dark peeking out from the front collar of his T-shirt. My guess was a tattoo. Of what? I couldn't tell. As it was, it resembled a big black blob. I screenshot it anyway, then turned on Sunset.

For once, morning rush hour traffic in Silver Lake moved at a decent pace. But this was still LA. Decent meant ten minutes to go two blocks. When I got closer, I saw why.

Someone was smack-dab in the middle of the street directing traffic. And unless the mayor had decided to exchange the dark blue LAPD uniforms for bright orange, that someone was definitely not a cop. He was about thirty-five-ish and five foot seven, with a slight but sturdy build that paired nicely with his blond hair and brown eyes. He'd probably play the best guy friend that the female lead ignores to spend ninety-plus minutes arguing with the leading man.

I got in the turn lane and waited for some indication that it was my turn to go. He let a few cars continue straight, then blew a whistle, gave them the "Talk to the Hand" / "Stop!" gesture, and motioned for me to turn left.

I pulled into a small store lot, got out of the car, and waited to cross the street. When all was clear, he gestured me toward him like the wannabe crossing guard he obviously was. I got within a foot of him, then stopped. "Aubrey, what did your mother tell you about playing in traffic?"

He didn't look at me, too focused on the task at hand. "The city refuses to put a much-needed traffic light at this location, Ms. Anderson. I am doing my best to alleviate the situation."

"Of course you are." A Prius whipped past me. The driver honked and Aubrey gave him a friendly wave. He must come out here a lot. Probably half the neighborhood thought he was homeless.

"Can you take a quick break so we can chat?" I asked.

He turned, giving me the full weight of his brown eyes. "It is rush hour, Ms. Anderson."

I took that to be a no. "Aubrey, you do realize you're not a cop anymore, right? And even when you were, I hope you weren't stuck directing traffic." I still hadn't gotten the full story on what had happened there.

"I may not be a police officer, but they cannot take away my rights as a concerned citizen."

It was clear he wasn't going anywhere. At least not until each and every one of his neighbors was at work safe and sound. That meant I'd have to risk my life to talk to him. Ironic. I got all up in his personal space. "There was a shooting last night."

That got his attention. At least briefly. Aubrey threw me a quick look before turning to tell a car to turn left. I pretended his hand motion meant I should continue. "A publicist named Lyla Davis was gunned down at an ATM after she left a party. Omari was there! Well, right before it happened. He's okay. The police already released a photo of the shooter."

I held up my cell, but Aubrey was too busy giving a Honda the right of way to even glance at it. So I moved it closer until it was about two inches from his eyeballs. The Honda would be okay without Aubrey's careful direction. "There are also witnesses, including her driver," I said. "The guy shot him *and* his car before running off when a couple pulled into the lot."

"That is very unfortunate." Aubrey left it at that. He was clearly not as interested as I was. Blurg.

I thought about how I needed to get him on board. Thought about Omari there right before it happened. Thought about poor Lyla there when it did happen. I ran through my Rolodex of "Reasons Aubrey does things" and came up with "They've specifically asked for the public's help to ID the guy."

I could literally see his ears perk up. There was nothing Aubrey liked more than being helpful. It was just that normally the cops weren't receptive to his assistance.

"You said she was at an ATM machine?"

Bingo.

We went to a nearby donut shop to do a bit more research and divvy up duties. Aubrey would canvass the neighborhood around the bank to see if anyone saw anything. He'd also speak with the two witnesses. I'd recruit my friend Emme and her elite computer skills to sharpen the released ATM footage for any additional clues. I'd also try to find the unnamed driver, which wouldn't be the easiest thing in the world without a name. Even TMZ was having trouble bribing someone to share that. To their credit, they had learned he was at Cedars-Sinai hospital.

When I got in my car, I emailed the video to Emme, then called her to explain what had popped up in her inbox. Once I shared all the details, she allowed me to come over. Yes, allowed. I'd once stopped by uninvited and spent ten minutes ringing her bell. She only let me in after I'd commented on her latest Facebook status.

I thought about the case while in the car. If I was being honest with myself, I was scared you-know-what-less to look into another murder. I used the drive to convince myself it would all turn out fine. They already had a picture of the bad guy. We just needed to find a name and hand it over to the police. If handled right, there would be zero interaction with any murderers of any kind. Been there. Done that. Had the emotional and physical scars to prove it.

Emme's door was unlocked when I got there, a good thing since she was engrossed as usual in a computer game. Any semi-decent interior decorator will tell you a room needs a focal point. Emme had chosen a huge desk with a computer monitor bigger than the TVs of most sports fanatics. The result was more command center than living room.

And at the center of it all was my Emme. At five foot seven and a size two with (real) blonde hair and blue eyes, she looked like a leading lady. Literally. Her twin sister Toni—the same one who was allegedly one half of Tomari—had two minutes and four Oscar nominations on her. Luckily, Emme didn't give a single iota. She'd retired from acting at age six.

Grownup Emme turned around when I walked in. "Omari's good?"

I nodded. "Yeah. He's even going to work. I asked him some questions but he didn't see anything."

Emme turned back around to resume playing the life simulation game where you happily run errands that no one wants to in real life. "The story's been trending on Twitter all morning." That was how she got her news. There were worse ways. "Video's almost ready, BTW."

I made small talk while we waited. "You given much thought to your birthday?" It was in a few weeks and it was a big one. Twenty-five.

"TBH"—to be honest—"nope," she said. Then, eyes never moving from her game, she opened a right desk drawer, grabbed a piece of paper, and handed it to me.

I took a look. It was a photo of a pair of ugly sunglasses with two yellow circles in each upper corner. She'd copied and pasted some marketing material. The brand name was Focals. The tag line: *Let's get visual!!!* Yes, with three exclamation points. Apparently it was some new gadget that let you record POV videos and send them directly to any social media app on your phone.

Someone had obviously been thinking about her birthday after all and knew exactly what she wanted. Emme barely left her apartment, so I wasn't quite sure why she needed sunglasses—even ones with a built-in camera. However, I owned lots of yoga pants even though I never went to actual yoga. Maybe these sunglasses were just as comfy and forgiving after you splurged on extra-large fries. "These will look great on you, Em!"

Emme had also listed the MSRP and five local stores where one could buy Focals, as well as their hours of operations and one other thing. "What are the links?" I asked.

"Google Map directions from your place to each location."

"Can you email this to me—" My phone buzzed before I could finish my sentence. An alert told me I had a new email from Emme titled *Focal Info*. "Thanks."

"NP." No problem. There was a beep. "Footage is done."

She pulled it up on her mega monitor. It was black and white and from a POV above an indoor ATM machine. A guy stood in front of the machine. With a start, I realized it was Omari. My breath caught. Lyla appeared a few seconds later, a dark bookbag hanging from her erect left arm. Omari left as she came in. They didn't speak but he held the door. Neither seemed to realize it didn't close all the way behind them.

That answered one of my burning questions: Why hadn't the police used records of the killer's ATM card to track him down? No way was I telling Omari that he may have helped the shooter get inside.

Lyla walked straight to the cash machine. ATM cameras are up there with DMV and passport cameras when it comes to making sure you don't look your best. But I was still able to make out the nails. Long, dark-colored talons, they were the only hint that she had some edge to her. She probably used them to offset the adorable freckles.

The killer came in a minute later, wearing a white T-shirt and what looked like a beanie on his head. He kept his head down and his hand over his face, making it impossible to identify any marks or features. I honestly couldn't even tell if he had a nose.

He made sure to shut the door firmly behind him. As soon as it was closed, he pulled down his beanie, transforming it into the aforementioned ski mask. He followed ATM etiquette by standing a few feet away, which conveniently also kept him away from the security camera. He waited patiently, head always down, as Lyla finished her transaction. It was only when she turned that he made his move, going for her cell phone first. Wrong choice.

I had to give it to Lyla. She didn't go down without a fight. It was uncomfortable to watch knowing the final outcome. But she put her mani to work, scratching at his covered face and exposed neck and arms, pulling at his white T-shirt. Unfortunately, she didn't get the chance to rip off the ski mask.

The footage stopped right before the really scary part. I was glad. The next clip started with the killer running out the bank's front door, Lyla's backpack at his side.

We replayed it again. And again. On the third viewing, I remembered the blob. In the still images the police had released, it looked like nothing more than a huge patch of dirt. But Emme's monitor gave a much clearer picture. "Em, can you pause this section and blow it up?"

During the fight, Lyla pulled at her attacker's shirt—revealing more of his chest. He definitely had a tattoo. But even with Emme's magic, we could only make out a few centimeters. It was definitely round and looked like it had cogs. It wasn't much but it was enough.

If I could match the top of the tattoo with the rest of it, then I could be well on my way to finding out who killed Lyla Davis.

Until then, I needed to talk to Lyla's driver. He wasn't anywhere on the security footage, but the front of his car was. We paused it again to get a good look. It was dark and obviously an SUV. The front grill had the Lincoln emblem: the one that looks like a compass has gone on a crash diet and lost twenty pounds more than it should have. There was a white California plate but one that didn't have the standard collection of numbers and letters. Not a shock there. Los Angeles, the home of vanity, was also the home of the vanity plate.

I hated them. Mainly because it always took me forever to figure them out. I'd once spent an entire hour stuck in traffic trying to decipher what the guy in front of me meant when he'd chosen BRN 2BWD. It took me looking it up on my phone to realize it was Born to be Wild. More like Born to be Confusing.

This one read 2N UP.

"At least the plate's easy to read," Emme said.

"Exactly." Two and up.

"Tune up," she said.

Oh. That definitely made more sense for a car. But still. I was close. Kind of.

Unfortunately, running license plates was a luxury reserved only for Los Angeles law enforcement, one of the many ways the state tried to protect celebs from the ever-present lens of paparazzi. Of course, Razzle had a database of five hundred-and-growing celebrity plates while the rest of us jumped through hoops to look up drivers who hit our car and took off.

"Tune up could be a company name," Emme said.

I nodded. "The SUV makes me think he's a professional driver. Not some Joe Blow doing it for extra money."

Emme opened a new browser tab and typed in "Tune-Up Car Service." Bingo.

The first hit was a site for a local car service. From the looks of it, a one-man shop run by a guy named Dante Brooks. The site had no pictures of him, but Emme took care of that in a few seconds by googling his name and the word "Instagram." His 2NUPCarzzz Insta account had lots of casual shots of Dante smiling in front of a very familiar Lincoln SUV. I pegged him for mid-thirties standard-issue white guy. He'd probably be an extra hired to blend into the background of a movie scene and pretend to have conversations. Basically, a guy you never notice.

Still wanting confirmation that Dante was our driver, I picked up the phone and called Cedars-Sinai. After a few minutes, I got connected to an actual human. "Yes, hi, I'm looking for the room number for Dante Brooks."

There was a pause. Finally, the person spoke. "We're only allowed to give information on Mr. Brooks to family members. Not to members of the press."

We'd found our driver. I just needed to figure out a way to sneak into the hospital and get him to talk to me.

# Four

I didn't have to worry about going all *Mission: Impossible* at the hospital. While I tried to come up with a plan to get into Cedars-Sinai, someone else came up with a plan to get Dante out of it. They'd released him in the middle of the night. Emme and I hadn't been the only ones finally able to suss out his identity. News crews had even done us one better and found his home address.

Omari got off set early, so I spent the afternoon with him but didn't spend the night. I was home with Sienna and Aubrey when TMZ broke the news. Aubrey had come over to share that he'd gotten nothing new from talking to the witnesses. He argued with me about going to the hospital right up until we realized we no longer needed to. Instead, we all watched a reporter stationed mere inches from Dante's front lawn. She was far from alone.

"Well, at least I know how to find him," I said. "Just look for the helicopters hovering above his place."

"Can you imagine having all those cameras outside your house?" Sienna asked.

It'd be horrible.

"It'd be amazing," she said.

"He probably is not there anyway," Aubrey said. "He might be residing at a friend's house until things quiet down."

He had a point. I thought about Dante's social media accounts, which I'd stalked like a sixth grader with her first crush. "He didn't seem the type to share every meal on the Internet but maybe he once tagged a friend we can look up."

I pulled up Dante's Instagram on my phone and narrated my findings. "Photo of a car. Photo of a car. Photo of him ... washing a car. Photo of a car. Photo of him waxing a car. Photo of a car. Looks like he has a round-trip airport deal if any of you are planning on taking a trip."

Aubrey piped in. "No thank you. I refuse to ride in airplanes."

For the 1,763,766,868th time, my sarcasm went right over Aubrey's head. You'd think I'd stop trying, but nope. I'd added *make Aubrey laugh* to my bucket list. Right after *sky diving* and before *chicken out of sky diving and tell everyone I did it anyway.*

"He's got a lot of comments." I looked at Dante's latest Instagram post. "All news reporters asking him to check his DMs to discuss an interview request." Not for the first time, I felt a bit out of my league. I forced myself to snap out of it.

"Guess they figured liking all his photos would entice him to give them an exclusive," Sienna said. "Living. The. Dream."

"Really?" I asked. "You'd want to get shot for said dream?"

She paused just long enough to make me think she might. "Depends on the number of comments."

"Over 1,000."

She peered over my shoulder. "Nope. I'd have to get at least a million." She pointed toward the screen. "His number is listed. We should give him a call."

I hesitated. "I'm sure Sam Jones from ABC 7 already tried that."

"Yeah, but you're way hotter than Sam Jones."

I didn't know about that. Los Angeles news anchors didn't look exactly like movie stars, but they did look like their body doubles. All tightened and toned and tanned. Not to mention bleached—hair and teeth. Probably other body parts too. Sienna was right, though. It couldn't hurt to call.

I dialed the number listed in Tune-Up's airport ad, then put the phone on speaker. It went straight to voicemail. I hung up right after the beep.

"At least we know he is checking his voicemail," Aubrey said.

"We do." I stated it as fact when it was really more of a question. "Because ..."

"Like you said, Ms. Anderson, chances are he is getting several phone calls. If he was not checking his voicemail, the mailbox would be full."

"Checking messages and returning them are two different things, though. What do you want to do?"

"I suggest we still head to his house and interview a few neighbors. If he is not there, they might know where he is."

Worked for me. Sienna had an audition and opted to stay in, so Aubrey and I went downstairs to my car. Once we took our respective seats, I tried to turn on the ignition.

Nothing.

The whole car-not-starting thing had become a huge pain in my derriere. Luckily, Aubrey handled the situation better than I did. "Where are your jumper cables, Ms. Anderson?"

"I don't have any." He gave me a look. "It's on my to-buy list!"

It wasn't, but still. The only thing that stopped me from banging my head against the steering wheel was that I'd gotten makeup on the horn the last time I attempted it. It took half a tube of Clorox wipes to clean off and I'd missed the beginning of a new *The First 48* episode. "How am I supposed to hunt this guy down if I can't even get my fudging car to start? It's not like he's going to come to me."

And then I thought about it. Maybe that wasn't such a bad idea. It was a long shot, but still. Desperate times called for desperate phone calls. I pulled out my cell and hit the number for Tune-Up Car Service. It went straight to voicemail again. This time I waited for the beep and went into my spiel. "Hi. This is Dayna Anderson. Our company's CEO is looking for a new driver and someone recommended your company. I was wondering if we could do a tryout. We have a flight out of LAX this evening."

Dante Brooks called back within the hour.

Aubrey and I were already waiting when Dante pulled up at exactly 6:00 in a silver Toyota Camry. The only way I'd gotten Aubrey to agree to my deception was promising we'd reveal ourselves as soon as we hit the 10 West. He told me that I should take the lead. Fine by me. My plan was to question Dante once freeway rush-hour traffic took him hostage. That way he couldn't kick us out. And if he did, he wouldn't get very far before we caught up.

I was surprised that he'd agreed to pick us up, considering the circumstances. You could certainly tell that something had happened to him recently. He didn't jump out of the car as much as hobble out.

And his left arm had been professionally bandaged. Otherwise, though, he looked pretty good to go.

In person, Dante had brown hair, brown eyes, and coconut-popsicle-hued skin with more hills and valleys than Runyon Canyon. His smile was gorgeous, courtesy of teeth that were straight but not so perfect that they were walking advertisements for his cosmetic dentist. Plastic surgery isn't some big secret around these parts. You hear about the fake boobs, the fake noses, the fake hair. But you never really hear about the fake teeth. Hollywood probably had more in a one block radius than a seniors' facility in West Palm Beach.

But Dante's? They looked God-given, like he'd never even had a retainer, much less braces or veneers. He flashed them at us when he smiled and then spoke, his voice as deep as the Grand Canyon. "Have to apologize for the car. Unfortunately, my main mode of transportation is currently unavailable."

Unavailable because it was currently in police custody, thanks to coming in contact with a few stray bullets. "No problem," I said, and Aubrey nodded in agreement.

He looked at me then. I knew the expression. It was coming. "We're not exactly the same age range, but I swear you look like someone I went to high school with."

There it was.

They say when you're on television, people think they know you. Well, when you *were* on television for thirty-seconds-a-pop commercials that stopped airing almost two years ago, people think they know you … from their hometown. I didn't want to get into the whole "I used to be semi-famous" tale of woe, so I just nodded, and then motioned toward his injured arm. "You good to drive?"

"Looks worse than it is. And I still have all my extremities." He wiggled all five fingers to prove it.

"Great! I'd give you a high five but ... "

He laughed. "Yeah, probably best not to."

He opened the back door for us and Aubrey and I settled in. I clicked on my seat belt and addressed Dante in the front seat. "You sure you're okay to drive?"

He held up his bandaged hand. "It's clearly been a rough couple of days but driving clears my mind. I was out anyway. Might as well make some money, right? And who doesn't love a trip to the airport? I know a shortcut that can get us there in fifteen minutes."

That would not do. At all. Under normal circumstances, I would love to know every single turn. Not this go-round. When it came to interviewing witnesses, it normally took me fifteen minutes just to think of a suitable question. We needed him trapped as long as possible. "Can you take the highway instead?" I asked. I'd get the shortcut directions another time.

We made small talk about the weather (it was so nice, we loved it) and *Judge Judy* (she was so mean, we loved it) until we got to the Robertson Boulevard entrance to the 10. We hit standstill traffic before we even made it to the main highway. Fine by me. "So what do you two do, exactly?" Dante asked.

I'd planned to ease into that topic one step at a time. Unfortunately, Aubrey dove in so fast I was surprised he didn't hit his head on a diving board. "We are looking into the murder of Lyla Davis."

So much for me taking the lead. If the car had been moving, Dante would have slammed his brakes. Instead, he whipped his head around. "You're reporters?"

I was quick to correct him. "Investigators. ASAP Investigations. We solved the Haley Joseph hit-and-run a few months ago. And yes, we're looking into Lyla Davis's murder." Technically, I hadn't lied about who we were. Aubrey *was* the CEO of our company.

Dante said nothing. I sent up a quick prayer that he didn't kick us out. It would take a Lyft driver at least an hour to get through this traffic to come get us on the side of the road and I surely was not walking the three-and-a-half miles home in four-inch heels. I spoke again. "Look, I'm really sorry for the airport mumbo jumbo, but we want to find out who killed Lyla—and shot you. We were hoping you'd help us get this guy behind bars."

Dante stared at us for an entire minute. I know because I counted. Then, thankfully, he finally spoke. "I need to see your license."

He didn't mean driver's. I'd made that mistake once before, when I'd first met Aubrey. I smiled—he wasn't kicking us out the car. My feet thanked him. "Sure thing. Aubrey, show him your license."

"I do not have it," Aubrey said.

I turned to Dante. "He doesn't have it with him." No clue why I was acting like a translator. It only felt like Aubrey spoke a different language.

Aubrey shook his head. "No, Ms. Anderson. I do not have one at all."

I looked Aubrey dead in his face. "You don't have a license? At all?"

He nodded, nowhere as concerned about this revelation as I was.

This was not good. In fact, it was bad. And not Michael Jackson dancing in an abandoned subway bad. "You never mentioned that."

"You never asked, Ms. Anderson."

"I didn't know I had to!"

I glanced up at Dante watching every moment with an amused look on his face. I gave him a tight smile. "So, no license, but my partner has over a decade of police experience. And we will be getting a license soon. Trust."

Aubrey had the nerve to roll his eyes next to me.

There was another in what had become a conveyor belt of pauses, and then Dante finally spoke. "And here I thought I'd landed a big account."

He smiled, and I joined in. "Even though we're not going to the airport, I can still tip you. Give you a great review on Yelp."

"Who would turn down a good Yelp review?" It was clear he was teasing. "What exactly do you wanna know?"

"Was this your first time meeting Lyla?"

Dante shook his head. "I drive for Uber when things are slow. I'd picked her up one time a couple years ago maybe and we hit it off. She started calling me directly when she needed a driver." He stopped to take in a huge breath. "I do want this guy found more than anyone. I'll do whatever it takes to help."

I was about to ask my next question when Aubrey beat me to it. "Did you get a clear view of the assailant when he walked into the bank?"

Good question. The killer hadn't pulled his mask down until he was inside. If he'd walked by Dante, he could have seen his face.

Dante shook his head as the traffic moved in dribs and drabs. "I didn't even notice the guy. I saw that actor coming out of the lobby and getting in his car, but otherwise I was focused on my phone. My girl was mad at me so she was blowing my phone up. I'm talking texts two inches long."

Been there. Sent those.

I shook my head compassionately as he continued. "I was doing serious damage control. Only looked up when I heard shots. She was still alive. I could see that. I jumped out of the car, got to the door, but you need a freaking card to get inside ..."

He paused then, and I hated myself for making him relive it all.

"I was too late," he finally said. "He shot at me as soon as he came out of the building. I ducked but he still grazed my arm. I played dead. Didn't move. Kept my eyes closed. Didn't open them until I heard the sirens."

He was beating himself up over what he'd done—or rather, didn't do. Save Lyla. I could tell it wasn't the first time, either. If driving helped clear his head, like he said, he'd probably logged hundreds of miles in the hours he'd been out the hospital. I leaned closer as I spoke. "I would have done the same thing because it was the right thing to do. You tried to help her. It was too late. You had to protect yourself. And you're helping her now."

Aubrey was quiet. We sat there as Dante spoke, even though he no longer seemed to be speaking to us. "This guy. He could've been anyone on the planet. It all happened in a minute tops. And by the time I realized I should've paid him some attention, I was more concerned with the blood coming out of my body. Never knew surface wounds had so much blood." He laughed then, even though it wasn't funny, and glanced back at me in his rearview mirror. "Anything else?"

I shook my head. "You can drop us back off. I have a Yelp review to write."

"It better be five stars. Have tips and check-ins and all that."

We were near the Overland exit, so Dante doubled back and took us back to my condo. Aubrey got out the car first but I stayed behind to give Dante one of our new business cards. "Please let me know if you remember anything else. My number's on there."

He glanced at it. *"ASAP Investigations. LICENSED investigators."*

Blurg. I'd already pushed the whole licensing debacle out my brain. "Can I have that back for a sec?"

When he handed it to me, I scribbled a few words on it and then gave it back. He read it aloud again. *"ASAP Investigations. Soon-to-be licensed investigators."*

It was only after Dante had pulled away that I realized I'd forgotten to ask him about the tattoo—and the shortcut to the airport.

I'd Internet-stalked Aubrey before. Several times, in fact. Left to my own devices, I hadn't found much. He had no social media—not even a leftover Myspace account he'd forgotten about like the rest of us once we all fully jumped ship to Facebook. So I had Emme do my dirty work as soon as I got back home. She sent over a full report within an hour. That's when I learned why Aubrey no longer worked in law enforcement.

Eighteen-year-old Lorna Rodriguez had been brought to the Malibu sheriff's department around 1:00 a.m. on a Thursday night. She'd been caught shoplifting a pack of gum from an all-night convenience store and "caused a scene" when caught. Cops were called. Lorna caused a bigger scene. She was arrested, causing her biggest scene yet. One worthy of an Oscar, if you believed the cops. The one who brought her in later claimed she was "highly intoxicated." Her car was impounded—her purse, cell phone, and wallet inside.

Lorna was booked and soon released on her own recognizance. The cops promised to get her car out of impound but she refused to wait. Instead, she chose to walk. It was her right. It was also barely five in the morning. The last anyone saw Lorna she took off on foot down Agoura Road, disappearing further and further into the inky black abyss with each step.

Her parents were furious, which was probably still an understatement. They spoke to the cops. And when they weren't happy with the answers, they spoke to journalists. Lots and lots of journalists. Asking them all to find out what had happened to their little girl. Questioning why the police just let her walk out in the dead of night. Inquiring why no one ever called them.

They currently had a lawsuit pending.

In contrast, the sheriff's department had stayed relatively mum on the topic, except to announce that the desk sergeant on duty that night had been reprimanded—and again to share that he had tendered his resignation. They never mentioned his name, but I knew who it was.

Aubrey had never outright told me his version of events, instead offering snippets here and there. It was clear he blamed himself. I, in turn, didn't blame him for not wanting to talk about it. I wouldn't have wanted to either. I figured he'd rather focus on the next phase of his life as a private investigator. Of course, I also figured he'd taken the steps to be licensed.

I hadn't read up on licensing procedures in California. There could be a chance that ASAP Investigations didn't need one. Maybe it was more of a suggestion, like when a waiter offers a wine that would pair great with your veal parmesan. (Apparently, you should order Merlot.)

I googled "unlicensed private investigator in California." First thing that popped up was an article about a guy charged with one count of false representation and one count of illegally working as a private investigator. It was only a misdemeanor, but still.

Licensing clearly was not a suggestion, like I'd hoped. It was a requirement.

It was weird Aubrey didn't have one. He tended to operate by the book. He hated when I checked my phone at a red light. He had to know what he was doing was illegal. Maybe he just hadn't gotten around to it. Luckily, he had me to rectify the situation.

I looked up license requirements. They were strict: complete an application, undergo a criminal history background check, and have at least three years paid investigative work experience. You also had to pass a two-hour multiple-choice exam and pay a crapload of random fees for things like "licensing" and "fingerprint processing."

If I was going at this alone, I'd be in deep you-know-what. I didn't fit the requirements by a long shot. But for Aubrey, it would be a piece of cake. Chocolate ice cream cake, preferably with those chocolate crunchies in the middle if you wanted to get specific. Aubrey could meet all those requirements and more. The license was just a mere formality. He'd get one and we could continue our plan of me serving as his apprentice.

I just needed to get to a Staples and print out the application. Preferably before either of us got arrested.

# Five

I definitely needed a new battery. Probably needed a new car. Quite possibly needed a new life. But until I got all that stuff, I needed a ride. I'd dropped my car off at a mechanic the next day and was swapping life stories with my Lyft driver when Mama called. Or should I say, FaceTimed. I'd gotten both my parents new iPhones. In typical fashion, Daddy hadn't even opened his while Mama had taken to it just like I knew she would. She Facebooked. She Instagrammed. She took quizzes telling her when she should get married based on her choice of a fast food lunch. She even posted the results.

Her texting game was even better than mine. Bitmojis. Ebrojis. Other types of ojis I hadn't even heard of. And based on the call, she was now finally FaceTiming.

I answered and saw a blurry white blob that had to be the ceiling. Her FaceTime skills were clearly a work in progress. "Boop." She used my nickname. "You there? We can't see you."

"You gotta turn the phone so it's facing you. It's like when you do your selfies."

The screen jerked a few more times before I finally saw my parents sitting cheek-to-cheek. They weren't being romantic. We didn't do that in our family. They were trying to make sure they were both in the screen. "Hey baby girl," Daddy said. "You look beautiful today."

I didn't but I'd take it. "Thanks!"

"What are you up to today?"

"Aubrey and I have a new case we're looking into, so I spent the morning doing research."

When I wasn't Yelping mechanics, I'd devoted a fair amount of time that day to looking up tattoos. The hope was to find one that matched what little we could see of the shooter's tat, then flash it around the neighborhood where Lyla was murdered.

But apparently he hadn't plucked the design from *Tattoo Designs for Dummies*. When I didn't find anything that remotely looked like it, I printed out what I could make of the tat from the still pics from the ATM. I wanted to talk to some tattoo artists to see if they'd ever seen something similar, with cogs on top. But of course my car was out of commission. I hoped Sienna would let me borrow hers so I could stop by any tattoo parlors near the crime scene. The killer could have been local.

My parents looked at each other. I knew what was coming. Mama spoke first. "I wish you'd get a real job."

She'd said the same thing when I'd told her I wanted to act. I, in turn, told her exactly what I'd said back then too. "This is a real job, Mama. One I'm good at."

"Because you solved that one little murder?"

"Yes, and a few other things. We helped locate a missing grandfather. And now we're looking into this woman shot at an ATM."

Mama sighed. "And how's that going?"

It wasn't really, but I sure wasn't going to tell her that. The tattoo thing was a reach. Even I knew that. But otherwise we were at a dead end. We hadn't had much luck with the witnesses. Omari saw nothing. Dante only confirmed the little the police had already released. And Aubrey hadn't gotten anything out of the other witnesses.

Luckily, I didn't have to answer her. Daddy jumped in. "Baby girl, what your mother's trying to say is that we just don't want you to get hurt."

"No," Mama said. "What I'm trying to say is that she needs to get a good corporate job and save that investigating stuff for the police. Just because you got lucky finding that poor girl's killer doesn't mean you need to make this a career."

I had nothing to say to that. Probably because deep down, part of me was scared she was right.

The Lyft driver pulled up in front of Omari's building. "I gotta go," I said. "But send me some selfies! Love you."

I hung up before either could respond. Pushing the convo to the back of my mind, I thanked my driver and got out.

When I got upstairs, I used my key to enter Omari's loft. Nothing greeted me but a closed bathroom door and a muted TV. I walked over to the bathroom and lightly knocked. "Marcus, I'm not wearing any pahnties."

My Eartha-Kitt-in-*Boomerang* impression was spot on, even if it was a lie. I was indeed wearing underwear, granny panties at that. I had a sexier pair I planned to change into later and pretend I'd worn all day.

"Who are you talking to?"

It was Omari. Unfortunately, he was behind me. I glanced at him, then back at the closed door, instantly embarrassed that someone had heard my attempts at sexy talk. "You're supposed to be in the bathroom."

"Am I? Because I'm not."

"Yes, I see that now. But if you're not, then who is?"

"Nina. Been in there a while, too. I kinda want to slip a match under the door with a note strongly suggesting she light it."

He always made me laugh. "She's forcing you to go to another event tonight?"

"Yeah, some magazine party at Chateau Marmont. She also wanted to go over Silver Sphere Awards logistics. When we should arrive. What I should wear. Who should I bring."

"What you should say when you win?"

I could see him light up at the mere thought but he opted to play it cool. "Not going to even jinx myself," he said, then went for a subject change. "We're thinking of having my mom as my plus one."

"She'd love that! It's a great idea." It was also probably Nina's idea. Omari bringing his mom had her name written all over it—in big block letters you could see from outer space. Bringing an adorable relative to an awards show was a publicist staple, like claiming two celebs were "just friends" when they were actually dating. "We'll have to get a designer to send her a dress and I'm sure Sienna's friend Fab can do her makeup," I added.

As much as I loved my fleeting, oft-times rocky relationship with fame, I'd quickly realized it was more a sugar daddy than a soulmate. I liked what it gave me more than how it made me feel. I had no desire to squeeze—literally, at this point—myself into a designer dress and spend three hours pretending to be interested when strangers were given yet another statue to put on their mantle. I was fine with Omari going with his mom.

"Nina's probably already on it, but I'll let her know." He glanced at his watch. "Gotta get dressed."

And with that, he disappeared upstairs. By the time Nina came out of the bathroom I sat on the giant purple people eater of a couch forcing myself not to replay the convo with my parents. Instead, I forced myself to be nice to Nina.

After all, she had a connection to the Lyla Davis case. I figured I'd butter her up, see if she had any insider info, and save myself pointless conversations with a kajillion and one tattoo artists. My aversion to needles was almost as bad as my aversion to exercise.

"I didn't realize that you used to work for the Silver Sphere org," I said.

She looked torn, her desire to not want to *ever* talk to me doing battle with her desire to want to *always* talk about herself. Vanity won. "I was their in-house publicist for five years, but I left after last year's show to build my own boutique entertainment publicity and image consulting firm. It was a hard decision because I loved it there. Gus and everyone is amazing. But I've wanted to set up my own firm for years and decided to just do it. It was finally time to branch out and have a more hands-on role with top Hollywood talent. *Blah. Blah. Blah.*"

That wasn't what she said, but it sure was what I heard. I'd stopped needing a publicist ten seconds after Chubby's ended my contract and I hadn't given what publicists do much thought since. I nodded with the occasional "Right" thrown in to make her think I was actually listening. When it looked like she was finally taking a breather, I made my move. "Well, I'm glad you were able to step in and help them. Have you gotten any leads on Lyla's murder?"

"Nothing I can share." She smiled, obviously loving not being able to tell me anything.

Blurg. I stood up. "I'm gonna go check on Omari."

When I walked upstairs to his bedroom, I found him staring at his shirt. One Nina had no doubt picked out. It looked like it could fit a five-year-old. I came from behind and draped my arms around his stomach. He leaned into me and spoke. "This is the exact reason I stopped letting my mom pick my clothes. I'm getting flashbacks."

He peeled it off, which proved difficult. Partly because it was so tight. Partly because I refused to let go of him. But he managed and went into the closet, playfully dragging me with him. Once inside, we picked something more age—and size—appropriate. "Excited for tonight?" I asked.

"Of course. I love walking around speaking to people Nina says I need to talk to, so someone can take a picture of us talking to each other. The conversations are all the same. *My agent is working on that. I just wrapped filming this. I bought a beach place in Malibu.* Blah. Blah. Blah." The blah, blah, blah was real this time, not just in my head.

I smiled. "If you're a good boy, I might send you a few pics while you're there."

"As long as they're pictures of you. Last time you said that you sent me photos of a milkshake."

"Not *just* 'a milkshake.' One rimmed with frosting and that had cotton candy, a lollipop, and that yucky rock candy stuck in it. I'm telling you, if I ever go to New York I'm getting one."

He gave me a look, so I kissed him. And then I did it again. And again. Then we were interrupted by the sound of someone coming up the stairs. Nina had struck again. I immediately pulled away. "I'm coming now," he called out and we heard her footsteps retreating down the stairs.

I gave him one final quick bird peck. "Bring me back something good."

"You know I always do. The bag from the Silver Sphere cocktail party is actually over there. Take whatever you want."

He motioned to a bookbag thrown haphazardly in the corner. It immediately made me think of Lyla Davis. Blurg. "Be safe tonight," I said as he stood up.

"The worst thing that's going to happen to me is that I might get blinded by camera flashes. I'll be back in a couple hours. Don't leave this time."

Within two minutes, they were both gone. I missed him immediately. Her? Not so much.

I forced myself to focus on the bookbag. To call it a gift bag would be an insult. Gift bags held sweet tarts and lollipop rings that kids took when they left and begged their parents to eat in the car. This was a gift bag on steroids and it was definitely not for children. In yet another attempt to make everything sound cooler than what it is, Hollywood had even given the bag its own name: Swag Bag, aka Stuff We All Get. It held products companies donated in hopes celebs would take them home and love them so much they'd not only use them all the time, but be photographed doing so. In Hollywood, even the gift bags had ulterior motives.

The freebies were housed in the black leather bookbag. I picked it up to give it a thorough once-over. I couldn't tell what was inside, but based on the weight, it was packed to the gills. Instead of the traditional side to side zipper, this had one that went from top to bottom—or vice versa if you were an optimist. The material was a quilt pattern that crossed to form line after line of diamonds.

It looked nice. It also looked familiar. Lyla had carried one just like it the night of her murder and the killer took it with him when he left the scene.

I looked inside. It was like someone shoved an entire high-end department store into a ten-by-fourteen-inch space.

A box of herbal lollipops. Mine.

A jar of Crème de la Mer face cream. Definitely mine.

Two bottles of new caramel-bacon-flavored Ciroc. Most definitely his.

A weekend getaway worth $1,500 to the brand-new Celebration Hotel in nearby Palm Springs. We'd take joint custody of that one.

A gift certificate valued at $2,000 for something called a vampire breast lift. Normally mine if I hadn't already gotten my boobs done.

And finally, a gift certificate from Wheelhouse for a free top-of-the-line indoor exercise bike and a year of complimentary online spin classes. All Omari's.

I fired off a text to Sienna. Within minutes, I was rattling off the bag's contents as we FaceTimed. "The killer's gotta be using some of this stuff," I said.

"You think his skin is that bad? I need to look at the video again before I can gauge whether a jar of Le Mer can truly help him out."

She was not helping. At all. Especially since she knew he wore a ski mask. "Probably not the Le Mer, but something. That's the point of a robbery, right? Take something so you can use it yourself. Unless we want to drive around LA looking through people's trash cans for an empty bottle of bacon-flavored vodka I figure our best bets are the bike and the trip."

"I agree. We can drive to Palm Springs and do a stakeout."

I'd finally got her on track. "Yes!"

"Go to the spa. Lay by the pool."

"No."

"He could also want to work on his tan so technically we'd be spying on him."

Good point. "Yes."

"And I'm in desperate need of a good facial and massage."

"No." I refused to let her get me sidetracked. "Let's just start with the bike."

Spin classes had been at the top of the Hollywood exercise heap for a while. I'd even been a hard-core devotee in my past life as an actress but I'd left it behind along with my career. Despite what the name might have you think, spinning has nothing to do with yarn or plates or even dancing. Class actually consists of a room full of people on stationary bikes all peddling in unison up pretend hills.

When it first came on the scene, some had assumed it would disappear like step aerobics, Jazzercise, and Tae Bo. But it didn't die. It multiplied. Studios popped up everywhere, all with owners who quickly realized providing a bike and some trendy soundtrack simply wasn't enough. So they did anything and everything to separate themselves from, well, the pack. There were rides in front of IMAX screens, leaderboards that let you compete against classmates, and hybrid classes that paired spinning with everything from yoga to strength training.

When it came to spin, SoulCycle was king. But Wheelhouse had made it clear it was coming for the throne with its latest venture—workouts done from the comfort of your own home. It was the one thing that hadn't been done before. Mainly because it wasn't yoga. You needed more than a mat and a fresh pedicure to participate. Unsurprisingly, most folks didn't have a spare indoor bike lying around. Realizing that, Wheelhouse sold specially equipped at-home bikes with a large touchscreen that let you stream studio classes in real time and even had the aforementioned leaderboard so you could compete against the rest of the world.

They apparently had such high hopes for the venture that they were giving them away to Hollywood's elite. Because who wouldn't want to work out next to Gwyneth Paltrow, even if she was thousands of miles away? They'd even came up with a catchy tagline: Wheelhouse in your house.

Sienna and I weren't in our house. Instead, we were in her car outside the studio's new West Hollywood location. Aubrey, however, was inside. Our plan was to start with the honest approach and go from there.

Since the Silver Sphere gift certificate let you buy the bike online or at their WeHo flagship, we'd sent Aubrey in to flash the surveillance photo. Hopefully someone with the same physical description and tippity-top-of-a-cog neck tattoo as our killer had come in to pick up a Silver Sphere nominee bike. If they said no, albeit in a friendly way, Aubrey would see if they'd let him look at the names and addresses of anyone who'd used the nominee gift certificate to buy a bike online.

Sienna and I stared at the entrance. There are the days I feel I can conquer the world before noon. And then there are days that I truly believe that if God wanted me to have to spend hours in a car, he wouldn't have given me such a small bladder. Today definitely fell into the latter. "Are you thinking what I'm thinking?" I asked Sienna.

"That I have to pee?"

"Yep. It's had to have been at least an hour since we last went." I glanced at my cell. "Or only fifteen minutes."

Aubrey had once suggested I bring a jar for stakeouts. It turned out that was easier said than done. Instead, I just Yelped nearby locations with public bathrooms and utilized the same approach I used at the movies. Run out when you have to go and hope nothing exciting happens when you're gone. In both cases, I normally had Sienna waiting to eagerly tell me what I'd missed and vice versa.

Aubrey came out and got in the backseat. "So?" I prodded.

"It was a dead end," Aubrey said. "The salesperson was a young woman named Sweetie who refused to share any information, even though I made it extremely clear that it was for an investigation of a celebrity."

Blurg. I knew it was a long shot. "So what now?"

I was antsy. I'd watched enough *The First 48* marathons to know that the longer it took to find a suspect, the harder it was to solve the case.

"I suggest we try again tomorrow or later today," Aubrey said. "Perhaps we will have a more cooperative cashier."

I didn't want to wait that long, especially without any guarantee that we wouldn't get the same result. But since I didn't have any better ideas, I pulled out of the parking spot to find a bathroom. We were turning into an Arco gas station when a J. Chris song came on the radio. I immediately shut it off.

Janet Christie was a movie star. She couldn't honestly be considered an actress. Last year she also suddenly decided she could sing and released an album under the persona J. Chris. The album went platinum, thanks in part to a duet with her hunk of a country star husband, Mack Christie. It was also the title track from Mack's acting debut. Sienna turned to me. "Do you think J. Chris is—"

She abruptly shut her mouth. Weird. I was going to press her for more, but then I got an idea. Despite the recording success, J. Chris hadn't given up acting. Though they'd never been in the same film, she and Mack had collaborated on music. The couple was up for Silver Sphere Awards for "Best Actress in a Movie," "Best Actor in a Movie," and "Best Song from a Movie." If that wasn't enough, they were also hosting this year's awards show. Which meant they'd probably been at the nominee party. Which meant they probably got the gift bag. Which meant the staff at Wheelhouse wouldn't be surprised if "Janet Christie," or rather her assistants, came in to pick up a bike.

After we used the bathroom, I explained my plan to Sienna, ignored Aubrey's protests, and called Emme to have her help out. Once we were all set, I called Wheelhouse and spoke with a woman. Then we dropped Aubrey off in Silver Lake, stopped by Omari's apartment to pick up his gift certificate, and drove back to West Hollywood. It took us a good two hours, which was perfect. My idea needed time to truly percolate.

Sienna and I fine-tuned our plan of attack during the ride over. I also changed the display photo associated with Emme's number on my phone. By the time we got back to Wheelhouse, we both knew exactly what to do.

"Remember, I'm bad cop this time," Sienna said as we strode into Wheelhouse's flagship. Yes, we took turns.

The store had two main sections. Up first was a showroom packed tight with Wheelhouse workout gear, cycling shoes, and branded weights. It also housed a few of their brand-spanking-new in-home bikes. Try before you buy and all that.

Beyond that was a hallway leading to the studio. I knew this because a sign said *Studio* and I could hear the faint hum of Beyoncé. A class was going full throttle somewhere off in the Wheelhouse abyss. We stopped in front of a retail counter. A woman poured over a magazine. The aforementioned Sweetie, if the name tag was to be believed.

"Ugh, Toni Abrams is really letting herself go. She looks like a hippo." Sweetie didn't look up while she spoke, although she was clearly talking to us. No one else was there. "If it's for a role, she better get an Oscar."

Spoiler Alert. Sweetie was not very sweet. I looked to see what she was reading. The infamous "Stars Are Just Like Us!" page of *Us Weekly*. Toni was outside Versailles restaurant off La Cienega Boulevard. She'd been tearing into a piece of garlic chicken and the camera had caught her mid-chew. It wasn't a pretty sight. At all.

Anyone would have looked bad in that type of pic. Movie star or not. Problem was, we were dealing with an "or not." It wasn't a photo of Toni. It was Emme. She was indeed the bigger of the twins. If you considered a size two to be big.

And people wondered why Emme barely left her house.

I pointed to the photo. "You think that's big?"

Sweetie still didn't look up. "Hey, if the shoe fits and the outfit doesn't . . ."

Geez, she was a cranky one. Perhaps because she'd been subsisting on kale, hot air, and judgement for most of her adult life. Any guilt I felt about my forthcoming lie went as ghost as Casper. "If that's a hippo, then you must think I'm Godzilla."

Sweetie looked up long enough to give me a once over. She didn't say anything. She didn't have to. Her expression said it all.

Since we were apparently judging appearances and what not, I took her in. It was a given she'd fit right in at the "Mean Girls" lunch table if only she wasn't twenty-plus years too old. It was clear she was still searching for the fountain of eternal youth. It was also clear that she hadn't found it. Her body was as fat-free as skim milk. Her skin happened to be just as pale. If it weren't for the perfectly ponytailed red hair, I'd have mistaken her for a skeleton. I wasn't impressed. In the least. "Now are we done with the critique so you can actually do your job?" I said.

Sienna glanced at me. We'd agreed she would play bad cop, but that was B.S.—Before Sweetie.

"You have to excuse my friend." Sienna reluctantly fell into her new role. "She got up in the wrong bed this morning."

"You mean wrong side of the bed," I said.

Sienna leaned toward Sweetie and whispered loud enough so I could hear, "I don't. She didn't even get his name. I told her not to have that fourth drink."

They both laughed and Sweetie looked ready to give Sienna the other half of a "Best Friends Forever" necklace. "How can I help *you*?" It was clear by her tone that Sweetie literally meant just Sienna. I wasn't offended. At all.

"We're here to pick up an order. Should be under Keila Somers." That was the name I'd picked for our cover story. Sienna held up the certificate. It was Omari's, of course, but that was need-to-know information. And Sweetie clearly did not need to know.

Sweetie pushed some buttons on a laptop, then stared at the screen. "You're all set." I already knew that, since we'd been the one to call and set it up. "You didn't even have to come in. It's scheduled to be delivered this evening," Sweetie said.

"Delivered?" I turned to Sienna, channeling my Sweetie-induced rage into the role. "You set it up for delivery?"

We had, but that had been part of the plan. Sienna played her role to perfection. "Of course not. I clearly told the girl on the phone it was a pickup. We all know J. does not do delivery. Not food. Not flowers. Certainly not bikes. There must be some mistake."

I addressed Sweetie but looked at Sienna. "Was there, Sweetie? A mistake?"

Out the corner of my eye, I saw Sweetie shake her head. "It's already on the truck."

"But *we* called and explained the situation, right?" Again, I directed my ire at Sienna. It was called method acting. Brando had won an

Oscar for it. Two, in fact. "*We* explained that our boss didn't like deliveries. Didn't *we*?"

"We did," Sienna said. We actually didn't. Another part of my plan. "Is the truck still here?" she asked Sweetie.

Sweetie nodded.

"Can't you just take it off the truck?" Sienna asked.

"We'd have to take every bike off, and we have a lot of deliveries."

"Can we talk to the manager?" I asked.

"That would be me," Sweetie said. Of course it would. With her sunny disposition she had to be the owner's second wife's third cousin once removed.

"I understand." Sienna turned back to me. "You should call her right now and explain the mistake."

"*I* should call her? And explain *your* mistake?"

Sienna nodded. "You're the executive assistant, remember? I'm just the personal assistant. You're the one always throwing your seniority in my face."

My phone rang right on cue. "Oh look, she's calling." I finally turned to Sweetie as I got out my phone, making sure she saw the caller ID pic. "It's our boss."

# Six

Sweetie's eyes bugged out when she realized who the order was for. Or at least who she *thought* it was for. I'd gotten the J. Chris pic off of Instagram—a "no makeup" shot posted thirty-four weeks back. I knew from past experience people changed their tune when they thought you were talking to an A-list celebrity, especially one with as bad of a diva reputation as J. Chris. TMZ kept a running log of how many cell phones she'd destroyed by throwing them at poor assistants and salesgirls' faces. I believe it was up to seventeen, but I hadn't checked in the last five or so minutes. The number could've grown.

I hit answer. "Hi, Ms. Christie. It's Keila."

"As in Tequila?" Emme asked from miles away. "You got your fake name from liquor?"

"No!" I said. "Not your personal assistant. That's Sheila. This is your executive assistant."

"Keila and Sheila? You knew they rhymed when you chose these names, didn't you?"

"Yep. We're at Wheelhouse but there's a slight issue with your bike."

"Should I yell now?"

"Not yet," I said. "They won't let us take the bike with us. They'll only deliver it."

"What about now? Can I yell now? Can I? Can I? Can I?"

"*Yes*," I said. "I did tell them who you were. They don't seem too concerned with keeping your business private."

Emme let me have it. "Look here Tequila. Brandy. Champagne. Whatever your name is. I gave you exactly one job to do. One!"

I pulled the phone away from my ear all shocked-like so Sweetie could hear. Every. Single. Word. "I have my interview with Gus the Gossip in a few hours," Emme continued. That is, J. Chris did. I'd checked. You can't say a girl doesn't do her research. "I can't be concerned with this. Tell them if that bike even drives past my house, I will destroy them."

Yes, it was melodramatic. It was also accurate. J. Chris had dropped a "I'll destroy you" during a disagreement with a flower place over being sent a white rose bouquet. I'd read about it—and every other detail—in a wrongful termination lawsuit filed by her fourth assistant.

"They won't let you pick it up? Who told you these lies?" Emme went on. "Give me their name. Now!"

I glanced at Sweetie, who shook her head frantically.

"I have to get her name. Let me call you right back." I hung up. "How quickly can we get the bike off your truck?"

Not bothering to wait, I walked to the back of the building. Sienna scurried behind me. Sweetie was right behind her yapping a mile a minute. "You can't go back there!"

I turned back to her. "I'm trying to save our jobs. All of our jobs. We'll look through the bikes. When we find it, you get it off the truck.

Or just rip the dang address label off it. I don't care. But that bike cannot make it to that house."

Within minutes the three of us were in the truck staring at boxes upon boxes of stationary bikes packed tighter than a freshly botoxed face. The labels were stuck in a top corner of each box for easy viewing. "VIP orders have a pink sticker," Sweetie said. "Let Jimmy know when you find it and he'll take it off." She motioned to a worker a few feet away who was paying us no mind. "I gotta get back to the front desk. Make sure you let Ms. Christie know how accommodating we were."

And with that, she was gone. I was surprised she'd leave us alone, but it wasn't like we could stick a 125-pound bike down our pants and sneak out.

Luckily, there were only about fifteen pink stickers, which was fine by me. I hadn't been this happy to be in the back of a truck since high school. "You know the plan," I reminded Sienna. "Take a pic of all the addys. We'll have Emme look them up later and see if any could possibly belong to our killer."

We worked in blissful silence. I recognized a few names and several streets. Nominees clearly weren't passing up the free swag. I had a great rhythm going when Sienna called out from somewhere in the depths. "Found it!"

She sounded confident. Almost too confident. I came over for a closer look. The box was addressed to a R. Jones who lived in Ferndale. "You sure?" I asked, just to be, well, sure.

"Have you heard of Ferndale?"

"Nope."

"Me neither. And if I don't recognize a place that means only one thing. No one famous has lived there. Ever. This is our guy."

I believed her, but still. "Let's look at the last couple. Just in case."

Five minutes later, we were walking back to the car. Unfortunately, we had to pass Sweetie, once again immersed in her magazine at the front desk. Glad to see she was working hard. "You find the bike?" she called out as we speed-walked by.

"Yeah, but she changed her mind," I said. "You can deliver it. She consulted her spiritual advisor, who said it's a good day for deliveries." The address they were shipping the bike to was Emme's apartment, anyway.

Three hours later, Sienna, the bike, and I were all crowded into Emme's living room. The delivery guy—a different one from Jimmy—had just finished setting it up. Emme stared at the bike, then looked at me. "IDK." I don't know.

"You said you wanted to exercise more," I said. "Now you can take spin classes and not leave your house. I figured you'd love it."

"Sigh," she said, in lieu of actually sighing. "Fine. You win." I didn't know it was a competition, yet I still treasured the victory. "I'll send you video of me on it from my new Focals."

"If you get them," I said, knowing full well she would get them and I would be the one buying them for her. She knew it too, which made it all the more frustrating.

"Right," she said. Then, "You have the addresses?" Emme had found some quite possibly illegal fancy software online that did instant background checks.

"I already know which one it is," Sienna said.

"Maybe R. Jones is someone's assistant," I said.

"Not a chance. Hollywood assistants are the ultimate wannabes. They aren't living in Ferndale. They probably live in ritzier neighborhoods than their bosses."

Touché, but still. I called out an address. Emme typed it in, fingers flying over the keyboard. But Sienna was faster. "That's Leo DiCaprio's Malibu house."

Emme nodded. "Right."

I gave her the next address. Once again, Sienna spoke up. "Reese's beach house."

"Ding. Ding."

It was a good party trick. I made a mental note to ask her to bust it out at our next get-together. I gave Sienna my phone. "In the interest of time, let me know if you don't recognize any of these addresses. While you do that, Emme can look up the Ferndale addy?"

I read it off. Emme tapped a few buttons, then spoke. "The R stands for Regina,"

Blurg. "Anyone live with her?"

"IDK," Emme said. "No one else is listed."

I'm the first to admit black people can definitely get creative with names, but it was rare even for us to name a boy Regina. Maybe she was someone's poor assistant after all. Emme motioned to a monitor. "No Facebook or Twitter. Did find her Instagram. It's private though."

I looked. The page was indeed locked. All we could see was her profile pic. On Emme's gigantic monitor, Regina looked almost life-size. She wore a tank top and on her arm was a tattoo. A rose that turned into a clock. The top featured some very familiar cogs.

Regina Jones must have been one of those people with her phone permanently attached to her hand because she accepted my follow request almost immediately. Of course, she didn't follow the Ms. Lady of the Red Vine fan account back. As Sienna pointed out, that was kind of rude. We needed as many followers as possible. Plus, she would miss out on some great shots.

Regina clearly wasn't the killer. She had boobs. The guy in the surveillance footage didn't. The first photo on her page was her cuddled up. Unfortunately, it wasn't with a man with a matching tattoo. It was with a statue. One made of dingy brown metal sculpted into a curly haired woman giving a side-eye for the ages. She had her legs crossed and arm casually propped on back of a bench. The bench was coincidentally made from the same material, which gave the effect that the woman had been waiting for something for so long that she'd mummified.

"It's Lucy!" I said. "They're in Palm Springs!"

Sienna and I had taken a trip out there a couple of years back and went full tourist. The Lucille Ball statue had been one of our first stops. We had the pictures to prove it, including one of Sienna thrusting her own boobs out right next to Lucy's as if comparing the goods.

I read the caption. "Mr. Wonderful got me going on vacay. #MrWonderful #Surprise #Vacay #Needed #ILoveLucy #ILove Him #TooBlessedToBeStressed #Love #ILoveMyLife."

Personally, I thought it was #Overkill but apparently one couldn't have too many hashtags, just like one couldn't have too many friends. Regina didn't hashtag where they were staying, but then she didn't have to. I was guessing it was the hotel from the swag bag.

"So, she's dating a murderer," Emme said.

"Looks like it," I answered. "The ink. The bike. Now the trip to Palm Springs. It all added up."

"We're going to Palm Springs!" Sienna couldn't mask the excitement in her voice and realized it too. She opened her mouth again, attempting to sound more solemn. "For work."

"Not yet," I said.

She motioned to Emme's Gigantor computer screen. "The photo was posted three hours ago. They're there. We need to catch him in the act … of tanning."

"We just need a photo or a name, which we can get from here. Let's keep checking her page."

We combed the rest of her Instagram in hopes of finding a photo of her beloved. We got zilch. Apparently, the only thing Regina liked more than hashtags was selfies—893 to be exact. And not in a single one did she bother to clean her bathroom mirror. Though there were quite a few mentions of Mr. Wonderful there wasn't a single picture. Regina also didn't tag his account or mention his real name.

"I guess Mr. Wonderful is a tad photo shy," I finally said.

"Are we sure he even exists?" Sienna asked. We'd had a previous experience with a make-believe boyfriend.

"Yep. This's one is on tape," I said.

Sienna smiled again. "Palm Springs it is!"

I still wasn't quite ready to go the confrontation route. "I'm gonna send her a DM."

It read: *Mr. Wonderful might not be who you think he is. Plz call.*

I included my cell number.

And with that, we parted ways. I headed to Omari's. Sienna went home to get ready to go out with her friend Fab. Emme went back to her simulation game. Our own versions of pure bliss.

Omari was home with no pressing party invitations, which meant I had him to myself. We went to bed very early, went to sleep very late, and woke up the next morning to his landline ringing. Yes, Omari still had a landline. He picked it up and mumbled a few words before thrusting the phone in my general vicinity. "For you."

I was instantly awake and in full panic mode. Had bill collectors tracked me down to Omari's place? I was tempted to just hang up.

Then I remembered I'd actually paid Sallie Mae. She had no reason to send her attack dogs after me. But still. "Who is it?" I asked.

"Nina."

That made me want to hang up even more. I took the phone anyway. "Hello ... "

"You know who killed Lyla." It was more statement than question.

I was instantly confused. "I have a lead. That's it. It might not even pan out."

"That's not what TMZ says."

"Let me call you back."

I hung up and opened the TMZ app on my phone. Sure enough, it was the lead story. *"No Chicken! Former Chubby's Spokesperson and Ms. Lady of the Red Vine Solve Publicist's Murder?"*

They'd even thoughtfully created a graphic of me holding a piece of fried chicken in one hand and a pair of handcuffs in the other. To make it even worse, they'd superimposed Sienna next to me, holding a piece of Red Vine licorice and a gun. She'd love it.

Omari looked over my shoulder, saw what I was looking at, and went right back to sleep. "Way too early for this."

It really was. Still, I trucked on, not even bothering with the article. My brain wasn't up yet. No way could I read anything longer than a sentence. Luckily, there was video. Sienna and Fab filled the screen as soon as I hit *play*. They walked out of a club and directly addressed the camera. The cameraman was off screen but I recognized the voice. Razzle.

"So Ms. Red Vine. Solve any more murders?"

Sienna just smiled coyly. That's why she was my girl. Unfortunately, Fab jumped in. "Stop being modest! She already found the guy who killed that dead publicist!"

Sienna's eyes bugged out, words tumbling out her mouth. "We haven't found anyone. We may have found someone connected to the guy."

Fab kept on like Sienna hadn't even opened her mouth. "His girlfriend. Thanks to Sienna, the police will have the guy behind bars in no time. Why send the police when you got Ms. Lady of the Red Vine?"

And with that, the screen went black. It was only eight a.m. and the article already had over 1,000 comments. Like an Ultimate Fails compilation, it'd gone viral.

Fudge.

I checked my phone. Fifteen missed calls from numbers I didn't recognize. Almost the same numbers of texts, all starting with variations of "I'm a reporter with ... " There was also one from Sienna. *So sorry! Begged Razzle not to use it. At least TMZ put a question mark at the end of the headline!*

I wrote back telling her not to worry about it. It wasn't her fault.

Of course, even though it wasn't her fault, it was a problem. I needed chocolate. Stat.

Sienna had an audition that morning, so I was on my own for lunch. I was narrowing down my choices when the phone rang. I assumed it was Daddy until I glanced at the caller ID. Private number.

When I picked up, the only thing that greeted me was lots of heavy breathing. I thought maybe it was a crank call. Then I remembered no one did that anymore. It was way easier to send an anonymous tweet or Instagram comment.

I was about to hang up when she spoke. "You obviously ain't sleeping with him yet or you wouldn't be contacting me."

"Excuse me?"

"You heard me." Indeed, I had. That didn't mean it made one iota of sense. "You're the one all up in my DMs and now you're acting all shy."

I realized I was talking to Regina Jones. And it didn't sound like she'd checked TMZ that morning.

"Oh yes," I said. "Mr. Wonderful."

"More like Mr. One Minute." Well, dang. "But you'll find out soon enough since apparently he can't wait to see you. Can't believe him. Leaving me to go and see some skinny-sounding heifer."

Skinny-sounding? Not gonna lie. That made me happy. I was about to thank her too when I realized she assumed I was Mr. One Minute's side chick. In my two months of PI-dom, I quickly realized one thing. There was no one more bitter in life—and "more better" in interviewing—than a woman scorned. They told everything to everyone. See above about his bedroom skills.

Of course, I also knew one thing a scorned woman hated more than her cheating significant other—the chick he cheated on her with.

I briefly flirted with going along with it. Best case scenario, Regina would want to meet in some parking lot and I could question her while simultaneously avoiding her trying to beat my butt. It would take some multitasking but perhaps I was up to the challenge. But what if I wasn't? I tuned back in to find Regina still on her tear. "Taking my car. Leaving me here. After he claimed he was taking me away because he loved me so much. Junior knows I gotta work tonight."

I latched on to the word *Junior* like a teenaged girl on to a boy band member. I had a name. Unfortunately, a very, very, very vague one. One probably not government issued and if it was, it meant he probably had three other names that went in front of it. First, middle and last. Unless I wanted to leave a message on the tip line that Lyla Davis was killed by Junior, who also went by Mr. Wonderful or Mr. One

Minute depending on how his girl was feeling about him that day, I needed his full name. I thought quickly. "I'm not his new girlfriend. I just need to confirm that he's the same person in our records. Can you just spell his full name for me so I can check if it's right?"

I smiled then, all proud of myself. Regina was not nearly as impressed. "He owe you money?"

"Not at all."

"You the police?"

I caved and went with the truth. "A private investigator."

But the only thing that answered me was complete silence. Regina Jones had hung up. Blurg.

# Seven

I replayed the conversation. It was clear Regina was still in Palm Springs and this Junior was not, which meant he was on the run or, more likely, back in Los Angeles. A Los Angeles that covered 503 miles and housed almost four million people.

If Regina wouldn't help me, maybe the Celebration Hotel would. I found their number online and called. It took three automated messages and two fulfilled requests to push two before I spoke to someone with a pulse.

"Welcome to Celebration, this is Janeen. Come celebrate with us!"

"Yes, hi, Janeen! Can you please transfer me to Regina Jones' room, please?" I'd used please twice, but one couldn't be too polite when one needed information to solve a murder.

There was a pause. I assumed Janeen was looking up Regina's name. Apparently, she didn't find it. "I'm sorry, but there's no one here listed under that name. Perhaps she's staying with someone else. Can you give me their name?"

Funny, I was going to ask Janeen the same exact question. "Sure thing. His name is Junior."

Another pause. I let it ride out. Janeen finally spoke first. "Junior what?"

Again, I wanted to ask her the same thing. "I don't suppose you can just search for any guest who is a junior and transfer me to one of those rooms. It doesn't matter which. I'll just keep calling back until I get the right one!"

"I'm sorry ma'am, but I'll need a name."

Since I (still) didn't have one, I said my goodbyes and hung up. It looked like my best bet would be to drive there after all. If I could talk to Regina in person, I might at least get a last name. I didn't need much more than that.

Palm Springs was a straight two-hour shot eastbound on the 10. It was in the desert, a fact they share with pride. Being a water girl myself—black girls not wanting to get their hair wet is a myth—I never saw the appeal of it. Judging by the number of visitors each year, others clearly didn't share my lack of enthusiasm for sand with no water next to it.

I was tempted to wait for Sienna, especially since I knew she had her heart set on a Palm Springs "stakeout," but she was still at her audition. I sent off a quick text asking if she was almost done and waited fifteen very long minutes without a reply. As much as I wanted to wait, I couldn't.

The longer I waited, the better the chance Regina would leave—or worse, make up with Junior. I could be there and back without Sienna even knowing I'd gone without her.

I gathered my purse and a snack or five for the road, then ran to my parking space. My car wasn't there. I started hyperventilating. The building's parking lot was underground and gated. Not to mention the car that parked next to me was a Porsche Boxster convertible with an owner often too lazy to push the button to put the top back up. Why steal a twelve-year-old bright pink Infiniti when you could steal a Porsche? Everyone, including aspiring car thieves, should aim high in their profession of choice.

I was about to call the police when I remembered something. My car wasn't stolen. It was still in the shop. Apparently my car issues were deeper than just a battery. Something about a corroded terminal. The mechanic had promised to have it fixed by five. Great for the long term. Not so great when I needed to get to Palm Springs right then and there. I needed a ride. Sienna was out. Both Omari and Emme would let me borrow their cars but that still meant I needed to get *to* them. And it could take an hour in LA traffic.

Luckily, I knew someone who could help. Dante picked up on the second ring.

"Hi! This is Dayna Anderson, you probably don't remember me—"

"The soon-to-be-licensed investigator. Yeah, I don't remember you at all."

"Good, because I'd hate for you to remember me for that." Talking to him reminded me I needed to print out the application and get it to Aubrey. "Any chance you can give me a ride to Palm Springs? I need to get to the Celebration Hotel. ASAP."

"Impromptu vacation?"

"Work actually. Lyla's case. Like I said, we really want to help find her killer."

I was more than happy to leave it at that. Dante, however, pressed on. "Glad to hear it, but someone told me you already found the guy."

"Just a lead. We don't have a name yet though know he may be in Palm Springs. His girlfriend definitely is. I tried to talk to her but she hung up before she told me anything more than the guy is called

Junior. I want to drive out there to speak to her. At least camp out in the lobby until they show up. How much for you to take me?"

"I couldn't charge you. I have a pickup at three, but let me make some calls and see if I can get someone to do it for me."

"That'd be great."

After we hung up, it was another forty-five minutes before my phone rang again. I spent the gap telling myself not to look at the clock and then glancing at it anyway. It made the time crawl by like the 405 at five p.m. after it's rained for longer than five minutes.

When the phone did finally ring, it wasn't even Dante. "I start work at seven. Meet me at 6:45. M&M's in Carson."

And with that, Regina hung up on me for a second time. Perhaps this was her version of chatty. She had even called from a non-private number. I wasn't going to question it. Just like I wasn't going to question why she'd suddenly changed her mind. Instead, I called Aubrey. When I got his voicemail, I left a message giving him a G-rated version of what I'd been up to. One that omitted anything that may inspire a lecture.

Sienna also hadn't texted me back. Either the audition had gone longer than she'd expected or she'd gone shopping after. It looked like I'd be meeting Regina on my own. I forced myself to look at the bright side.

Unlike Palm Springs, Carson was only about twenty miles away. And I'd have my car, with its newly uncorroded terminal. I texted Dante, letting him know I no longer needed a ride. He had that appointment at three and the mechanic was in walking distance. Then I pulled up the M&M's menu. Since I was going down there anyway, I might as well get dinner.

I spent the entire forty-five-minute car ride brainstorming ways to get Regina to talk. While driving east on the 10, I came up with idea number one. I'd already asked Regina to confirm Junior's full name. I could stick with that thread, asking her again while pretending I had it already written on a piece of paper. I dubbed it the "If it ain't broke, why fix it" option.

When I merged onto the 110 south, I came up with my "Molly, you in danger, girl" option. Make her think the police were on to her and she needed to let them know about Junior or risk going to jail herself. Could be true for all I knew. After all, we'd found her from nothing more than a bag full of free stuff. Of course, that plan only worked if she really wasn't in on it. I hoped for my sake that was the case.

By the time I took the exit for the 91 West, I came up with the "Help a sister out" option. I knew Junior did it. I knew she—fingers crossed—had nothing to do with it, but if I'd found her it was only a matter of time that the police would too. Give me his name and I'd keep her out of it. No one would know she snitched.

I got to M&Ms fifteen minutes early. The restaurant was nestled in a bland beige and white strip mall so close to the 91 I could smell the exhaust. Its neighbors were a UPS store and a Starbucks. Though the parking lot was sprinkled with cars, I only saw one human and even then it was just a body part—an ample rump bending over as its owner leaned into some pitch black Mercedes with tacky bright gold hubcaps and random etchings in the dark black windows.

I went inside and placed two to-go orders. When I came back out, the car was gone. The butt's owner, however, was still there. I recognized the neck ink before the rest of her. I blamed not seeing her through the foggy lens of a dirty mirror like in her endless selfies. I walked over, a smile plastered on my face to show I came in peace.

"Regina, hi? I'm Dayna Anderson."

She said nothing, opting instead for a nod of recognition. I handed her a card. She took it without even glancing at it and I had no doubt it would be in the garbage before I got out of the parking lot.

"Sorry, I saw you talking to someone so I ran inside."

"Yeah, rich folks are always getting lost on the way to the StubHub Center." Her voice was matter-of-fact.

I nodded, not because I cared about lost rich people. I was busy reviewing my carefully planned-out investigative options. Now that I'd seen her in person, I decided "Molly, you in danger, girl" would be my best bet. "I know you're wondering why I wanted to me—"

"Javon Reid." Again with the matter-of-factness. It took me a second to realize what she was telling me, the name on Junior's birth certificate. I wanted to do the time-out sign so I could cartwheel around the parking lot. I didn't even care that she could have told me the name on the phone. Besides, if she had, I wouldn't have gotten dinner so …

"So Junior's real name is Javon?" I wanted to be 110 percent sure.

She nodded. "That's what you wanted, right? When you tried that 'confirm the spelling' BS."

It was indeed what I wanted. Despite my enthusiasm, I made a note to self to permanently strike "If it ain't broke, don't fix it" from my investigation techniques since apparently it was broke. Very broke at that.

"You want his number?"

I did. She rattled it off and I quickly plugged it into my phone. Not that I'd call him. It wasn't because I hated talking on the phone. I hated talking to possible murderers.

"We done here?" Regina asked before I could get out as much as a thank you.

We weren't. Why was she suddenly being so forthcoming? I was torn between asking her that or just asking her more questions. I went with option B. "So, you know what Javon did?"

She shook her head. "Junior's always doing something. Didn't even bother to ask why he had those marks on him. I'm sick of it. Just like I'm sick of him. You know he never came back, right? He can stay his butt at his grandmother's house. She lives right on my block, but I can't come over though because she doesn't like me. He can take me to Palm Springs. Tell me that he's got some surprise coming to *my* house. But he can't take me to see his grandmother? Who lives right on my block."

She laughed, but she sounded as bitter as the runner-up to Miss America.

"Men," I said, because really, what else needed to be spoken. Then I got serious. I needed confirmation Javon/Junior was the right guy. "Do you know where Junior was the night of the 9th?"

"Not with me. Maybe ask his grandma. I don't wanna know about whatever he's involved in."

I mimed zipping my mouth closed and throwing away the key. She'd learn soon enough anyway.

"I learned early on not to ask too many questions," she said. "But I'm not stupid. Trust that. Didn't expect him to steal my car though."

"You call the police?"

Regina looked at me like I was the one who was stupid. "What if they arrested him?"

I figured that was the point but I wisely didn't say that. Instead, I let her keep talking.

"He's always said he'd rather die than go back to jail. No way I'm gonna have that on my conscience. He's ruined my life enough already. Anything else?"

I was tempted to ask for a picture but realized I might be pressing my luck. It was probably online anyway. Instead I shook my head and she walked away without so much as a high five, which was more than fine. My takeout was probably ready.

Javon "Junior" Reid's photo was online all right, but while his girlfriend preferred selfies, he preferred mug shots. I counted five for various counts of robbery and petty theft. He was nothing if not consistent. I definitely wouldn't have cast him as Thug #5 or anything like that, though. He had a baby face through and through, from the large eyes to the cheeks that looked like an overblown helium balloon. He looked just as high in his most recent mug shot. It did a little, but not much, to lessen the impact of the baby face. I bet when he smiled, he flashed dimples. Made you wonder if the not very threatening face was a factor in the very threatening lifestyle choice.

The tattoo must've been recent because it wasn't in any mug shots. Maybe it was a "Please baby please" gift from the last time he made Regina mad. A last-ditch effort to apologize.

Matching tattoos were apparently the twenty-first-century sign of true love. My college boyfriend had wanted us to get each other's names tatted on our respective chests. The only thing that stopped me was my fear of needles, which was a godsend. Otherwise, my dating pool would be permanently limited to men named Dontrell. It would have made me destined to die alone.

Junior and Regina obviously felt differently. Of course, I'd never have the chance to confirm it with him because I had no plans to ever talk to him. Confronting a killer was way above my pay grade. Been there. Done that. Passed out in front of a group of tourists immediately afterwards. Definitely something I planned to keep as a once-in-a-lifetime experience. Kind of like getting an STD.

I scanned Junior's photos once more as I continued my convo with Aubrey. I'd finally gotten him on the phone for an update.

"So Ms. Jones just volunteered his name without any persuasion?" Aubrey said when I'd finally shut up. "Why?"

I'd had the same thought myself. It didn't stop me from being annoyed. "Because I'm a crack investigator?"

"You are clearly not a modest one, Ms. Anderson."

"Honestly? She realizes he's involved but at the same time doesn't trust the police. Doesn't want to snitch. It's easier to tell me and have me tell the police. It's like we're her snitch surrogates. Call it trickle down snitching if you prefer that term instead."

"I do not," he said. "In fact, I do not like any of it."

At the moment, I didn't like him. I was sky-high, floating on my inflated ego, and he was doing his utmost to bring me back down to reality. "Look, we got the name. Maybe only because his girlfriend is mad at him. But who cares? This isn't the movies. Sometimes people just give you the name." I took a deep breath. "I need to go and call the tip line."

It wasn't the best excuse I'd ever given anyone—that was reserved for Sundays growing up when I didn't want to go to church and would magically have a "big test" I needed to stay home and study for. For Mama, the only thing that trumped the Bible was my science textbook. As much as she loved Reverend Stewart, he wasn't personally giving out college scholarships. Not when he had a church building fund.

After I hung up, I realized I'd once again forgotten to tell Aubrey about the application for the PI license. Fudge. I made a mental note to finally go get it printed out.

I waited to finish eating before I called the tip line. I told myself it was because I was hungry. In reality, I was avoiding the Voice. The Voice was one of the people who manned the Crime Stoppers toll-free tip line. I'd never seen her in person. If I did, I'd probably cross the street. She was up there with Regina when it came to sunny demeanors. We hadn't spoken since the Haley Joseph hit-and-run case. I'd only called the tip line on a few occasions since then and had lucked out and gotten someone, well, nice each time.

But that didn't stopped the sense of dread I felt every time I had to call the number. It was like the climax of a horror movie, except I was clothed when I called. Usually. Whenever the female lead opened a door, she never knew if the bad guy was waiting behind it. Well, whenever I called the 800 number, I never knew if the Voice would answer.

I dialed and waited. It rang. Once. Twice. Three times. Just when I thought I'd have to leave a message, someone picked up. "Tip line."

It was her.

I took in a breath, then dove in. "Yes, I have a tip regarding the murder of Lyla Davis."

I waited. She said nothing. Just loudly chewed her gum. So I waited some more. Maybe she'd blow a bubble. Spice things up. Finally, she spoke. "What are you waiting for?"

"Oh. I thought you had to read me my rights before I gave you any information." I'd made this mistake with her before.

"Aren't you that annoying chick who solved that hit-and-run? The one who kept calling, accusing everyone and their mama of doing it? I recognize your voice."

I should have been flattered. For some reason, I wasn't. "That's me: 1018. Anyway, I think I've been able to identify a suspect in the Davis case. Javon Reid. Goes by Junior. I have a phone number for him."

I rattled it off and quickly got off the phone.

It took the police exactly fourteen hours to confirm my tip and distribute Junior's most recent baby-faced mug shot to the broadcast stations as a "person of interest," which was police speak for "he definitely did it but we don't want to get sued." The news soon spread over social media, with enterprising Internet snoops even uncovering a long dormant Twitter account. By that afternoon, Junior had gained 20,000 followers. I wasn't one of them.

Luckily, no one connected him to Regina and her social media accounts, though I did notice she'd made them private. She also didn't answer my *You okay?* text.

Omari had the day off, so we'd spent the day sleeping together. Literally. We'd both had really long days at work. I was mid-nap number two when my phone rang. It was Sienna. I ignored it. When she immediately called back, I knew it had to be of dire importance. Either there was news about Junior or she needed help picking a new nail color. "They found him?" I asked when I picked up.

"Nope. Still on the run." She paused dramatically for ten seconds. I counted. "He's live-tweeting taunts to the police."

"No!"

"Yes."

Beside me, Omari played on his tablet. I practically snatched it to go on Twitter. #NOTSCARED and #COMEGETIT were trending in LA. Once I checked Junior's feed, I knew why. *Popo running up on my grandma. Scaring an old lady like they're tough. YOU REALLY TOUGH THEN RUN UP ON A GROWN MAN. #NOTSCARED #COMEGETIT*

He followed it up with a second tweet.

*Just know this. No way I'm going back to jail. #NOTSCARED #COMEGETIT*

"It's not smart to taunt the police," I said.

"It gets better," Sienna said. "There have been sightings. People posting photos on their Twitter, Instagram, and Snapchat. Apparently he's in a gray Honda Accord."

"Is he alone?" I thought of Regina. She still hadn't texted me back.

"One person claimed he stole his Chihuahua. So maybe not."

We went back and forth a bit more, then got off the phone. Omari and I spent the rest of the afternoon glued to our respective social media, alternating between Twitter, Insta, and Snap and calling to each other when we uncovered news.

But after his initial flurry of tweets, Junior went radio silent for the next few hours. Not that it stopped the online hunt, which had gone from legit possible sightings of gray Accords to someone photoshopping Junior's mug shot in a white Ford Bronco.

I texted Regina a couple more times to no avail. I even called her at M&Ms, but the lady who answered said she wasn't at work. I was lying in bed staring at the ceiling when Omari rushed upstairs. "He tweeted."

He showed me Junior's message: *Bye Pigs.*

"Crap," Omari said, and pointed to something on the screen.

For the first time all day, Junior had turned on his Twitter location. He clearly wanted to be found.

# Eight

They found him at two a.m., despite the location for his tweets being relegated to just longitude and latitude. Luckily the LAPD, all four local news stations, and about a kajillion Twitter users were all more adept at deciphering coordinates than I was. Junior was hiding in a residential neighborhood in Mid-City.

A couple stations dispensed news crews and helicopters so the world could watch in real time. Based on the social media activity, it did. Omari and I were no exception. The place Junior had picked looked dark and deserted, the only light emanating from a streetlight the next house over. It was soon joined by cadres of flashing cop cars. The overall effect was bad rave party.

Lights flicked on in the house, first in an upstairs window, then on the lower level behind the front door—all providing a visual trail of someone's movements inside. His or her final stop was the front door, as evidenced by the porch light turning on even though we didn't need it.

Standing in a formation that would make a Rockette proud, a row of officers were armed and ready. I'd prefer them to kick, not shoot. I didn't know if Junior was inside and if he had hostages. I still hadn't heard from Regina.

It took a moment for the door to open. A foot peeked out, clad in a fuzzy slipper. It was soon joined by the rest of her. A woman I'd never seen before came out with her hands up. Smart lady. This was clearly not Junior, but that didn't mean he wasn't inside. SWAT went to check, leaving one member to drag the woman to safety.

Within five minutes, one of the SWAT team came back out. There were several discussions, some involving the homeowner. Some not. It was a stark reminder this wasn't a movie. If it were, we'd have been able to hear every word.

Suddenly two broke off from the group and headed to the side of the house. As they walked, they were joined by others. It was like some weird flash mob, if flash mobs carried a battering ram and wore protective helmets. They reached their destination.

The garage.

Except they didn't stop. The battering ram reduced the cedar garage door to nothing more than wood chunks. A flash-bang was tossed inside, causing the garage to light up. What followed was lots of movement. Lots of chaos. Lots of questions. And lots of waiting.

It took another hour for "sources" to confirm to KTLA a body was inside, one they had "reason to believe" was Junior. He'd left the car running and the garage door shut. It wasn't clear how he'd got inside, but we would probably never know because he was dead.

Regina was opting to ignore my texts after all. I was relieved. I'd never been so happy to encounter bad manners.

After an hour of watching KTLA put the garage door footage on repeat, Omari and I accepted there wasn't going to be any more news and turned the TV off. That should've meant that I went to sleep. I couldn't.

I lay there flat on my back in the dark, eyes staring up at nothing. One person had died, which was more than enough. Junior shouldn't have died as well. I definitely hadn't intended for him to. I figured he'd be arrested and spend the rest of his life in jail too afraid to bend down for the soap.

"It was his fault." Omari spoke from somewhere next to me. I couldn't see him in the inky blackness. "No one told him to rob that publicist. No one told him to bring a gun. No one told him to shoot two people. No one told him to hide out. No one told him to run from the police."

I didn't say anything. I couldn't say anything. So Omari kept going. "And no one told him to kill himself, Day. No one."

Then he made the biggest sacrifice he could. He let me snuggle. While I hated PDA, Omari wasn't a cuddler. Normal protocol was that he stayed on his side of the bed. I was expected to do the same. So this was a big gesture. I took full advantage and we just stayed like that, me draped on him like a cheap curtain until I finally spoke. "How'd you know I was awake?"

"You weren't snoring."

"Yes, you snore, but just a tiny bit. It's more like a wheezing, like you were a cat with a really extreme case of asthma. It actually sounds exactly like when you're walking up a set of stairs."

Sienna truly thought she was making me feel better.

"Good to know," I said. "Just curious, how long has someone gone without sleeping?"

"Want me to google it?" Sienna pointed at the store model laptop she was playing with.

We were at the Staples on Wilshire where I was finally getting all eighteen pages of the Los Angeles PI license application printed. There had been no news about Junior since they'd found his body, and I'd successfully buried my guilt under a pile of Snicker wrappers and empty bags that once held marshmallows.

My phone rang. It was Aubrey. I took a few steps away so we could chat in private. "Hey! I was just thinking about you." I'd actually been thinking about how I needed to buy more Snickers and marshmallows, but he didn't need to know that. No one did. "I have something for you."

I knew I was overly perky, but, besides food, it was another way I dealt with bad news. I waited for him to ask what it was. He didn't. After thirty seconds, I pretended like he had. I waved the folder holding the PI application even though he couldn't see it over the phone. "Look, I'm gonna be honest here. I know we don't always see eye to eye. We've had our bumps in the road. But I need you. And if you really think about it, you need me too. And I think we need to make things official. A real partnership."

I paused then, which was Aubrey's cue to speak. Once again, he didn't. So I did. Again. "Yeah, I know it's a lot to process, and so let's make a date to discuss it in person. Tonight work?"

"I am afraid I am busy, Ms. Anderson."

Busy? Aubrey had no life outside of investigating. And as I clearly just mentioned, he needed to be including me if he had a case. "Okay … what about tomorrow? We can do dinner."

"I have to go, Ms. Anderson."

He hung up without even telling me why he'd called in the first place. I walked over to Sienna. "You think Aubrey has a girlfriend?"

Sienna thought about it. "I mean, he *is* sexy."

I literally gagged. Sienna turned to me excitedly. "That's exactly how you sound when you snore."

I got to Omari's a little before five to give myself plenty of time to nap. I debated if I should record myself. Part of me wanted to find out if I did indeed sound like an asthmatic kitty cat when I slept and part of me was quite content never, ever having that info confirmed.

I'd just started the *record* feature on my cell when it rang. I checked the ID. *DNA*. Short for "Do Not Answer."

So, of course I did. DNA was usually reserved for exes and I was never one to pass up a chance to curse out an ex. I'd even hunted down Dontrelle's number just so I could add it to my phone with DNA listed.

"Good afternoon." Even from across town, Nina's voice sounded like nails on a chalkboard. Ugh. "Omari mentioned you might be able to help get his mother ready for the awards."

I decided to play nice. "Yep. I have a friend who is a makeup artist."

"Great! I really appreciate you being so onboard with this. Anyway, I never thanked you for helping solve Lyla's murder. Of course, the police are dragging their feet on officially closing the investigation."

"Yeah, LAPD just doesn't take your word for it that someone's guilty. They actually expect twelve other people to agree with you, to the point of offering an actual conviction." Considering how many people I'd falsely accused during my first case, this was definitely a good thing.

"He's dead," Nina said. "There's not going to be a trial, so why wait? I figure you can pick up the reward check tomorrow."

I'd forgotten that the Silver Sphere Organization was offering a reward. But now that I remembered, I was instantly suspicious. "Why the rush?"

"It's like they say, the show must go on. I want to get this unpleasantness out of the way so we can focus on having the best Silver Sphere Awards ever. It is the biggest party of the year, after all."

They always talk about PR professionals "spinning" the story. Nina was spinning harder than a Beverly Hills trophy wife in the front row at Wheelhouse.

"You can just pick up your check at the Silver Sphere Award Nominee Conversation Series," she added. Her voice was so casual that it took me a second to realize what she was talking about.

"Oh, the press conference."

"No, the Silver Sphere Award Nominee Conversation Series, where our nominees have a chance to sit in front of a rapt audience of journalists and answer their most burning questions."

"Like they do at a press conference ... "

It used to be a luncheon. But some accountant realized that a bunch of actors weren't going to eat anyway, and so the Silver Sphere Award Nominee Conversation Series was born.

"I thought it would be quite fitting to present the reward to you and your friends then, so you all can be properly thanked for your contribution to bringing justice for Lyla," Nina said. "Lyla's driver has already agreed to come."

My eyes narrowed. The whole thing reeked of a publicity stunt, and not even a good one at that. The tip line was supposed to be anonymous, yet Nina wanted to use my tip for promotion. I guess waiting for the LAPD to officially close the case was not helpful to Nielsen ratings. She had a show to promote, and handing over a nice check would be a great photo op.

"Yeah, that's going to be a hard pass from me." I still felt guilty about Junior's suicide. The last thing I wanted was to be applauded for it.

"We'll just do a quick bit about Lyla and then present you with the $500,000 check, take a few pictures, and you can be on your sweet little way. You won't have to say a word."

At least that's what I think she said. My brain stopped working after it heard $500,000. I knew there was a reward, but I assumed it was along the $15,000 or so the LAPD normally offered.

My mind flashed to what I could do with the money. After Aubrey, Emme, and Sienna got their portions, I'd still have a good amount. I could help my parents with their house, give some to charity, rebuild my savings, buy a new car, and, most important, give some to Dante and Regina. If she ever responded to my text.

It was settled. "So what time is this Conversation Series?" I asked.

It turns out I do snore. However, Sienna was wrong. I do not sound like a cat with breathing issues. I sound like a dog toy being drowned in Jell-O. I wanted to make amends to anyone I'd ever slept in the same room with, starting with my parents, continuing on to Shanna Monroe, whose house I was at every weekend in sixth grade, and not stopping until I personally apologized to Omari. I'd have to sleep naked in hopes of distracting him from the wretched noise emitting from my mouth.

I brainstormed other distraction methods as I made my way to Aubrey's place. He was a fourth-generation Angeleno, which made him almost as rare as an actress with all her original parts (body parts, not roles). An elder Adams clan member had purchased a plot of land off a hill in Silver Lake and even had had the wherewithal to build three apartments into the side of it. The apartments were topped off with what was the main house. Aubrey rented the house and two of the apartments out, opting to stay in the studio squished like a bug between them.

It saved him money, but it also made it hard to avoid visitors. As I knocked on his door, I could see his shadow moving around inside and heard him walk the ten steps to answer it. He was holding his bike helmet and looked surprised to see me. "Ms. Anderson, what do I owe this pleasure?"

"You owe it to not returning any of my phone calls. If I didn't know better, I'd think you were avoiding me."

He clearly looked on his way somewhere, so I handed him an envelope. I'd shoved the license application inside it, which made the contents bulge like the Rock's muscles. With the Conversation Series the next day, I wanted to at least be able to say that ASAP Investigations was in the process of being licensed, if anyone asked.

"What is this, Ms. Anderson?"

"Open it and see! You got my message about the Silver Sphere press conference?" Aubrey was the only person I knew who actually checked voicemail. "I figured we could go together."

"I am going to pass," he said. "This was really your case, Ms. Anderson. You should be the one at the press conference. Now if you will excuse me, I am running late."

He placed the envelope a counter, shut the door behind him, and walked to his bike. Aubrey didn't run late. He was gone before I could even ask him where he was going. Something was up. Once again, I flashed on the idea of him investigating without me. Maybe he realized he didn't need me after all.

I was late, but in my defense, it was nearly impossible to find parking. It didn't help that a tour bus took up four spaces in the already too tight parking lot. I was pretty sure it belonged to one of the hosts, Mack Christie—the down-home Texas boy apparently so scared to fly that he traveled everywhere in a deluxe apartment on wheels.

Once inside, a PA rushed me backstage since they'd already started. The Silver Sphere Award Nominee Conversation Series setup looked more like a Broadway production than a press conference. It didn't help that it literally took place on a stage. One that had a gray rug and a row of life-size Silver Sphere Awards anchoring both sides of the stage. Someone had also set up a six-foot-tall portrait of Lyla's face.

SSO President Gus the Gossip held court at a podium in front and waxed poetic about Lyla's life. Sienna and I watched from offstage right. Emme had refused the invitation. Dante stood a few feet in front of us. He'd dressed up for the occasion, wearing a black suit with a matching black arm sling. I didn't recall him having it before. That had to be Nina's idea. Sienna wore red, of course. I'd opted for yellow. It was as close to a signature color as I had.

"Lyla was a valued member of the Silver Sphere Organization, and in her honor the award for Best Director will now be rechristened the Lyla Davis Award for Best Directing," Gus said.

The crowd of journalists all clapped. Normally this would have been quite unprofessional, but conveniently they were all Silver Sphere members. Nonmembers could watch the proceedings on television like the rest of the mortals. Gus waited for the applause to die down and proceeded. "But we're not here just to honor the life of a great woman, we're here to honor the everyday heroes instrumental in bringing her killer to swift justice."

More applause. "First, I'd like to introduce Lyla's driver, Dante Brooks, who heroically took a bullet to the arm in an attempt to save Lyla's life."

Sienna and I watched Dante walk onstage and shake Gus's hand. As they posed for a photo in front of Lyla's six-foot face, I second-guessed my decision to come to this thing. Nina rushed by, walkie attached to her ear. I stopped her. "Do I have to stand in front of Lyla's photo?"

"That a problem?"

"Well yeah, it's kinda weird to receive a check while the dead girl literally looks on."

Nina sighed, then looked at me like I was the one in bad taste. "Lyla was a publicist. This is how she would have wanted it. You are going to go out there. You are going to smile. And, most importantly, you are not going to forget to stop on the black X so the camera guys can get the right angle."

And with that pep talk, she was gone. Onstage, Gus continued. "And now, our final featured guests, the people responsible for identifying the murderer: Dayna Anderson and Sienna Hayes." Gus looked over at us expectantly.

Sienna ran onstage like she was competing in the 100-meter dash. She would have gotten gold in the last Olympics. I took a bit longer, reminding myself the money would help a lot of people, my parents included. Gus continued his spiel. "These two beautiful women linked Javon Reid to Lyla's tragic demise thanks to a tattoo and our Cocktail Party swag bag. I always said those bags were good for more than just freebies."

The audience laughed on cue even though it wasn't funny. At all. Gus turned to us. "We'd like to invite you to be our very special guests at this year's awards. You will come, right?"

Most definitely not. Luckily, Gus didn't wait for us to answer.

"You all are simply amazing! And I'm not the only one who feels this way. This is the first year our hosts are also nominees. They are two of the biggest stars in the world and one of Hollywood's greatest love stories. And they'll finally answer all our prayers by starring in a film together when *$3000* begins shooting next month. Ladies and gentlemen, Mack Christie and his equally talented wife Janet Christie, aka J. Chris."

Yes, the same J. Chris we'd used in our Wheelhouse scheme. They came from stage left. At first I thought J. Chris's red glitter bomb of a blazer had me so blind I was seeing things because it looked like they were each holding one side of the biggest check I'd ever seen. Then my eyes cleared and I realized they were indeed holding a check like the ones they give lotto winners.

I stood there dumbfounded while Mack and J. Chris handed the check to Sienna and me, then stood on each side of us like extremely attractive, extremely famous bookends. The journalists went full paparazzi, yelling J. Chris and Mack's names in hopes they'd look directly at their camera phones. The collective flash made the deep red of J. Chris's blazer pop. She smiled, rocking her signature red lip. She wore no other color.

"J. Chris, over here."

"Mack, look this way."

Sienna instinctively turned in whatever direction the Christies did while I just stood there wishing for my new second-most-wanted superpower. The ability to blink my eyes and be magically transported to my bedroom. After a few pain-filled minutes, it was over. "Now it's time for questions with our heroes and hosts," Gus said.

Questions? Nina had promised me I wouldn't have to speak.

On cue, a few stage hands brought a set of three chairs. There were six of us onstage. Since this was a conversation series, not a press conference, Nina had bypassed the normal setup of a row of chairs in front of a long table, instead opting for higher director chairs. The stagehands set two next to each other and angled them so they faced the third. I briefly wondered if they expected us to play musical chairs for a seat, but I didn't have to worry. The chairs were clearly not for us. Gus took the single while the Christies took the other two.

I guess us "heroes" were expected to stand behind them. Not knowing what to do with the check, I tried to hand it to a stagehand. He ignored me, impressive considering I was waving a three-foot piece of cardboard in his face. "Let's get this conversation started!" Gus said. "Let's start with questions about the tragic incident. Ernest, you go first."

Ernest stood up. "Yes. Janet, did you get a chance to personally thank Dayna and Sienna for their role in solving Lyla's murder?"

She didn't. "I did. I couldn't resist giving them both big hugs."

Yeah right. There were rumors J. Chris hated if non-celebrities did two things: touch her or look her directly in the eye. Maybe she thought we were all Medusa and she didn't want to turn to stone.

"Lyla was a close personal friend and we still can't believe she's gone," J. Chris added. "It's such a blow, but I know she'd want the show to go on."

She sounded so much like Nina that I briefly wondered if Nina had given her talking points.

"When was the last time you spoke with her?"

"At the Nominee Cocktail Reception. I gave her a hug and told her what an amazing job she was doing. I've been involved with SSO for years and Lyla was by far the best publicist they've had."

That clearly was not in any talking points. Nina would have had her say "second best."

It went on like this for another ten painful minutes, the journalists peppering J. Chris and Mack with questions while the rest of us stood in the background like movie extras. Finally, I saw Nina doing a wrap-it-up motion off to the side. Gus must've had eyes in the back of his head because he said, "That's all we have time for. Up next we'll have a quick roundtable conversation with our Best Actress in Television nominees."

The Christies stood up and smiled as more cameras flashed, then we all formed a line to walk offstage. Mack, J. Chris, Sienna, the check, me, and Dante. Sienna was in a super good mood because she instinctively reached out and gave J. Chris a hug. I gasped as camera flashes went off all around me.

I fully expected J. Chris to disengage from Sienna's impulsive embrace as quickly as possible so she could launch her cell phone at her, grenade-style. But J. Chris didn't pull away. Instead, she hugged her back. The attendees ate it up.

After what felt like a minute, which is like two days in hug-time, Sienna was the one who disengaged. J. Chris shocked me again by grabbing Sienna's hand and leaning in. "Thank you again for finding Lyla's killer."

Maybe the gossip mill was wrong about her. It wouldn't be the first time. See: Tomari. I watched, happy, as she and Sienna strode hand-in-hand backstage.

As soon as we were five feet from the cameras, J. Chris pushed Sienna, causing her to bump her thigh on yet another life-size Silver Sphere Award the stagehands were bringing onstage. Sienna bounced off it like a basketball.

J. Chris spoke. "Touch me again and I will sue you for assault."

# Nine

I was poised to pounce in defense of Sienna's honor, but J. Chris yelled before I had a chance to yell first. "Nina," she screamed. "I thought my people made it clear in my rider that I was to be the only one wearing red!"

And with that she was off, leaving us alone with her husband. I happily turned my ire on him, but he must've been used to dealing with people upset about his wife being upset first. "I'm really sorry about that," he said. "She's really been stressed lately."

He was about to say more, but J. Chris called his name and he scurried after her like a rat in the subway. I glanced at Sienna, who had her skirt hiked up and was peeking at her injured thigh. Thankfully, there was no blood. "You'll probably bruise." I said.

"God, I hope so. I want to take a pic of it and frame it. Think she'd autograph it?"

Something told me the answer was no. "Maybe if you offered to use your blood. I'm sorry that happened."

"It's fine. Like Mack said, J. Chris is probably stressed out about Anani's big blind." Realizing what she'd said, Sienna slapped her hand over her mouth. "Sorry." Her voice was muffled. "I said the A-word."

The A-word was Anani Miss. Sienna was as obsessed with the blog as I used to be, so it was a testament to how much she loved me that she hadn't mentioned it. I knew she probably was dying to when Anani had done her big blind a few weeks before. Anani was known for her weekly blind item day where she shared gossip about celebs. These were usually more juicy than scandalous, but she still wouldn't name who it was about. It was way more fun to guess.

The big blind was an entire different level, which meant it got its own separate post. It had become an annual tradition on the site, always happening around the same time and always the most scandalous piece of gossip you'd find on the site all year long. Unlike a lot of the posts on blind item day, Anani always revealed the people in her big blind, normally after returning from her annual month-long hiatus. I knew Sienna had probably been dying to discuss it.

"Fine. Tell me, what is it?"

Sienna happily removed her hand from her mouth. "It's about an A-list singer who's been using someone else's voice their entire career. The popular guess is J. Chris."

I refused to be interested. "Well, the attitude is real even if the voice is not."

"Amen."

Dante walked up just then as Sienna continued on. "You're coming to the Silver Sphere Awards with me, right? Since Omari is bringing his mom." She could sense my hesitation because she grabbed my arm and gave me puppy dog eyes. "It'll be fun. We'll get our hair and makeup done. I know you used to love that."

I did, but still.

"And imagine the sightings," she said. "You're going to be laughing all night."

I would, but still.

"And what if Omari wins? Don't you want to be there to see it?"

I did, but still.

"I really want to go but I don't want to go by myself. I want my best friend to come with me. Please."

I glanced at Dante, who wore an amused expression like a well-tailored suit. I turned back to Sienna. "Fine." I'd do it, but only for her.

She smiled. "It's settled. You coming to the green room? There's food in there."

"No, I gotta find Nina and trade this for the real thing." I held up the check.

Sienna left us in the name of celebrities and snacks. Dante still had that slight smile on his face. "Didn't think you'd cave so quick."

"Resistance is futile when Sienna wants something," I said. "Plus she's right about the sightings. You and I can sit in the back of the auditorium and laugh at everyone."

"Thanks but no thanks. Only way I'm going anywhere near that thing is if someone pays me to drive them there." He pointed at the check. "Thought you were about to use that check to commit assault with a deadly weapon."

"Oh, I was."

"I drove J. Chris here. What you got was her best behavior. First, she wouldn't let me drive my own car. I had to drive one of theirs. Then she went ballistic because it was too hot. Then went even more ballistic because it was too cold."

"I would have left her on the side of the road."

"I was tempted, but then I remembered my thousands of dollars in hospital bills."

I motioned to his sling, which held a heavily bandaged arm. "Thought it was just a surface wound."

"It is. Nina thought it'd be better if I wore this. Something about keeping with the mood." He looked at me, then. "Did I thank you yet? For finding the guy who did this?" He motioned to his arm.

I, in turn, motioned to the cardboard megacheck. "I want to give you part of the reward." He looked at me like I had three heads. "Well, not part of this check, exactly."

He laughed. "I figured. Still, I couldn't do that. I didn't do anything."

"Except get shot."

"I definitely got shot. Still, I can't take it."

"You can and you will." I let him know exactly how much I wanted to give him.

He let out a whistle. "You're right. I can and will take that."

"Great. I'm going to find Nina so I can get our money. Maybe I can do direct deposit. Have the money for you tomorrow or the day after."

He nodded and we said our goodbyes. Backstage was a mass of people, half of whom probably didn't have to be there. The publicists. The assistants. The managers. The random hangers-on. I found Nina standing outside the green room, where they kept talent happy at these sorts of events.

Nina spoke into a walkie. A woman stood next to her. If I had to cast her, she was a shoo-in to play the action star's surly teenaged daughter. Bad hair. Worse skin. Body shaped like a pink highlighter. She was practically the same color, too. Of course she actually didn't look much like a seventeen-year-old up close, but then neither did the people Hollywood always cast to play them.

"We need the Best Actor in Television nominees onstage in five," Nina said. "Anyone have eyes on Grant?"

"Right here."

Omari came up behind us. I would've kissed him but it would have been classified as a public display of affection. Knowing my thoughts on that, he didn't even try. Instead, he glanced at the check in my hands. "You bringing that to my place tonight?"

"Not if I can help it," I said. "Nervous?"

The journalists out there were also conveniently the ones who would be voting for the Silver Sphere Award winners. This was Omari's big chance to impress them. He shrugged. "Brandon Marlowe's won four times in a row. They're going to make it five."

The fact that he'd studied his competition said more than his actual words. I didn't point that out, though. "Maybe they'll want to spice it up."

"Maybe, but they love him. Probably because he's like an open book. You know I don't talk about anything private."

"Then go semi-private. Give them some cute soundbite, like how you're bringing your mom to the show because she made so many sacrifices for your college fund, how happy she was when you got that degree in drama."

Actual drama, not the type you saw on reality TV shows.

Omari laughed. "She did bring that huge 'Congrats Omari' sign to graduation."

"Yes! They'll love that. Don't think of it as sharing too much about your private life. Think about it as honoring your mom."

He didn't respond, but I could tell by his smile he was thinking about it. He glanced at me again, this time giving me—not the check—a once-over. When he looked up, he wore a naughty smile. "You looked great out there, by the way."

I blushed. Just as he was about to say something else, Nina practically yanked him away. "He needs to be onstage now. Kitt can take him."

Someone clearly wasn't a fan of public flirtation and I had a sneaking suspicion why. Tomari. I rolled my eyes, then covered it with a smile when I realized Omari was still eyeing me. I'd promised myself I wouldn't let him know how much Nina annoyed me, and I'd almost slipped up. He glanced over his shoulder at me as the woman next to Nina—apparently Kitt—led him toward the stage. "Let's do Chinese tonight."

Nina watched until Kitt and Omari were nothing more than specks, then tried to get around me.

Like I was going to let that happen. I casually blocked her with the three-foot reward check. Glad it was handy for something. "So where can I trade this in for the real thing?" She just stared at me, so I tried to explain. "The reward money. I know you don't expect me to fit this in my ATM."

"Oh, about that ..."

Nothing good ever starts with "About that ..."

"We haven't gotten in all the donations from the nominees, but we will," Nina said. "And as soon as we do, it's all yours."

She smiled then, like she was doing me a favor and hadn't used false pretenses to get me there for free publicity. I was not a happy camper. "How long are we talking?"

"Couple days tops. I'll call you. In the meantime, you can keep that as a memento."

And with that she was gone, leaving me and my useless fake check. This was not good. I needed sustenance, preferably covered in chili. Since I was at the green room, I left the check in the hall and went inside. Let it be someone else's memento.

Sienna was right. The room was a mishmash of well-known actors, their "people," and a vast array of snacks. I saw Sienna standing near a movie star trying to covertly take a selfie with him in the background.

Spoiler alert: the green room, where the stars gather before a show or some other event, is hardly ever green. Someone once told me it got its name because it used to be where money changed hands for a gig. This one was black and featured formations of couches and chairs in what I'm sure the designer called "conversational clusters." There were also flat screens on two walls showing the live feed of the stage for those interested. I definitely was, but first I needed sustenance.

I kept one ear on Omari's live feed as I beelined to the food table. It wasn't worth the trip. The food choices were about as diverse as the nominees, all stupid healthy stuff that looked like it came straight from Gelson's. A waste. Tommy's would have been happy to "sponsor" the green room. Sure, J. Chris and her ilk wouldn't have touched a single burger but I would have eaten enough for all of us and happily taken the rest home. Instead, I picked up a carrot stick and tried to pretend it was a French fry.

I was thinking of lodging a formal complaint when something interrupted my train of thought. That something was Gus's booming voice. Even from a sixty-inch TV screen, he was loud and obnoxious. He asked Omari a question. "Why are you so private about your personal life? You don't even admit you're seeing someone."

Great question. I expected Omari to give the usual canned response: he kept his personal life private because of blah blah blah.

"I'm definitely seeing someone," he said, and I almost choked on my carrot. I've had nightmares of dying due to food but it always involved overdosing on chocolate or drowning in melted ice cream. Not this. "My girlfriend is the most amazing woman I've ever met. And I don't talk about her not because I'm private. I don't talk about her because I'm selfish. I don't want to share her or what we have with the world."

By that point my mouth was wide open, carrot spewing out like hot lava.

Take that, Nina.

I headed back to M&Ms that evening to try to catch Regina on her shift. I wanted to let her know about the reward money, and she still wasn't answering my texts. In a fit of desperation, I'd even called her number—and we all know someone has to be really desperate to actually want to speak to another human being on the phone.

I had the radio cranked up and was singing along to Kandy Wrapper, but the song went off right when I found my groove. It was replaced with a familiar voice. "This is Gus the Gossip and here's your daily gossip report. The Silver Sphere Awards are known as the biggest party in Hollywood. Every year the nominees come together beforehand for an intimate Conversation Series, where they share personal details of their busy lives and reveal new projects. This year's conversation was no exception."

The radio cut to another familiar voice—Omari's. "My girlfriend is the most amazing woman I've ever met. And I don't talk about her not because I'm private. I don't talk about her because I'm selfish. I don't want to share her or what we have with the world."

When I'd suggested he share a bit of his personal life, I hadn't expected that. Not that I was complaining. At all. I wanted to roll down the window and ask the person in traffic next to me if she was listening. And if she knew he was talking about me. But I refrained.

The broadcast cut back to Gus. "That was Silver Sphere Award Best Actor in Television nominee Omari Grant, talking for the first time about his girlfriend..."

Dayna Anderson!

" ... Toni Abrams," Gus said.

Wait, what?

"The two have been inseparable the last three months, but this was the first time Grant dished details on his relationship."

Tomari had struck again.

I suddenly lost all interest in the radio.

When I finally made it to M&M's I was still in a bit of a mood, so I forced myself to think positive. Solving Haley Joseph's murder hadn't been a fluke. And now I'd done it again. Despite what my parents—and, if I was being honest, sometimes myself—had thought, I was good at this. I was even getting compensated for it. Money I planned to share with Regina, who despite her less-than-stellar-quality traits had turned in her boyfriend. It couldn't have been easy. If she could handle dealing with Junior, I could handle my own the-public-thinks-my-hot-boyfriend-dates-someone-else problems.

When I finally went inside, the restaurant had a nice crowd. An older waitress still greeted me. "How many, hon?"

I plastered a smile on my face. "I'm actually here to speak with Regina."

"Ain't here."

"I thought she worked evenings."

"She did, until she quit Thursday."

"I saw her that night. What happened?"

"You a friend?"

I nodded. I wanted to be one. Close enough. The woman still looked suspicious. "I'm surprised she didn't say anything. Left so quick she didn't even give notice. Rumor is she came into some money."

I flashed on Junior and wondered if Regina had been involved after all. "Legally?" I asked.

The woman relaxed. "You must be a friend because you obviously knew Junior. Carol told me that Regina told her someone gave her a nice chunk of change just to give that fool's name to some lady."

Needless to say, some lady was really surprised to hear that.

# Ten

"It could very well have been a Good Samaritan, Ms. Anderson. Though I will admit that does not make much sense. The tip line is anonymous. They could have just called themselves."

Aubrey was on his futon, looking at printouts of evidence from the case. His studio wasn't much—the futon, plus a desk and kitchen alcove with a tiny bathroom off it—but it was clean. I had to give him that. After I'd left M&Ms the night before, I'd called to update him on what he'd missed, and we agreed to meet bright and early the next morning. For once I was on time.

"Maybe someone really hated Junior but didn't trust the cops," I said from the corner Aubrey called a kitchen. I grabbed a bottle of Arrowhead from his fridge. "Not even for an anonymous tip. Of course, that doesn't explain the whole paying Regina thing."

"Someone clearly wanted us to turn Junior in," Aubrey said.

But who? And why? I moved back into the main room and sat down next to Aubrey. He jumped up and took a seat in the office chair by his desk, where I noticed the envelope with the license application. It wasn't opened. "Okay, what's going on Aubrey? You're acting weird. Well, weirder than normal."

He looked surprised. I kept on him. "You've avoided my calls. Now you're acting like you don't want to even be in the same room as me. If you don't want to work with me anymore, just say so."

"Pardon me, Ms. Anderson?"

Was he really playing dumb?

I motioned to the unopened envelope. "You haven't even opened the license application."

"What application, Ms. Anderson?"

"We talked about this. Making things official, having a real partnership. Don't you remember?"

"Yes, but ..." He trailed off. For the first time since I'd known him, he looked embarrassed. "I assumed you were discussing dating each other."

I let this sink in. "You thought I was hitting on you? So what did you think was in that envelope? Oh my God. You thought I'd written you the world's longest love letter. Eighteen pages filled with hearts and Dayna Anderson-Adams-Parker in cursive. I have a boyfriend, Aubrey."

Men.

I laughed. Just a bit. Then a lot. He had the nerve to look hurt, like he was offended I'd rejected his rejection of me.

"I obviously misread your intentions," he said.

"Obviously." I wiped my eye. "Now that we've established neither of us wants to date each other, can we get back to the case?"

He looked relieved. "I suggest we drive by Ms. Jones's house. Maybe she will be home."

"Let's go." I still had Regina's address in my phone from our little outing to Wheelhouse. I wiped the final tear and got up, grabbing the

PI application as we left. "I will say this, though. The next time a woman does express her undying true love, maybe handle it better. At least don't be so obvious you're avoiding her."

"I will definitely keep that in mind, Ms. Anderson."

Aubrey was quiet our entire drive over, busying himself completing the application. Regina's neighborhood was quiet and well tended, featuring small one-story houses with ample green grass between the front door and street. When we pulled up in front of her place, a lone older woman picked up trash a few houses up. All the action seemed centered a few doors down, where a jumble of cars were concentrated around one house.

Aubrey looked up just as another car joined the pack. A woman got out looking somber and holding a casserole dish. "Someone must have passed away," Aubrey said.

"Must be Junior's grandmother's house. Regina mentioned she lived on the same block."

"Perhaps we should stop by if we cannot reach Ms. Jones."

I'd kept a running tab of places I'd never take Aubrey. The movies. The strip club. Into the general vicinity of my parents. I mentally added "home of a grieving family" to that list.

"Perhaps ... " I said.

Regina's driveway didn't have a car in it but then I wasn't expecting one. Not so much because I didn't expect her to be there—more because it was probably impounded as a crime scene since Junior took it from Palm Springs. I parked, blocking her driveway, and we both got out.

We walked up the stairs, opened the black metal screen door, rang the bell, and waited. When that didn't work, we knocked. Both garnered the same result. Nothing. The door remained closed. Aubrey watched as I went to a window, got on my tippy-toes, and pressed my face against it to double check.

"She's long gone. She knows better than to come back here," a voice called out.

I recognized it—the voice of that one woman in every neighborhood who has too much time on her hands and therefore knows everyone's business. Back home, that woman was my mother. Thanks to her, news in my Augusta neighborhood traveled faster than a video compilation of cute dogs.

I turned and smiled. Nosy Neighbor's black-don't-crack age put her at around fifty-five, which meant in actual years she was at least seventy-two. The only giveaway was the crown of gray-black hair pulled in a bun at the nape of her neck. She was skinny, probably from all the walking, with smooth brown skin the color of cardboard. If she were to be cast in a movie, she … wouldn't be cast at all because, hello, she was black and a woman over fifty.

She held one of those mechanical grabbers in her left hand and a trash bag in her right. Having two decades of up-close experience with the neighborhood gossip, I knew exactly how to play the situation. I sure wasn't going to pretend like I was a friend. Nosy Neighbor would know that she'd never seen my car.

"Hi! We're actually investigators and believe Regina might have some information that might help us. I'm Dayna, but everyone calls me Day."

"Ruth Reid. Everyone calls me Mama Ruth."

The last name was the same as Junior's. Could it be? I decided to assume, regardless of what it made of you and me. "I'm so sorry to hear about your grandson, Javon."

Mama Ruth nodded her thanks. She must have slipped out her house for a walk.

"It's all that girl's fault," she said, waving her trash bag in the general direction of Regina's place. "I've been calling the police. They won't call me back. I know *that girl* called the cops on my grandson. There's a special place in you-know-where for those who helped get him killed. Regina and all the rest."

I just nodded. No need to mention we were part of "all the rest."

Aubrey, however, spoke up. "Ms. Ruth, I am Aubrey S. Adams-Parker. We have reason to believe that Mr. Reid—"

It took everything not to cover his mouth with my hand. I interrupted with a quickness, throwing him a look. "We have reason to believe that Javon got a bad rap. In fact, that's why we came by. We wanted to ask Regina some follow-up questions because her story didn't check out."

Mama Ruth nodded. "I can't believe people would think Javon could so something like this ..." She paused and I was ready to dismiss it as classic Grandma-in-denial-her-grandson-is-a-sociopath. Then she continued on. "Something like this on his own. Someone put him up to this. Probably Regina."

Someone put Junior up to this? I tested out the theory. It felt good in my hands, especially when you factored in the "Good Samaritan" who'd wanted Junior out of the way.

"I know the boy ain't a saint," she continued. "Doesn't mean I loved him any less. He stayed with me sometimes, had this hiding spot he thought I didn't know about in the shed. I went out to check it and that's where I found the money and the phone."

"Did you give this information to the police?" Aubrey asked. I was too surprised to talk.

"I tried. None of them want to call me back, like I said. I'm about to throw the lot of it away."

"We'd be happy to take a look at it." I glanced over at Aubrey, who nodded.

She left her tools on the sidewalk and we followed her back to her house. We could hear the voices inside. I noted she ignored the front door like an email from a Nigerian prince and walked directly to the back. The shed wasn't much to look at but at that moment it was the most beautiful thing I'd ever seen. Within seconds, Mama Ruth had opened Junior's hiding place—a makeshift hole below a broken piece of tile on the floor.

There was indeed a cell phone and a wad of cash, all hundreds, at least two inches thick. There was also a *Black Tail* magazine, showing a back shot of a woman squatting in nothing more than heels and a headband. I ignored it, too focused on wondering if the phone still had any prints. Aubrey, however, did not. I hadn't pegged him for a dirty magazine type of guy.

"Is this Junior's phone?" I asked, but I already knew the answer. He hadn't seemed the type to have a pink flower phone case, and the police had made it clear that he'd stolen Lyla's personal cell phone.

"Don't think so. Doubt the money is his either." Mama Ruth grabbed the phone. It was dirty as all get-out. She wiped it off on her T-shirt.

Bye-bye prints.

I was about to say something when Aubrey handed the magazine to me without a word. Inside was a piece of paper and on it someone—I guessed Junior—had written a date, time, address, and the word "anonymous."

I'd been eating, sleeping, and drinking Lyla Davis's murder investigation for almost two weeks. I knew the details better than I knew my social security number. It was the day, time, and location of Lyla's death.

"Mama Ruth, can we take this?"

She just nodded.

Once back in the car, we each threw out theories like yesterday's trash. "So someone tells Lyla to meet them at the ATM, where they send someone to kill her," I said. "And that same person uses us to ensure that the guy is apprehended."

"How did they know Mr. Reid would not turn on them?" Aubrey asked.

"Junior was adamant he wasn't going back to jail. He told Regina. Even tweeted it right before he died. Maybe the person knew the same thing. Figured Javon would get killed. Or, in this case, kill himself. The only thing I don't understand is why would someone put a hit on someone as well-loved as Lyla? Even J. Chris liked her."

"All types of people have secret lives, Ms. Anderson."

"What about the 'anonymous'? You think they wanted it to look like a botched robbery? Which it did." I pulled up outside of Emme's building.

"This is not the police station," Aubrey said.

"Correct. It's Emme's. You've been here before."

"I thought we were taking the evidence to the police."

"We will. I just want Emme to look at the phone first." It was clear from Aubrey's look that he didn't approve. At all.

Emme ran out her door as I continued my plea to Aubrey. "Just give us the time it takes to drive to the police station. Once we give the phone to them we'll never see it again. If someone's out there thinking they got away with murder, partly because of us, I want to know who it is. The phone might be the key to finding them."

Call me old-fashioned, but I preferred my "accessories" to be necklaces, not to murder. I also felt silly that I'd been proud of myself, thinking I might actually be good at this, when someone had been pulling my strings like a puppet. Maybe my mama was right. I'd been lucky with the Haley Joseph case.

"I will give you and Ms. Abrams five minutes," Aubrey said. "It will begin now."

Yay! "I'd make a joke about kissing you but you'd think I was in love with you again."

He didn't laugh, just stared at me as Emme jumped in the backseat. I'd texted her the details when we left Mama Ruth's house so she was prepared. Looking solemn, she glanced at Aubrey as she put on her seat belt. "This is a horrible idea, IMO." In my opinion.

"Save it." I pulled out to head to the police station downtown. "He's letting us check the phone."

Emme smiled and pulled on a pair of rubber gloves. "In that case, where is it?"

I handed it to her. It was in a resealable plastic sandwich bag with illustrated snowmen and candy canes on it. She gave me a look. "Professional."

"It was all Mama Ruth had at her house. I charged it on the way here but it's passcode protected. Don't you have something that can break it?"

Emme nodded. "It can take a while, though."

Aubrey spoke. "You have four minutes, thirty seconds." He was seriously keeping track.

"Hopefully not longer than four minutes and twenty-nine seconds," I said.

Emme checked something on her phone, then pressed a few buttons on Lyla's phone. "Done," she said. "It was her birthday."

Of course it was. I should've checked that first. Saved myself the gas. "Let me see!"

Aubrey literally put his hands in his ears like a child. Hear no evil and all that. We were stuck in traffic, so I turned around as Emme showed me the screen. It consisted of the standard-issue iPhone apps and Gmail. That was it.

What self-respecting woman in her twenties had an iPhone with no extra apps? It wasn't like the Stocks app let you filter your selfies to the point where you looked like your very own Madame Tussaud's wax figure. "Scroll to the next screen," I said, then tacked on a *please* at the end like my Mama always told me to. "Please."

"Isn't one." She swiped as proof. Sure enough, the screen remained the same.

I felt as confused as I'd been in Calculus senior year before my mom let me drop the class. There had to be a good reason for this. "Maybe Junior deleted them."

"He'd have to know the password. And why not just wipe the phone completely?"

"Three minutes," Aubrey said. He really wasn't helping.

"Let's just check her Gmail then." I glanced at the phone again. It listed 5,257 unchecked messages. Great.

Traffic started moving, so Emme sat back. It took her thirty seconds for her to talk. I counted. Aubrey did too. "Hmmph," she finally said.

Someone saying "hmmph" was never a good thing. It was right up there with the word "interesting." At that point, I just pulled over, Aubrey-the-human-countdown-clock be darned. Emme leaned forward and showed me what had her so perplexed. The inbox was empty. "Where are all the messages?" The Gmail app notification claimed there were thousands.

"Maybe Lyla had more than one account," Emme said. She tapped the icon in the upper left corner. The email address was a Viv3000. Emme clicked the down arrow, and the list of available Gmail accounts popped up. There was indeed another one listed.

AnaniMissBlog@gmail.com

"Time's up," Aubrey said.

# Eleven

The best way to describe my reaction was shock and *aww*, as in aww crap, I did not see that coming.

"Why are we not driving?" Aubrey asked.

But it was hard to drive when your jaw was dropped so low, it could have hit the gas pedal. "Lyla was Anani?" I said, more to myself than anything.

"What are you talking about, Ms. Anderson?" Aubrey asked.

"The email account on the phone is for a well-known yet anonymous gossip blogger."

"Oh, I see," Aubrey said.

"Oh you see? That's all you can say. Don't you get what this means?"

But of course, he didn't. He shrugged. "Like I previously said, everyone has secrets, Ms. Anderson. Now that we have uncovered Ms. Davis's, we can figure out what to do next."

I'd spent a significant portion of my waking hours trying to guess the actual person behind Anani Miss. During one four-hour road trip to Vegas, Sienna and I concocted some ridiculous fantasy that Anani was reality star-du-jour Joseline Hunter turned Smith turned Miller turned Jones turned No Last Name Needed. Or so her "momager" claimed. The official reason was that the Joseline "brand" no longer required it. In reality, after four mini-marriages in a two-year span, it was hard even for Joseline to keep up with the latest hyphenated addition—much less the general public.

But Anani wasn't a disgruntled A-list reality star with a mother who thought it was a good idea to Facebook Live her breast augmentation. She wasn't even an A-list publicist. Lyla had been an assistant up until a few months ago. Nina's assistant, at that. It had been a lot more fun when I thought Anani was a celebutante—and still alive. Because overexposed celebrity or not, Lyla Davis was dead.

"Where should we start, Ms. Anderson?" Aubrey asked.

"I honestly don't know. Anani had tons of enemies. Enough for her. Us. The entire mainland population of China."

"You mentioned wanting to kill her yourself just last month," Emme said.

Indeed, I had. Not that it was relevant.

"We need to uncover who hired Javon Reid," Aubrey said. "I will continue to look into Mr. Reid and see if we can uncover the person on that end."

We didn't have a name, so I'd secretly dubbed the person Geppetto, since they were pulling my strings like I was Pinocchio's black cousin with equally wooden dance moves and a nose that also didn't always cooperate with the rest of my face.

"You should pursue the anonymous blogger angle since that is more your field of expertise."

Fine by me.

Sienna stared at Emme's computer monitor like it was a visitor from outer space. One who came in peace straight from Krypton and had the glasses and cape to prove it. "No," she said.

I nodded. "Yes."

"No."

"Yes."

Sienna shook her head. "Maybe Lyla was a superfan like us and hacked her password."

"The password that happens to also be the same as Lyla's lock code?" I asked.

"Which is?" Sienna asked.

Lyla's birthday, but I certainly wasn't going to tell her that. "Nice try," I said. Giving her untethered access to the Anani account would have led to the world's first gossip overdose. How would I have explained that to Sienna's family?

"Figured it was worth a shot. I just wish you could have kept the phone."

We'd dropped it—and Aubrey—off at the police station before texting Sienna to come to Emme's place. We'd thought it best that Aubrey dealt with the cops by himself.

"Emme checked it out while Aubrey was busy critiquing my driving," I explained. "There was nothing on there. No texts, phone log, or even web browser history. Looks like she only used the cell to check her email."

"At least we know why she was never outed all these years," Sienna said.

She was right there. Anani had kept things sparse. Besides the blog, her presence on social media was slim to none. No official Facebook page. No Instagram. No Snapchat. And definitely no LinkedIn. She did occasionally tweet but not often enough. I spoke. "The lack of apps on her phone had to be on purpose, not because she'd forgotten her Apple ID."

"Like you?" Sienna said.

She was right. Thank God for small favors and the fingerprint option.

"And we *do* have access to her emails." I decided to go with a glass half full approach. "There's definitely a clue there. We just have to find it. It'll be easy."

Sienna stared at the open inbox on Emme's screen in complete and utter reverence. "Can you imagine what secrets are in there?"

I only cared about one.

"We might be SOL," Emme said from next to me. "There's gotta be 10,000 messages in here. At least."

As proof, she kept scrolling. And scrolling. And scrolling. We watched in horror. I finally took mercy on our collective souls and physically stopped her from scrolling any further.

Blurg. I hoped the glass was half full of vodka. It was becoming very, very difficult to stay positive. "Hypothetically, how long would it take to go through all these messages to find any threats?"

Sienna raised her hand. "Me! I volunteer, as a tribute! Even if it takes me days and days and days. I will read each and every message because I am that dedicated to solving this case."

Emme and I looked at her, then looked at each other. I spoke first. "So how long ..."

"IDK," Emme said. "I could do a search for *kill* or *dead*."

Sounded good to me. If someone threatened Anani, chances were they would use either of those words. And use it they did. Emme's searched yielded over 1,000. It'd take time to go through each one. We needed an easier way to narrow them down.

I combed my brain for another key word we could search for in the Anani inbox and found the crime scene photos in a crevice. Lyla and Junior crossing paths hadn't been a bad twist of fate like we'd originally thought. Someone had wanted them at the same place at the same time. Someone who'd want to know exactly where Lyla would be at the exact moment before she died. Someone who'd have to make sure she was there. Of course, Junior could have just followed her from the party, but Omari would have seen him. He hadn't.

"Could you look up the word *bank*?" I asked.

Emme tapped the screen a few times. "Only thing I see is something about Kandy Wrapper having sex in a Wells Fargo vestibule."

Sienna literally gasped. "Blind item #4. March 13th, two years ago. I knew it was her."

She went to grab her cell, probably to message Fab. We were all silent for a bit. Sienna text-gossiping. Emme tapping buttons. Me lurking behind her like she was a message board. Finally, I thought of something else. "There were two email accounts, right?"

Emme nodded. "Second one was empty."

"Did you check the trash or sent messages?"

"Not yet." She was already logging into the account. The password was, wait for it, Lyla's birthday. A kajillion thoughts flashed through my brain in the .0761 seconds it took for the inbox to load. As with the casts of *The Bachelor*, they were all variations of the same thing: *Please let us find something.* A clue buried in the confines of a sent folder. A key bit of info hiding in junk mail. A lead playing hide-and-go-seek in the archives.

Instead we got nothing. Nada. *Rien* (thank you one year of high school French). Not even an invitation for a penile enlargement.

"Who doesn't even get spam?" I asked. It was an inalienable right, along with life, liberty, and the pursuit of happiness.

"No spam means it's probably a new account," Emme said. "Would also explain why there's not much here. Just a draft from a couple weeks ago."

She pulled it up. It was written the same day as Lyla's murder. The problem was that it wasn't addressed to anyone. Not even a subject line, a la *Why do you want to kill me {Insert First Name of Killer} {Insert Middle Initial} {Insert Last Name of Killer}?*

In fact, it only said one thing.

*Hello ...*

It was clearly something she'd started but never gotten around to finishing. "Remind me of the name of the second email account again?"

"Viv3000."

It was random. In fact, *Viv* wasn't even a word. At least not one that could stand on its own. It could have been short for vivid. It could have been initials. It could have been a nickname. It *should* have been a lot easier to figure out. I'd done enough posthumous online stalking of Lyla to know her middle name wasn't Vivian or Viva or anything that even started with a letter at the end of the alphabet. It also wasn't the name of any family members. And nothing about the word *vivid* or the initials V. I. V. related to Anani. The same with the numbers on the end.

I glanced over at Sienna, who wasn't paying us one iota of attention. Her eyes were glued to her phone, probably texting Fab how unfair we were being.

I began pacing, chasing a lead that didn't seem to exist. "So basically we have an email account with too many messages and an email account with no messages. Let's figure out a plan to go through the inbox and sent message folder of the main Anani account. I'm going to—"

"Now can I get the Anani password?" Sienna practically shoved her cell in my face. Her Twitter app was open to an Anani tweet that was just a couple of weeks old. I read it out loud.

*"Pretty funny when your big blind has people so pressed you're getting death threats. #Yawn #RevealDayisComing #SorryNotSorry"*

# *Twelve*

*Well, hello my pretties. It's that time again. Anani has to say bye-bye for a bit, but you know she always leaves you with a parting gift. This is the best one yet. By far.*

*Picture it. LA. Last month. Sunset. A pretty big-time producer in town for one thing only: to meet someone Anani will call Piper. Piper's a super well-known, super pretty, super busy A-lister who's been any and everywhere these past few years. Your TV. Your radio. Your favorite website (wink wink). Talk about pipes. Even Anani has to admit she was singing along each and every time a Piper song was playing. She may have even downloaded one or two. All legally, of course.*

*Mr. Producer knows what working with Piper would mean for his career* and *his bank account. Arrangements are made for a quick meet-and-greet at a place they both should feel at home: a studio. Things go pretty dang well. They talk. They vibe. They bond. Mr. Producer's excited. So excited, in fact, he wants to get started right then and there. He asks Piper to step inside the recording booth.*

*Only one problem: Piper can't sing.*

*And Anani doesn't mean Piper can't sing that night. Piper can't sing. At all.*

*You read that right. That voice you sang along to on the TV? The radio? Those annoying awards shows? Turns out Piper was singing along too.*

*My little birdie told me Piper couldn't get out of there fast enough. Pretty sure Mr. Producer wasn't expecting that. So much for that epic collaboration, but you gotta keep the secret so the money continues to flow in and the sun doesn't set on the career.*

*Mr. Producer should consider himself lucky. Anani's heard Piper actually sing and boy oh boy, it sure ain't pretty. Not only will this one be revealed, but Anani has a first: audiovisuals. See you in a month. Until then ...*

"Kandy Wrapper! Rosey Hartl. Vanessa Heffernan. Oh, and of course J. Chris."

Sienna screamed out names faster than I could write them down. We sat in the bloset after our mad dash home, facing the one wall not covered in shoes. Instead, it held my beloved whiteboard, which was getting quite the workout. I dotted the *i* in Chris, then stepped back to examine my handiwork. "So that's at least ten A-list singers we wouldn't be surprised lip-synced. We need to narrow it down."

"I say we start with J. Chris."

Sienna sounded adamant. I wasn't quite on board. Not yet. "Her voice isn't even that great. Like if I'm going to lip-sync, I'm borrowing an amazing voice. Not a just okay one."

"It's better than yours. And mine."

Having spent a lifetime listening to my own shower concerts, I wasn't going to argue that one. "Let's say J. Chris is Piper. Then what's the 'pretty' connection? Besides, you know, just looks. I mean, they're *all* pretty. They wouldn't be A-list if they weren't. But the word itself must be significant. Anani—Lyla—used it five times."

Anani loved to plant clues via word choice. Not that I kept track or anything, but during her (extremely inaccurate) Tomari blind, she used *fine* three times. A reference to Omari's *LAPD 90036* character Jamal Fine. She chose her words carefully. Fun when you were trying to decipher gossip. When trying to decipher murder? Not so much. "Do any of them have something with pretty in it? Song title. Lyric. Favorite color of MAC lipstick. Something,"

Sienna thought it over and shook her head. "MAC has a shade called Pretty Please. But it's pink and we know J. Chris isn't having any of that."

Sure wasn't. J. Chris even wore red lipstick in her "no makeup selfies." "Can you read it again?"

I sat down and closed my eyes, figuring it might help me think better. Maybe I'd have a flash of brilliance. Or maybe I'd fall asleep and wake up to find someone had solved the thing during my naptime.

Sienna read the entire thing, her voice taking on the exaggerated pronunciation of a newscaster. "*Mr. Producer should consider himself lucky. Anani's heard Piper actually sing and boy oh boy, it sure ain't pretty. Not only will this one be revealed, but Anani has a first: audiovisuals. See you in a month. Until then.*" Sienna stopped reading and returned to her normal voice. "Boy oh boy, this is pretty hard."

My eyes flew open. "That's it. The blind is about two people. We're assuming pretty is a reference to Piper. What if it's referring to Mr. Producer?"

We spoke at the same time. "Pretty Boy!"

Pretty Boy was a bigtime Jamaican-English record producer. You could always tell his songs by the heavy use of dancehall samples and the annoying screech of some woman yelling "He's such a pretty boy." Rumor had it that it was his mama. That was all I needed to know about that relationship. God bless his girlfriends. Past, present and future.

"But isn't he based in London?" I asked. "The blind specifically mentions LA."

"I saw him at XO a few weeks ago. He definitely was in town. That's a new spot on—"

I cut her off. "Sunset, right?"

She nodded, but I already knew I was right. I'd retired from going out soon after I'd retired from acting. But I'd partied enough in the three years prior to know how the LA club scene worked. The names changed. The locations did not. A handful of places took turns being the "hot spot of the moment." Their average shelf life was that of a baby carrot. When it expired, the club simply got a fresh coat of paint and a new name and went to the back of the "hot spot" line to patiently wait its turn again.

I thought about it. Clubs weren't the only thing I knew off Sunset Boulevard. "She mentioned pretty five times and sunset twice. Has to be another clue."

"Jim Henson is on Sunset and La Brea."

The Jim Henson Company Lot with its collection of stages and recording studios, is best known as the place they recorded "We Are the World" back in the day. It's seen a lot of celebrities. What it doesn't see is a lot of commoners. Like with most businesses that cater to a celeb clientele, you can't just walk on the lot and say hey to Kandy Wrapper. You have to be on the list. Hollywood lives and dies by them. Whether it's a club VIP list, People's Sexiest Bachelors, or the top ten movies of all time, you're on a list or you're no one. Studios were no exception.

Which meant Jim Henson probably had a record of everyone who'd been on the lot, including Pretty Boy and Piper aka Geppetto aka person I needed to find before they had anymore nicknames. "If we can get our hands on the visitors' log—or better yet, security footage—we'd have what we need."

Sienna perked up. "We should drive there. Pretend we're delivering flowers. I could distract the guard. You could sneak on the lot. Find the security office."

I nodded. "Which would probably be locked. Which means I'd have to pick it." I made a mental note to order a lock picking set immediately.

"At that point, the guard would probably get a phone call about an alarm."

"Which I wouldn't realize was there. And I'd only have like sixty seconds before it automatically called the police."

"And it'd totally go off. But we would figure that would happen. So, we'd have a plan. When they got there. I'd distract them. With something other than my boobs."

I nodded appreciatively. "Which would give me just enough time to turn on the computer and figure out the password. It'd be something simple like JimHenson1234* because they all insist you have a freaking symbol now. Like it can't be your choice to have a password that's quote-unquote weak."

Sienna had heard the "my password, my choice" rant so many times that she just ignored it. "Right," she said instead. "You'd type it in. Then find the security footage, which would be neatly labeled by date. You'd look for the week or so before the blind item. Pull it up. And bam. Visual proof of J. Chris meeting Pretty Boy."

"Or one of our nine other choices." Sienna ignored that, so I continued on. "Whoever it is, she'd be running out the lot after Pretty Boy asked her to sing. I'd steal the tape so we could take it to the police. Brilliant."

"Yes!" Sienna said. "We could do that."

"We could totally do that!"

"Totally. Or we could just check his Instagram account."

"Or we could do that too."

My phone was already out. I pulled the app up and found Pretty Boy's username within seconds, no lock picking required. Not that it mattered. I was still ordering that lock pick set ASAP. Pretty Boy's Insta put Junior's girlfriend Regina's to shame. Every thought. Every selfie. Every meal. All shared with the world. I'm no math genius, but a cursory glance at his account seemed to show a five-posts-per-day average. And a whole lot of posting on his part meant a whole lot of scrolling on mine.

I'm not ashamed to say my thumbs were the body part that got the most work out. My personal record was being 262 weeks deep in Omari's college girlfriend's account. And I have never accidentally hit a like button. Not even once. It was a God-given gift.

It didn't take us long to find what we needed, posted a mere four days before the Anani blind item. He'd gone with a filter. Lark, if I had to make a cursory guess. I was a Clarendon girl myself. It made the red in Sienna's outfits pop.

The photo was taken inside, yet Pretty Boy had elected not to remove his sunglasses. He probably needed them to not be blinded when the light hit all the diamonds on his neck. And his wrists. And his ears. And, perhaps most importantly, his pinkies. While he treated diamonds like he'd purchased them on sale in a bejeweler kit, his photo-mate only sported one rock. Of course, the solitaire diamond on her left ring finger was probably bigger—and more expensive—than all Pretty Boy's combined. Her diamond was embedded on a ring as platinum as her hair. It was—

"J. Chris! I knew it." Sienna's scream was so loud they probably heard it in Calabasas. "Look at her. You can tell her voice is about as real as her nose, boobs, hair, lips, teeth, butt, nails. You need to call the tip line. Right now."

And with that, she glided off and left me with my thoughts. I wished she hadn't. I almost took her advice and called the tip line immediately. It's what I'd done in the past. But something stopped me. Or should I say someone.

Geppetto.

What if we were wrong? What if it wasn't J. Chris? As much as I'd love for the whole thing to be over—again—I had to wonder if this was still all part of Geppetto's plan. Just like they'd wanted me to hand Junior to the cops. Maybe they wanted me to hand them J. Chris as well.

I was not going to let them pull anymore of my strings. It would take more than just a blinged-out Instagram photo before I was ready to jump back down that rabbit hole. I couldn't see myself calling the tip line any more than I could imagine Pretty Boy's Instagram post being introduced as Exhibit 23 in trial.

I decided to sleep on it. It was still on my mind when I woke up the next day—alone, since Omari had a late call. There had to be something more concrete, I decided—preferably from Lyla / Anani herself. Or her source. Anani and her "birdie" communicated somehow. I was betting—hoping—it was buried somewhere in her email account. I got on my laptop and logged in.

I did a search for J. Chris and Janet Christie. There were a couple of blind items but none mentioned lip-syncing or any clandestine meetings with Pretty Boy. He also didn't come up in any searches.

Blurg.

I took a time-out, figuring I could google either of their real names. Or a friend or disgruntled ex-employee I could look up as a source.

I started with J. Chris and her Wikipedia, which had obviously been heavily edited by her publicist. It stated she was born Janet Malone and moved to LA at 20, which meant she probably was closer to 23. A stage age—one that shaved at least three years off your real one—was a Hollywood must, along with a weave, teeth whitening, and a nose job. I got so used to telling people my stage age during my Chubby gig that I still hesitate when I need to fill out my birth year on official documents. Maybe J. Chris had the same problem.

She'd started off with modeling and turned down a gig working in a music video for a debut country artist named Mack Christie. Mack may not have gotten the girl, but he did get a number one single. His career rose while Janet was cast on a soap opera. From there, she climbed the celebrity alphabet until she reached A-list with a role as the adoring wife in an Oscar-nominated Leo DiCaprio film. A couple of years later, Mack came back in her life when friends—read publicists—set them up. Hollywood's latest It Couple was born.

Despite repeated claims that their next collaboration would be a baby, it actually was some movie called *$3,000*. I had no clue what it was about but I doubted I'd be seeing it. You might be able to lip-sync a three-minute song. But an entire movie role? Not so much.

I did some more research but came up with nothing of interest. I was more lost than a bunch of teenagers midway through a horror movie. On one hand, chances were the source would probably contact "Anani" again. Somehow. Some way. I just didn't know when or how. And I had no desire to wait.

I needed to call Aubrey, if nothing more than to talk things out. My instincts were saying to put figuring out Piper's true identity on the back burner and focus on finding the source. But I wasn't sure. Geppetto still had me feeling shook, and I was treating my instincts like a cheating boyfriend who swore up and down that he'd changed: I didn't exactly trust them though I'd never admit that to my friends.

Also, I needed to talk to Aubrey about when he could take the PI exam, since I'd dropped the application off in the mail on the way home from Emme's yesterday. Once his application got approved, he would be eligible to take the exam and I didn't want to waste any time. A quick Google search let me know there were over 2,000 possible multiple choice, Q&A, and True / False questions covering everything from state labor codes to post office manuals. Another site claimed only thirty percent of applicants passed it. Blurg.

The one thing I did know from the last few days was I needed Aubrey more than ever. I just hoped he remembered half the stuff he'd learned at the Sheriff's Academy. To be safe, I found a site offering a study guide and printed out the info before heading over to his place in Silver Lake.

He must have just gotten home because he was standing next to his bike taking off his bright yellow helmet. A police scanner was mounted to his bike. It squawked. Aubrey's version of fun.

"We have a Code Six. Adam."

"Roger that. Forty-five will be in route."

"Oh no!" I put both hands to my cheeks *Home Alone* style. "A Code Six! Their lunch delivery isn't here yet?"

Aubrey wasn't amused. "The patrolman has arrived at the location, a Code Six, but they might need assistance—Adam."

Maybe we didn't need to spring for a study guide course after all. "You going to help out?" I grabbed a bottle of water from the cooler on his sliver of a patio. "Super Aubrey to the rescue."

"No, I just came back from Ms. Ruth's home. She let me examine her grandson's room. I did not find anything of note, but she did provide contact information for some of her grandson's associates."

I nodded appreciatively. "You have any luck when you gave the cops the phone?"

"They claimed they would look into it, but we shall see," he said. "What about you, Ms. Anderson?"

"Well," I said, "I did maybe find a motive through the Anani angle."

I updated him on what Sienna, Emme, and I had uncovered. He didn't speak until the end. "Forgive me, Ms. Anderson, but I find it hard to believe that alleged lip-syncing is a strong enough motive for a murder."

"That's 'cause you're looking at it from the point of view of a regular person. Being a celebrity is as much a brand as Coke or Pepsi. It's a legitimate multi-million-dollar enterprise. You make money for managers, publicists, execs at movie studios. Which makes them all invested in every aspect of your career and life. Chubby's had someone whose job it was to monitor my Twitter account and I was nowhere near the level of a platinum-selling singer. So this is not like me mouthing the words to Mariah Carey in the car. This has the potential to ruin a career and lose a lot of people *a lot* of money. And isn't money one of the prime motives for murder?"

If I had a mic, I would've dropped it. Instead, I settled for taking a sip from my Arrowhead bottle. I almost spit it out when Aubrey spoke.

# Thirteen

"I stand corrected, Ms. Anderson." It was the first time Aubrey had ever admitted I was right. "So what do you propose we do now?"

I'd come here to ask *him* that. "Sienna's working on getting J. Chris's schedule but it might take some time. Linking J. Chris to the blind is a dead end for now. So maybe we should possibly look into finding the source." I hated how hesitant I sounded.

It took a good thirty seconds for Aubrey to respond. I counted. "You said no one has ever linked Ms. Davis to this Anani Miss alias, correct?"

I nodded. "The blog is on its annual hiatus and always reveals a big blind item when it returns, right after the Silver Sphere Awards."

"The source probably does not know Anani Miss is dead, which means he or she will attempt to contact her again. I would not waste much time on that for now. Instead, we should look into finding the proof that Ms. Davis alluded to in her blog article."

Of course, I'd completely forgotten all about the audiovisuals. Blurg. "If we get that, we don't need a source or a threat. I should have thought about that."

"There is no question that you would have, Ms. Anderson."

I smiled then, appreciating his lame attempt to make me feel better. "Lyla seemed so focused on covering her tracks that I see her keeping a copy on her desktop or a flash drive. Not in her email or the cloud. Worst case scenario, it's in a safety deposit box and we're screwed. Best case, it's in her apartment."

"Well then, we should operate on best case scenario. What is Ms. Davis's home address?"

It took ten minutes to get in the car and less than that for Aubrey to work my nerves.

"I know you are not texting and driving, Ms. Anderson."

"Of course not." Aubrey made a point to side-eye the cell in my hand. "Technically, I'm GPSing and driving."

Which I was. Emme had found Lyla's addy in minutes. She texted it to me along with a reminder I only had a few days to get her birthday gift. I was lying to my GPS app Waze about being the passenger—like Aubrey, they too were serious about the whole distracted driving thing—when Aubrey jumped in with a PSA.

"You do know that a law firm estimated there are 300,000 injuries every year from accidents caused by texting while driving?"

"I did not know that. I do have a question, though. How do *you* know that? You have a flip phone so I know you didn't google that statistic on your cell." I stuck my tongue out at him.

"How old are you, Ms. Anderson?"

"Twenty-four." I automatically gave him my stage age. "Wait, no. That's wrong."

"You take this lightly, but 33 percent of drivers who were using their mobile phones during crashes were in their twenties, according to the federal government's distracted driving webpage."

I had to smile. Yes, Aubrey was a walking, talking footnote, but he was my walking, talking footnote. And my partner—when he took care of getting ASAP Investigations licensed. "By the way, I dropped the PI license application off. Next step is the exam. They test six days a week, so yay."

He nodded. "I will let you know as soon as I hear from them."

"Good."

We drove past the Paramount Studios lot off Melrose before hitting a red light at Van Ness. Across the street was a huge digital billboard that looked like someone had taken a movie screen showing before-the-movie ads and placed it four stories up. Image after image flashed, most promos for movies and TV shows, including Omari's *LAPD 90036*. Conveniently, the show was filmed at Paramount across the street. I'd bet good money I didn't have that all the billboard ads were for productions that shot on the Paramount lot. That meant the subjects on said billboard saw them on their way to work and were probably overjoyed Paramount was giving its all to promote their careers.

The latest ad for a sitcom featuring a chubby white guy and his ridiculously hot wife was replaced with an advertisement for the Silver Sphere Awards. *Live only on CBS!* It was a shame Lyla wouldn't be around to see it.

We started moving, only to stop again a few streets up. I used the time to review everything we knew, the facts continuously scrolling through my mind like sports scores on ESPN. When I got to the Viv3000 email addy it was like someone hit pause on the DVR. Its presence didn't make much sense. I could understand the secret Anani account but why have two? The only reason people needed a secret—

well, more secret—email was to sign up for yet another free Netflix trial or a porn site.

Or so I was told.

Lyla was meticulous about having the bare minimum on her Anani phone, so it wasn't there by accident. If she wasn't using Viv3000 for free porn, she had to be using it for something else. And that something else could be the Piper blind. It could be how Lyla and her source contacted each other, especially if Lyla didn't want to wade through the massive daily injection of new emails in the Anani account.

We were still at a stoplight. I glanced at Aubrey. He was distracted by someone attempting to jaywalk. A big no-no in LA. Aubrey rolled down his window and yelled out, "You know you are breaking the law, correct? You are risking a $250 ticket. I suggest you turn around right now and wait for the light."

It was a risk, but I took a chance. I logged on through my browser. It took a second but I opened it and navigated to the Viv account.

Still no new emails. Blurg.

I stole another peek at Aubrey. He was paying me no mind since apparently, the jaywalker wasn't following his advice. "I do not want to call the police and report you."

Feeling brave, I went to check the Anani account when my cell was wrenched from my hand. Aubrey started awkwardly tapping on my touchscreen like a three-year-old at his first dance class. I lunged for it and he proceeded to play a game of Keep Away. "We're at a stoplight!" I said. "If you don't give me the phone back, I swear I will be in my nightgown the next time I take you anywhere."

Aubrey looked at me as if wondering if I was bluffing. A dumb California law didn't allow women to drive in housecoats. Aubrey knew it too. "How much is that fine?" I asked him.

He handed my phone back to me without a word. The Viv inbox was not only empty, but he'd also somehow managed to delete the unsent draft. He was worse than my two-year-old cousin, who we dubbed the "Magician" due to her ability to delete apps from cell phones she hadn't even touched.

"Incensegrand can wait, Ms. Anderson."

My brain tried to calculate what he'd said. It hit me. "I'm not on Instagram. I'm working on the case."

I used the rest of the trip to explain why I'd checked my phone. He didn't seem convinced. We were still chatting when we finally pulled up to Lyla's address and got out. She lived in Hancock Park, an old-school rich-people neighborhood smack-dab in central Los Angeles. Nat King Cole and his family had integrated it in the '40s, much to the chagrin of some of his all-white neighbors.

The lawns were big. The houses were bigger. Huge two-story numbers with landscapes that resembled parks. Lyla's house was a classic Tudor and had a "Guest Cottage Available" sign staked in the front yard, right next to trash bags sitting at the bottom of the driveway. Someone didn't waste any time.

A woman opened the door before we could even use the doorbell. I'd cast her as the gentle old white lady neighbor who sexually harassed the hot male rom-com lead and cursed like an old-school rapper for cheap laughs. "Hello, are you here about the apartment?"

"Yes," I said, because I was.

Of course, "Honest" Aubrey spoke at the same time. "We are looking for the former residence of Ms. Lyla Davis. Would this be it?"

The landlord's smile deflated like my ex's tire after I may or may not have stabbed it with a knife. Aubrey didn't notice the reaction he elicited—nothing new there—and introduced us before launching into a barrage of questions. "Did you notice any suspicious visitors lingering outside over the past few weeks? Did Ms. Davis seem frightened or was she acting strangely?"

"No," the woman said, and left it at that. All righty then.

"Do you think we could take a look at her possessions?"

"Gone," the woman said. "Her parents asked me to box up all the personal crap and send it back to Ohio. Told me I could donate the rest. They promised to reimburse me for shipping but they haven't sent a check yet." She gestured to where the two trash bags sat next to the state-issued garbage bin. "And I got two bags of stuff of hers just sitting out here the past three days. The Salvation Army said they'd pick it up but so far no one's showed up. I'm not paying someone to haul it off. Especially if her parents aren't going to reimburse me."

Well, that stunk. For her. It was pretty good for us.

"We can take it for you," I said. Right after we went through it.

I'd thought maybe good manners would make her refuse and then we'd play the back and forth game of "I couldn't bother you." "It's no bother." "Really?" "Really." "Well I suppose, if you don't mind."

Instead, she just gave us a mumbled thanks and slammed the door before we could even tell her she was welcome. I turned excitedly to Aubrey. "License to snoop!!!"

And with that, I practically skipped to the street. It was the most exercise I'd gotten all month. Not able to contain myself, I pulled open the first bag, imagining years and years of diaries and printed-out death threats.

That was not the case. At all. Aubrey joined me and peered down at the bag's contents. "Ms. Davis was apparently a movie fan," he said.

That was putting it lightly. There were assorted personal odds and ends but mostly the bag was stocked full of DVDs. The other one held more of the same.

Blurg.

For a split second, I was tempted to just jump in the car and leave them be. But I was already risking bad karma with my "texting" and driving. Aubrey and I hauled both bags to my car.

"I have an appointment tonight," Aubrey said once we were back on the road.

"Want me to drop you off?"

"I am just letting you know that I will not be able to go through the DVDs with you."

Was Aubrey suggesting we ransack Lyla's DVD collection for our own benefit? I thought it over. I *was* coming up at the end of my (fourth) free Netflix trial. I would be in need of some entertainment.

He continued. "You can ask your friends to help you search for the one with the lip-syncing proof on it, correct?"

Oh. That sounded more like Aubrey. He actually had a point though. If Lyla did indeed have audiovisual proof of Piper's identity—like she'd claimed in the blind—she had to keep it somewhere. If she was old-school enough to have DVDs, maybe she was old-school enough to keep the proof on a DVD. And maybe she hid it in a movie case.

I immediately sent out a text. *Wanna go to an opening party?!*

I made sure not to do it while driving.

"You know you are wrong for this, Dayna."

When I was young, a dead giveaway my parents were really mad was when they called me Dayna. And if they used my full name—Dayna Olivia Anderson—I was really in for it. Daddy tells the story of how when I was two he wrote my full name out on a chalkboard and when he told me what he was writing, I solemnly told him it was my "bad name." Not much had changed in the ensuing twenty-ish years. Though I wasn't expecting Sienna to give me a whooping, I wouldn't have been surprised if she put me in time-out.

After getting my text, she'd assumed the opening was to celebrate a new store or art show. Oops. She was decked out in a red sequin dress so short that the sequins and dress were practically the same size. Of course, she looked amazing, even while standing in the middle of the hundreds of DVDs I'd unceremoniously dumped on our living room floor. I'd already gone through the other stuff in the bags and determined they weren't helpful to the investigation.

"In my defense, this is a party," I said. "And we will be opening movies."

"What's your defense for telling me 'movie night' at your place?" Omari asked from behind me. He was clearly Team Sienna in this argument.

"My defense is that if there is a movie in here that catches your fancy, we can definitely watch it." I lifted up the bowl I'd placed on the side table. "I made popcorn!"

They exchanged a look, but neither made a move toward the snacks or the DVDs. I resorted to begging. "Look, help me out this one time. Please. We just need to look for any DVD that doesn't match the cover. Sienna, don't you want to be the first person to see proof of Piper lip-syncing?"

She didn't respond, but she did grab a handful of DVD cases and move to the couch. Omari, however, stayed in place. I looked at him. "And do you ever want to have me spend the night again?"

He sighed but picked up a handful and moved to the area of the couch that Sienna wasn't occupying. I was glad they were both finally on board, but I still sat on the floor close to the door just in case either tried to make a run for it.

We all got to work. It wasn't the worst party I'd been to—that distinction was in eighth grade when I accidentally got pushed into a pool mere hours after Mama plopped down $75 to get my hair pressed. But it was close.

I was pretty sure I'd dozed off with my eyes open when I heard the magic words. "Bingo!"

Omari held up a case for the tenth anniversary edition of *Reality Bites*. Young versions of Ben Stiller, Winona Ryder, and Ethan Hawke were plastered on the front.

He dramatically opened the case. The DVD inside indeed had no writing. It could have been bootleg, but bootleggers normally made a semi-respectful effort to trick you into thinking it was the actual DVD. They at least pasted the movie name on in a fancy font. Or so I'd heard.

I stood up as if possessed and practically floated toward him. My thoughts hopped, skipped, and jumped to watching contentedly as Geppetto did a perp walk while an unseen news anchor intoned how they'd hired Junior to kill Lyla Davis and thought they'd gotten away with it. And how the proof all came down to a DVD that ASAP Investigations—I paused and mentally rewound my fantasy—the *newly licensed* ASAP Investigations had uncovered when they realized they'd been used as pawns in the killer's deadly game of chess.

I composed my official statement while we popped that sucker into the DVD player. By the time we hit *play*, I could hardly breathe. The screen was pitch black. Then, as suddenly as a car crash, we heard a female voice humming. It didn't sound like J. Chris, but then, if she was lip-syncing, it wouldn't have.

I leaned in closer just as the image came in focus.

Our jaws all dropped in unison.

# Fourteen

It wasn't J. Chris. It was reality star Joseline. And she was humming all right. Just not on a mic. There was also an organ she played with. I'll leave it at that. The home movie featured a very naked Joseline and husband number two or three. The marriages were so close together it was always hard for me to remember which one had come first.

The camera went black, only to come back moments later in what had to be a bathroom. Joseline stood on the side of a tub as confidently as if it were a stage. Though she'd switched from humming to moaning, she still wasn't wearing much clothes. Her hands were wrapped around a shower rod. His hands were wrapped around body parts.

I had one thought and one thought only: Joseline probably killed it doing pullups during high school gym. Her upper arm strength was amazing—especially considering what else was going on.

Although it was all very interesting, it wasn't very helpful. At least not to my investigation. Joseline was not the type to kill over leaked sex tapes. If anything, she'd leak it herself.

I shut the TV off and snatched the DVD out of the player. We'd only watched thirty seconds but it would be thirty seconds that was burned permanently in my brain. I glanced over at Sienna and Omari, only to see them staring at the now-black screen with looks of wonder.

I gave them both a tight smile. "So that's a wrap for movie night."

I shoved the remaining DVDs back into the trash bags and Omari and I headed to his place, where we opened them over Thai food, beer, and Lyla's copy of *Do The Right Thing* playing in the background. The rest of the DVDs all were in the correct cases. I should've been disappointed. I wasn't. After stumbling across Joseline's sexcapades, I was happy more than anything else.

Neither of us mentioned Joseline's sex tape, though I did force myself to watch it again, fast forwarding to make sure there was nothing on there related to the Piper blind. There wasn't, but I'd give the tape to the police just in case.

That decided, I made a good go of pushing it out of my mind—until I had to use the bathroom. I found myself glancing at the shower rod more and more with each subsequent visit. By my final trip before bed, I couldn't hold out any longer.

I stepped up on the tub to get a closer look. Thanks to Joseline's home movie, it had gone from innocent apparatus used to prevent water from splashing on your floor to something of infinite possibilities.

I listened for my boyfriend. Realizing the coast was clear, I reached up. Tentatively at first, then more confidently. The rod felt cool—and flimsy. I gently pulled, making sure not to yank too hard. The last thing I needed was for the entire thing to come crashing down. No way to explain that one. I had to hand it to Joseline. There was no way I could do it. I suddenly felt bad for all the times I'd underestimated her.

I washed my hands again—as if that could also scrub any impure thoughts—and headed into the bedroom. Omari was in bed, talking to another woman. Nina's voice tinged through the iPhone speaker: "We have to be there exactly at three on Thursday. I'm helping out at Silver Sphere until they can find a permanent replacement for Lyla, so I'll be coming from the office."

As much as I hated Nina's constant intrusions, the mention of the Silver Sphere office gave me an idea. I slipped out of the bedroom and grabbed my phone from the coffee table in Omari's front room. Despite the late hour, Aubrey picked up on the second ring.

"Hello, Ms. Anderson. Did you find anything with the DVDs?"

There are two people on this planet I would never, ever, ever talk to about anything remotely related to sex. One was in Athens, Georgia, where she was still insisting I was basically a virgin birth. The other waited for me to answer his question.

"Nope. Nothing at all." I quickly continued talking in case he could hear me blushing through the phone. "I still think the audiovisual proof is somewhere. Maybe she thought it was more secure at work. I figure I'll go over to the SSO tomorrow and ask about the reward money so I can check. That makes sense, right?"

I waited for him to validate my idea. When he didn't say anything right away, I panicked. "Right. I mean, I could also do something else. Try to get hired as a temp assistant."

Aubrey interrupted me. Thank God. "That will not be necessary. Your first thought to check the office is spot-on."

Like Angela Bassett, I exhaled. But I still didn't feel like I had my groove back. Not quite yet. "You sure?"

"Yes. Please let me know how it goes."

We hung up. By the time I walked back into the bedroom, Omari was off the phone. I slid in next to him. "Think I'm gonna stop by the Silver Sphere office tomorrow after I get Emme's birthday present."

"Great. Tell her it's from the both of us." There was a pause and the next time he spoke, he didn't look at me. "You check the shower rod?"

I paused oh so briefly. Had he heard? "Nope!"

"Me neither."

And then he smiled.

I consider myself a smart woman. One who knew I'd never be able to show my face at Emme's place or, more likely, on her iPhone screen, if I didn't get her Focals sunglasses in time for her birthday.

It helped I knew exactly where to go, thanks to the list of stores she'd thoughtfully printed out. Samy's Camera was closest so I drove over to Sepulveda Boulevard in Culver City to pick it up. The store occupied the corner of a shopping center. When I walked in, I saw cameras. I did not see Samy, or at least anyone who looked like one. I did see everyone else and their mama.

The place was packed. I stopped a sales associate as she tried to fly by undetected. "Excuse me, where are your Focals?"

"Follow the crowd."

I should have known these things would be popular since Emme wanted a pair. But still. My mother had dragged me on enough Black Friday Walmart excursions to know what to do. Elbows out. Knees bent. Stay low and focused. Grab and run. And no matter what you do, do not make eye contact. With anyone. It was an obvious sign of weakness.

I followed the rules to a tee and was in line to pay in the time it took to say, "I would drop kick a nun for that Furbie." You'd think a store that sold electronics would have the ability to let you pay with your mind—or at least with your iPhone. You'd be wrong. Samy at least provided great, and free, WiFi. I passed the time watching videos of cake being frosted. No judging.

After one particularly pleasing video involving buttercream and basketweave, I forced myself to be productive and check the Anani email accounts. I had to log in to both. For some reason, I found it impossible to remember to select the button letting my email keep me logged into the account. I could remember Oprah's entire "All my life I had to fight" monologue from *The Color Purple,* yet had to fight to remember that.

The Anani account had "only" 427 new emails. A cursory glance turned up that most was spam mixed with the occasional bit of fan mail. The Viv3000 account was as empty as my wallet. I wasn't sure what I was expecting but a girl can dream, right?

I exited the browser, paid for Emme's gift, and made it to Hollywood Boulevard in thirty minutes. Not too shabby.

Despite what the name may have you believe, Hollywood Boulevard is not, in fact, the epicenter of the entertainment industry. If you want to find a movie set, you have to look north to the Valley, south to Culver City, and east to Los Feliz. Since 2001, the street has been home to Hollywood & Highland, a complex offering tourists three levels of the same chains they can find much cheaper at home and offering actors the opportunity to get dressed real fancy-like and pick up an Oscar or two at the Dolby Theatre.

Oscar night aside, you could definitely still find stars, both literal (the Hollywood Walk of Fame) and fictitious (two Batmen per one block radius extending from Highland Avenue to points east and west).

It was also home to the Silver Sphere Organization, which occupied an entire level of fourth floor real estate in an office building a few blocks west of the Dolby. I stepped off the elevator and was greeted with a large-and-in-charge version of the Silver Sphere Award itself. At least six feet, it was taller than the average Hollywood actor sans shoe lifts.

The waiting room was big. It was also empty. The reception desk sat unmanned and a glass door—probably locked—protected employees from any random crazies who were pissed that Tom Cruise had been shut out for his heartwarming portrayal of Jack Reacher. The supersized Silver Sphere was left all alone to fend for itself. Guess they figured no one would have the balls—or upper arm strength—to steal a six-foot award replica. I sure didn't.

I was tempted to press my head against the glass door and make ridiculous fish faces until someone took pity on me and let me in. Either that or knock. But then I saw the sign and a phone that looked like the Batphone that Commissioner Gordon used to summon Bruce Wayne. It was planted firmly on the empty reception desk and the printed-out instructions next to it suggested I pick said phone up and hit 3.

The phone didn't even get out a full ring before someone answered. The voice was female and cheery. "Hello! Welcome to the Silver Sphere Organization! Please state your name"—there was a brief pause and I wondered if she did a back flip—"and who you're here to see!"

Not a problem. I'd known my name since I was at least two, and also who I was here to see since I'd come up with my cover story earlier that morning. "Hi, I'm Dayna Anderson of ASAP Investigations. I was told I could stop by and pick up a check."

A lie but at least a good one. Nina had indeed told me I could stop by the office to pick up the check. She just didn't tell me when. For all I knew, the check could actually be ready.

"Hi Dayna. It's Kitt!"

The singsong tone made me think I should remember who Kitt was. Problem was I didn't. I felt bad so I employed the "fake it till you make it" approach. "Oh hey, Kitt, I didn't recognize your voice." Just like I probably wouldn't recognize you! "Can you buzz me in?"

"Of course! When you get in, turn left and walk down the hall. I'll meet you and show you to Nina."

Once inside the hallowed halls, I turned left and was met by the blonde woman I'd seen backstage at the Conversation Series. So this was Kitt. She seemed happy to see me. "Sorry I couldn't come get you but we're expecting Todd Arrington today. Things are always hectic when nominees stop by the office."

Todd Arrington, of course, was Hollywood's action star-du-jour thanks to the *Man in Danger* series. His second film, *Man in Danger 2: Man in More Danger,* had had the biggest opening weekend in the past five years last fall and they'd already greenlit the follow-up: *Man in Danger 3: Man in Serious Danger*.

"You've met him?" Kitt continued. "I'm sure we could arrange an introduction if you wanted."

I did not want. Mainly because I had indeed met him during the Haley Joseph investigation. Sienna and I had just so happened to break into his house after a slight misunderstanding involving a perceived break-in-turned-kidnapping-turned-none-of-the-above. As a result, I hoped to never cross paths with Todd again. "Thanks for the offer, but think I'll pass."

Kitt nodded and gave me a tour. For a show known for sometimes unpredictable award winners, their office décor was pretty run-of-the-mill. Lots and lots and lots of beige. The only thing stopping it from being "any old office" was the oversized candid photos of winners' reactions when their name was announced at past Silver Sphere ceremonies. Kitt said each winner's name as we passed while I nodded appropriately and feigned interest. It must've worked, because she seemed pleased. We made it to Nina/Lyla's office with no incidents and she turned to me just as she was about to drop me off. "Gus talk to you yet?"

I shook my head, which she accurately took as her cue to continue. "He put your Conversation Series appearance on his site and it got major hits. I suggested he interview you guys and Dante for his live web show."

No way I was doing an interview with Gus the Gossip, not with Geppetto out there thinking he or she had pulled a fast one. I nodded anyway. Better to say yes now and ignore calls later. I'd learned that from my manager. "We'll see what we can arrange," I said. "I'll try to stop by before I go."

She smiled, then knocked on the closed door. Lyla's name was still on it. At least Nina wasn't tacky enough to remove the nameplate just yet. I'd give her another week.

"Dayna's here," Kitt said.

I heard a mumble, which we both took to mean it was okay to enter. Kitt gave me a quick hug, then disappeared down the hall. I opened the door and found Nina sitting behind her desk turned Lyla's desk turned her desk again. She made a point to stare importantly at her computer, which I couldn't see from my vantage point. She was too busy looking important to say hello, so I took a seat across from her and smiled. "That Facebook post must be really interesting."

She jumped ever so slightly, an indication my Spidey senses were indeed correct. "Let me finish this email and then we can chat," she said.

I resisted the urge to give her an exaggerated "yeah right, you're looking at email" wink. Instead I looked around. The Silver Sphere Awards publicist didn't warrant a corner suite, but the office was nowhere near closet-sized. I had to give Lyla credit. She'd bypassed pretty pictures of pretty people accepting their Silver Sphere Awards. Instead she'd gone for pictures of the actual movies, not just their stars.

It was the same eclectic mix as in her DVD collection. She had the original poster for one of Todd Arrington's first big hits: *Memorial Day.* He was dirty and shirtless and running from a burning building with a kitten in one hand and a baby in the other. I quickly turned away. Even seeing a photo of him gave me retroactive embarrassment. Another wall featured the poster for hooker-with-a-heart-of-gold romcom *Pretty Woman*, with a suited Richard Gere leaning precariously back on a young, vibrant, and thigh-high-patent-leather-boot-wearing Julia Roberts.

Though there were movie posters, there weren't any actual movies. Not even a bookcase to hold DVDs. Blurg.

I eyed the computer and wondered if they'd had a chance to wipe it yet. Much like Obi-Wan and Princess Leia, it was my only hope. I just needed to get my hands on it.

Nina must have liked her daily quota of Facebook status updates because finally she looked at me. "So, you're here for your check."

"You told me to stop by."

"I also told you I'd call you to tell you when to stop by."

I nodded, because she had in fact done just that. I decided to go for flattery. "I figured I'd save you a phone call. I know how busy you are ... chasing after your two clients."

Make that *kind of* flattery. Her eyes narrowed. "We're still in the process of raising the funds. We should have the final donations in a couple more days."

She turned back to her desktop. I'd been dismissed, when I wanted to dismiss her. I needed a way to get her out the office, stat. Short of pulling a fire alarm, I wasn't sure what to do. I pretended to grab something from my bag to buy myself some time. Out of the corner of my eye I saw the photo of Todd Arrington. It gave me an idea.

"Cool. I'll just stop by Gus's office. He wanted to talk to me about a possible interview but someone was in with him when Kitt gave me the tour. It kind of looked like Todd Arrington."

I was lying but Nina took the bait. I saw her glance at her watch, apparently cursing her luck that Todd Arrington was the one Hollywood celebrity actually on time. "If that's all?" she asked.

"Well actually, I wanted to see if we could get Omari on the phone and discuss his mom—"

"We can discuss that later."

"You sure? I want to make sure Miss Erica has everything set for the awards."

I said a silent apology for bringing my boyfriend's mother into my trail of lies, but I knew she would understand. Miss Erica was cool like that. Nina stood up. "I've got it all handled."

I reluctantly followed her out. At least to the door. Nina was so set on Todd that she didn't look back to see if I was behind her. She walked down the hall and disappeared into an office, then shut the door. I waited a few more seconds and then did a 180 and went back inside. No one even noticed.

She hadn't closed the door behind her when she left but I took care of that. I even locked it for good measure. Luckily she was so pressed to see Todd she hadn't even locked her computer.

Her Facebook page was still up. I resisted the urge to update her status. I had a video to find and two minutes tops to find it. Never one to discount the obvious, I checked the videos folder on her PC first. It was empty. I wasn't surprised. I'm not that lucky.

I had to go more in depth. Having asked Emme how to search a PC for videos, I'd come prepared. She'd texted me detailed instructions and they actually didn't seem that complicated. Maybe I was that lucky.

I opened up File Explorer, making sure the current directory was on This PC. Then I typed "kind:=video" in the search bar. Emme had promised me that this simple request would bring up all the video formats on the computer.

It yielded nothing. Like I said. Not that lucky.

I exited out of everything and got out of there to go visit Emme, who was downright chipper when I stopped by. At least chipper for her, which meant she made actual eye contact when she said hello. I was glad one of us was in a good mood. I plopped on her couch and filled my mouth with the remnants of a Snickers bar I'd found abandoned in my backseat. Thank God for small favors.

"Operation Office was a flop!" I sounded a tad too dramatic but I made no apologies.

I expected Emme to share some insight I didn't want to hear because it was true—like maybe that I was at a dead end. Instead, I got, "She probably has it on the cloud somewhere. I just need to figure out the account. We'll find it. Don't worry."

She turned to me and smiled. The eye contact. The smiling. The lack of acronyms in her speech. Something was definitely up. "There a new video game unexpectedly out?" I asked.

Emme shook her head. Another glance in my direction. Another smile from her. Another frown from me. For a second, I thought maybe she was her twin Toni and they were playing some sick joke. My only hesitation was I'd seen them impersonate each other and they could be spot on. This was not spot on. This was highly suspicious.

"You win a lot of money playing online poker?" I asked.

She shook her head.

"Have a good nap in that life emulation game you love so much?"

She shook her again. Still, I was a bit creeped out. We went on like this for a few more minutes, me throwing up what amounted to Emme's bucket list, all of which could coincidentally be completed from the comfort of her own home, and her cheerfully rejecting each suggestion. Finally, I gave up. Maybe she was just in a really good mood for no reason at all. It had happened to me once in college.

"I'll keep searching her accounts and let you know if I find the video," she said.

I gave her a quick hug and bounced, closing the door behind me. I got halfway down the hall before I realized what was up. I ran back and knocked like I was the police.

She opened the door as alarmed as she should have been.

"Who told you?" I gave her my best serious private investigator stare-down. The one I may or may not have spent weeks perfecting in the mirror.

I obviously still needed to work on it because she said, "IDK what you're talking about."

"Don't play dumb. We just had a ten-minute conversation and you never once brought up Focals. So who told you?"

The jig was up. Emme knew it too. She plopped into her computer chair. "You logged into the Anani accounts from Samy's."

"You can tell when someone logs into the account? And from where?"

Turning back to her computer, Emme signed on to the Viv3000 account via her web browser and pulled up something called "devices and activity." "Gmail lists all the sign-ins. A lot of the time it's a mobile phone. But if you use WiFi, it lists the IP. And I just happen to know the IP for Samy's. Don't ask." I had no plans to. She continued on. "But it lists everything. See, you logged on last night too, when you were out and about."

"No, I didn't."

We both looked at each other. "Sienna," I said. "You gave her the password?"

"No! You're the one who lives with her."

True, but I hadn't given it to her either. Of course, I didn't put it past Sienna to figure it out. There was only one way to settle this. I FaceTimed her. This was not something that could be done over text. I wanted to look into her eyes, even if they were on a small four-inch touchscreen.

"Hello!" Sienna was as chipper as Emme had been, but she was always chipper so this was nothing out the ordinary.

I was tempted to butter her up but decided to just get into it. "How'd you get the password to the Viv3000 account?"

There was a pause. I'd have to give it to her, she looked genuinely confused. "I didn't."

I glanced at the list again. There were a variety of IP addresses. "So you haven't been logging in like every hour the past two days while you were running errands?"

"Nope. If I was going to steal a password, it would be the Anani account," she said. I didn't mention that the passwords were one in the same, just let her continue. "Not some random account that she probably used for her porn subscriptions."

"And Netflix trials," I said. Then, "If not you, then who? The only other person who had access to the account was Lyla."

"Unless you're wrong," Sienna said. "Someone else clearly has access to it."

"But who?" I was genuinely confused and, if I was being honest, scared.

Emme hit a few buttons on her laptop. "Someone at the Coffee Bean on Platt Avenue."

"Great. We don't know who it is but at least we know what coffeehouse they prefer. Can you check the account?"

She did. I was hoping against hope that perhaps just maybe there was an email waiting for us. Or at least one sent out. But there wasn't. It looked exactly the same as it did this morning. Nothing in the inbox. Nothing in the sent message folder. Just the lone unsent draft.

"Would Aubrey have access?" Sienna asked.

I shook my head but then remembered something. "Wait! Aubrey deleted the draft from my phone this morning."

Emme's eyes narrowed. "Either we have a phantom message or someone left Lyla a note."

Huh?

Emme clicked on the Drafts folder, then on the draft itself. The message was simple and to the point.

*Why are you ignoring me?*

# Fifteen

Emme's expression was one of true love. A smile so bright I swore I saw her wisdom teeth finally erupting. I half expected her to drop to one knee and propose. And if Gmail had a pulse and a Netflix account, she probably would have.

"Brilliant. Just. Plain. Brilliant."

"Exactly," I said, even though it was clear she wasn't speaking to me. Or to Sienna for that matter, since we'd already gotten off the phone with her. "Just remind me why."

"Google is the Internet equivalent of God. All knowing. All seeing. All *keeping*. You send an email, it's in the ether. Even if permanently deleted, it's out there somewhere."

"Like in a galaxy far, far away."

She ignored my pitiful attempt at humor. "Only thing Gmail doesn't keep are drafts. It saves just the latest version. Delete one without sending. Poof. It's gone. You're SOL if you want to get it back."

I suddenly got it. Emme was right. It was brilliant. Just. Plain. Brilliant. "So Lyla and her source opened a joint Gmail account because it was the only way they could talk without anyone finding out."

Emme looked at me, all proud-like. And I was about to make her even prouder. "And the source doesn't know Anani is dead. No one does. So they've been waiting to hear from her for like two weeks."

I could use that to my advantage. In fact, I *would* use that to my advantage. "They're gonna log in again, aren't they?"

Emme nodded. "I'll create an alert for anytime someone logs in to the account. We'll know when they respond and we'll ping the IP. Find their location."

Worked for me.

I had expected to hear from Viv3000 the next day. I just hadn't expected to hear from them right after my manicurist—Alice, according to the nametag—had wrapped acetone-soaked pads covered in foil on the digits of my left hand. I was in desperate need of a mani-pedi. But when I heard the ding indicating I'd gotten an alert, I quickly snatched my hand away. Someone had logged into the Viv3000 account. Yes! The sooner we found their location, the sooner we could find them.

The plan wasn't to roll up on them for a confrontation, per se. I just wanted to know who they were, you know, just in case. I was about to text Emme but she beat me to it. The IP was another Coffee Bean. This one in Los Feliz. It would take me an hour to get there but Aubrey lived within spitting—or should I say, biking—distance. He could get there.

I put up one foil-clad finger to Alice, then dialed Aubrey. She sighed loudly. When he picked up, I quickly explained the situation. "So how soon can you get to the Coffee Bean?"

"I am not home but I am not far. I would estimate it would take me thirty minutes."

That could be enough time. "They might still be there," I said.

"You can always stall them, Ms. Anderson, until I can get there. You say you have some high technology way to communicate with them, do you not?"

I did, though those weren't my exact words. Thank God. "I suppose I could pretend to be Anani. Message them long enough for you to get there." Pre-Tomari-gate, I'd visited Anani's blog almost as much as I visited the bathroom. If there was anyone I could emulate, it was Anani. "But what should I say? I can't press too hard. I'm not sure how honest Lyla and her source were in their convos. Honestly, we're assuming Piper is J. Chris, but what if she's not? What if Lyla actually referred to Piper by her real name?"

"You are overthinking this, Ms. Anderson. One thing I learned from my time with the sheriff's department is that as long as you act like you know what you are talking about, the other person will assume you do. I suggest you keep it vague and let them fill in the blanks for you."

"I could do that." We hung up, though I wasn't ready to give up completely on my mani. I smiled at Alice. "I'll just let this soak off. You can start someone else."

She was already motioning the bottle blonde standing at the front desk to come over. I took a seat at the empty station next to her and pulled up the Viv300 account with my right hand. My left was still covered in foil.

Please let them stay at the coffee shop.

I checked the draft. The message from yesterday was still there. *Why are you ignoring me?*

Deleting it, I wrote, *I'm not. Can you chat for a few?*

I tapped the refresh icon five times before Viv responded. Luckily, I wasn't expecting a college essay of a response because I would have been disappointed. It was one line. *Thought you'd changed your mind.*

They were still there. Good. Of course, that meant I actually had to talk. What did I need from them? I thought it over. First step was to confirm Viv3000 even had anything to do with Piper. Second was to finagle Piper's true identity—J. Chris or not. Third was to convince Viv3000 to stop hiding behind an email account and go talk to the police. I wrote: *We only have a couple weeks to the reveal. Definitely still going through with it.*

Viv3000 wrote back almost instantly. *She might know. She mentioned Piper to me. She'll kill us if she knew we were talking.*

And that was all I needed. I had to get to Los Feliz to talk to Viv face to face. Hopefully Aubrey would make sure Viv didn't leave before I got there. I ripped the foil off my left hand, paid full price for my half manicure, generously tipped Alice, and went to my car, where I reread the message.

Might know. Piper. Kill us.

Not quite new information, but at least it confirmed my assumption. The Viv3000 account was set up about the blind and it was in fact a secret someone would kill—and had killed—to keep.

I finally responded with fingers that still reeked of acetone. *You're right. Might be good to take precautions. I can make sure a copy of the video gets to the police.*

The response was instantaneous. *Thought the DVD was copy protected. You made copies?*

Fudge. My response was just as quick. *It is. Meant my copy.*

Viv wrote back right away. And much like dino porn, it wasn't anything I wanted to read. *Maybe this isn't a good idea after all.*

I fired off a quick apology. *Sorry if I made you think I made copies. I didn't.*

I hit refresh a kajillion times. Nothing from Viv.

The only thing stopping an impending sense of doom was that Aubrey was still on the way. I called him. He picked up immediately. "I just arrived, Ms. Anderson. No one is in here."

We'd lost Viv.

Fudge.

Two days later and my apology was right where I'd left it. Viv3000 hadn't even logged in to the email account. I kept checking, as if willing them to do so. Emme said there was no way to track a person's IP unless they log in. I just hoped they responded and when they did, it'd be from a private IP address.

Day One wasn't so bad. I knew the day would creep by if I just sat around alone waiting for Viv to write back. Instead, I decided to pass the time by bugging Aubrey. I was at his house as soon as rush hour let me get there.

He was landscaping. I decided to supervise. "Any luck with Junior's friends?"

He shook his head. "They relayed to me that Mr. Reid was extremely vocal about coming into some money. However, he did not share who gave him said funds and they did not ask. The police have his cell phone but Ms. Ruth is getting me her grandson's latest bill."

The bill was also online. Emme could help with that but I didn't dare suggest it. Instead, I decided to whine. "I keep thinking how I messed up. Again. Viv will respond, right?"

"It has only been a day, Ms. Anderson. You need to give it time."

"So that's a yes?"

"That is a 'you need to give it time.' If they respond, that is great. If not, we will figure out another way to find them."

Hearing him use the word "we" was instantly reassuring. I jumped up. "I'm gonna get a water. Want anything?"

He shook his head and I strolled into his apartment like it was my own. I noticed the unopened envelope on the way back from the kitchen. It was brown, flat, and rectangular, like most envelopes. Also like me prepuberty. The return address was stamped *Bureau of Security & Investigative Services*. I took it outside, waving it in Aubrey's general direction. "You didn't tell me you heard back from the licensing people."

Aubrey barely glanced in my direction. "I did not realize I had."

I ripped it open. Aubrey was not happy. "You know it is illegal to open someone else's mail, Ms. Anderson."

"You know snitches get stitches, Mr. Adams-Parker." I pulled out a slim handbook, study materials, and a letter congratulating Aubrey on his private investigator license application being approved. Skimming it, I gave Aubrey the highlights. "They're happy your application has been accepted. Blah. Blah. Blah. Next step is to call the number in the enclosed handbook to schedule the exam."

He just nodded. For someone so concerned about breaking federal mail-tampering laws, he was in no hurry to reclaim his package. I continued on. "Testing is six days a week in a wide variety of locations to fit your schedule and traveling needs. Ooh, there's one in downtown. That's not far." I gave him a date. "Does that work for you? I can pick you up."

"That will not be necessary, Ms. Anderson."

"Great. Let's call them now!"

After we got Aubrey all set up with his test, I bugged him for another half hour and then finally let him be. I spent the rest of the day cleaning Sienna's and my apartment, talking with my parents, having dinner with my boyfriend, and generally managing to resist stalking an email account.

It was all good ... until Day Two with no response.

That's when I went into full panic mode, which normally involved sitting on my bed. In the dark. Trying to break a World Record for how many Oreos one could stuff in one's mouth. My current best was nine. And that's exactly what I did, alternating between downing Oreos and searching Google for references to Viv3000. The hope was I'd find some clue of Viv's identity. They had to be somehow connected to Piper if they were close enough to not only know about any lip-syncing but also have access to proof of it.

I started off just searching Viv3000. Besides an unrelated outdated Flickr account, nothing came up.

So I added Viv3000 and J. Chris to spice things up, all while trying to avoid getting Oreo remnants on my new bedsheets. I typed in the names and hit enter. Google being Google, it offered a suggestion: *Did you mean Vivian J. Chris $3,000?*

I did not, but I'd still take it. Clicking on the suggestion, I was shocked at how many links popped up—all with variations of the same headline: *Singer-actress Janet Christie signs on for $3,000 remake.*

I picked one article at random and clicked on it. J. Chris had signed on to play Vivian (ding ding) in a version of the movie *$3,000*, which apparently was a "dark drama" about a "down-on-her-luck" streetwalker who gets offered $3,000 to spend the week with a rich, successful businessman.

It was a remake. The original hit theaters in 1990, but not before Hollywood had stripped it of its dark elements, changed the title to be reminiscent of a song about a lady walking down the street, and gave it the requisite Happily Ever After. The movie itself had its own happy ending—*Pretty Woman* became one of the biggest romantic comedies ever.

My mind flashed to the Anani blind item. Lyla had mentioned "pretty" five times. Sienna and I were right in assuming it was a clue. It led us to Pretty Boy, after all. We just hadn't realized it had another meaning.

Lyla had hidden Joseline's sex tape in a *Reality Bites* case. Did she have a similar sick sense of humor about the J. Chris audiovisuals? I was pretty sure I'd seen a copy of *Pretty Woman* somewhere in her vast collection. Luckily, the two bags of DVDs were still stuffed in my backseat. I'd yet to donate Lyla's stuff.

I'd love to pretend that I kept them because my Spidey senses told me I'd need them one day. In reality, I'd been "meaning to" stop by the Salvation Army in the same way I'd been "meaning to" drink more water.

Of course, when Past Dayna had shoved the DVDs back in the bags before she'd shoved them back in the car, she'd neglected to put them back in any semblance of order, which meant Present Dayna had go through both bags to find it. I could've taken everything out in an orderly fashion, one thing at a time so not to make my Infiniti any more of a mess than it already naturally was. Instead I dumped the first bag all over the backseat and went scavenging as if for gold.

I threw the random junk and non–*Pretty Woman* DVDs into the front passenger seat, not caring where they landed. That was a problem for Future Dayna. Coming up empty, I moved on to bag number two and repeated the entire process.

*Pretty Woman* wasn't the last DVD I checked, but it was close. I opened the case. The DVD itself had the iconic photo of Julia Roberts and Richard Gere on it. Not a surprise. Someone would have noticed if it didn't. But I still wasn't ready to give up. Not just yet. Lyla had been nothing if not sly. Sliding the DVD jacket out from the case, I hoped for some additional clue. Maybe she'd written the source's real name or exactly where she'd left the lip-syncing proof. No dice.

Deciding to watch the DVD anyway, I went back upstairs. Sienna sat on the couch playing with her phone. I gave her an update. When I told her about the J. Chris connection, she practically did a seated cartwheel and proceeded to scream "I told you so!" eleven and a half times—the half only because I finally managed to cut her off with an apology. "I will never doubt you again," I said.

We both knew this was a lie, but we still went with it. I practically jammed the DVD into the player and waited for the thing to load. The screen went momentarily black. I held my breath until the menu screen popped up. I should've just breathed. It was a regular DVD menu.

I selected *play movie* as I spoke. "Maybe she got super slick and hid the proof in the movie. Maybe Lyla knew that one day someone—me—would look for the proof and that someone would see the menu. Maybe she hoped they would just give up—thereby keeping her secret safe."

"Or maybe it's just straight *Pretty Woman*." The movie started and Sienna spoke again. "Oh hey, it looks just like the beginning of *Pretty Woman*!"

I had no plans to give up that easily. Ever. I hit the fast forward button. Once. Twice. Three times. The movie jumped forward in fits and bursts. Thoughts of Geppetto flashed through my brain just as quickly as bits and pieces of movie images flashed on screen. I recognized a few scenes as they flew by. The thigh-highs. The singing in the bathtub to Prince. Vivian wearing the red dress. Him snapping the necklace case shut.

"Stop!" Sienna yelled.

# *Sixteen*

I got excited. "You see something?"

"Nope, this is my favorite part."

So we sat and watched Vivian tell the super mean saleslady about herself. It really was a good scene. So good we watched it twice, Sienna parroting the words with Vivian. Me playing the part of the stuffy sales lady. Once we finished our lines, we continued to fast forward. Within ten minutes, it was over and I had nothing to show for it.

I stared at the DVD cover. "I've seen this somewhere before."

"Maybe VH1 played it."

"No, not like that."

I racked my brain, mentally replaying the past few days. When it finally came to me, it still felt like a long shot. But still. I turned to Sienna. "I need you to be a distraction."

She jumped up. "Let me just change into a lower-cut top."

"Distraction for Nina."

"Oh, I don't think she's a boob girl but I can definitely still try."

We heard Nina before we saw her. I recognized the voice immediately. It was the same one from my nightmares. In a repeat performance from my last visit to the Silver Sphere offices, Sienna and I did the whole "use the Batphone to call since no one is in reception" bit, but only after Sienna took a few selfies with the oversized Award statuette in the lobby. I made a note to add it to her Insta account as soon as we got back home.

"I cannot wait until we go to the show," she said.

Blurg. I'd forgotten about that. I hadn't even bothered to shop for a dress yet. Sienna must have read my mind. "I got us dresses. Fab is bringing them the day of the show."

"He knows my size?"

"He's bringing every size. We can just return the rest."

"Works for me. Thanks!"

That settled, we called inside. Neither Batman nor Kitt answered the phone. An anonymous female voice let us in instead. The voice belonged to an intern, who met us on the other side of the door and led us to Nina's office before scurrying off. I didn't blame her.

I immediately understood why Kitt couldn't come to the phone. She was too busy being yelled at by Nina. The door to the office was closed, yet I heard her as clear as day. A Los Angeles day. Not a Seattle one. "We promised Toyota that Todd Arrington would be there. And he'd take a pic with the car. You told me you took care of it! It was your one job."

"I did. I swear. But his assistant said he changed his mind," Kitt said. I could hear the growing panic in her voice.

"They always change their mind. It's your job to change it back."

Part of me wanted to save Kitt from Nina's wrath. The other part wanted to eavesdrop in case I overheard something good. Compassionate Me won and I knocked. Nina stopped mid-scream. There was a pause and when she spoke again, it sounded like she'd transformed back into human form. "Who is it?"

I smiled even though she couldn't see me. "Dayna and Sienna."

She sighed so loud I heard it through the two inches of metal and ten feet of office space separating us. "I told you I'd call you when the check was ready."

Sienna chose that moment to be helpful. "We're not here about the check."

"Then why are you here?"

Nina still hadn't bothered to come out. We were literally talking to a closed door. It was for the best, since Sienna turned to me. "Give her a reason we're here," she hissed.

"The reason was the check," I told Sienna. "You knew that when you volunteered that we weren't here for the check!"

She had no answer to that, but then neither did I. So we just stood there giving each other panicked looks, willing the other to come up with a good idea. We stood like that for so long that Nina finally spoke again. "Thank God they're gone. I need to see Gus, then get over to the hotel."

She clearly wasn't talking to us. "He's not here," Kitt said.

"Of course he isn't."

The door swung open and we were finally face to face with Nina. Both Kitt and the *Pretty Woman* poster were a few feet behind her. So far, yet so close. I needed in there. Pronto. Nina looked at me. "Were you standing outside this entire time?"

The good news was I'd finally figured out an excuse for our presence. "Yes. We were waiting for Kitt. We need more details about the

Gus interview." I'd forgotten about it, along with the fact that I was going to the awards show. I looked past Nina to Kitt and threw her my most innocent smile.

Nina wasn't having it. At all. "You don't want to talk to me?" She had the nerve to sound put-out, like she hadn't just tried to wait us out by hiding in her office.

I ignored that. "Kitt, you have time to go over a few more details about the interview?"

"Of course!" We both smiled at each other, pretending like a fully grown human wasn't blocking our way. Never one to miss out on being in the spotlight—one she'd tried to extinguish a few minutes prior—Nina looked at me and smiled. "Will Omari be coming tonight?" I had no clue what she was talking about. This was clear, too, because she clarified. "Tonight is the 18th Annual Silver Sphere Awards Official Gift Lounge Presented by the Brand New Toyota Prius."

Next to me, Sienna started practically shaking in excitement.

"The 18th Annual Silver Sphere Awards Official Gift Lounge?" I repeated. It would kill her I hadn't included the entire title.

Nina fell for it. "Presented by the Brand-New Toyota Prius."

A mouthful for what basically amounted to a conference room, albeit a really nice one, packed to the gills with people and stuff. You have your swag bags—well, gift lounges are swag bags to the hundredth power, an awards season staple along with questions about "Who are you wearing?" and the orchestra playing lesser-known winners offstage before commercial breaks.

With gift lounges, celebs can come, peruse the goods, take a few publicity pics, and just leave with whatever catches their fancy. Anywhere else, this would be considered stealing. Here it's considered a good business opportunity. Yes, companies pay thousands of dollars for the chance to give their stuff away free.

Needless to say, it was not Omari's thing. At all. He was begrudgingly doing the parties and interviews because he wanted to win—even if he didn't admit it. But this was pushing it. I took a little too much glee reminding Nina of that. "Yeah, I doubt it."

"He *has* to come," she said. "You need to make him come."

I was about to remind her I wasn't Kitt. She couldn't just boss me around. But Sienna jumped in first. "I can make sure he gets his ticket if you want to give it to me."

She sounded convincing. In reality, there was no way Omari would even know the ticket existed. Nina barely glanced in her direction. "There are no tickets. Just a list. One he's already on." She checked her Fitbit, then turned to Kitt. "I'm heading to the lounge. Talk to Todd's people. And remind Gus he promised to run that exclusive this afternoon."

And with that, she was gone—leaving me alone with Kitt, Sienna, and her open, empty office. I needed to get rid of Kitt ASAP. Sienna and the office could stay right where they were. Unfortunately, Kitt resisted my attempts to will her to just walk away. "So you guys are going to do the interview!" she said.

This is probably why people suggest you not lie. It's hard to keep track of them. Not that I would let that deter me from doing it again. "We actually just wanted more info," I told her. "I know Nina gave you a big to-do list. Just send us the details."

"I can multitask. Let's go chat in the conference room."

Ugh. "I have to use the bathroom. You and Sienna get started and I'll join you in a sec."

"Yes, let's go." Sienna made a point of adjusting her top and thrusting her boobs in Kitt's general direction. Kitt didn't even glance at them. Guess she obviously wasn't a boob person either. Women could be weird like that. Probably because if they ever wanted to see boobs, all they had to do was look down.

Sienna and Kitt took off in one direction and I in the other. One byproduct of always having to use the bathroom was you never forgot where one was. It was like some sixth sense. Some people never forget a face. I never forget a lavatory location.

When I got back from my bathroom break, Nina's office was still open—and empty. There were people around but I paid them no mind. They in turn paid me none. I'd once crashed an audition a friend had told me about, and despite a serious case of the nerves, I'd forced myself to walk in like I belonged there. It worked. The poor assistant checking me in assumed the mistake had been on her end. I didn't get the part but I *did* get a good life lesson. If you act like you belong somewhere, no one questions if you don't.

I walked into Nina's office with the confidence of Tyra Banks on a runway. I paused in front of the *Pretty Woman* poster, did a quick turn, and gave it my best *smize*, aka smile-with-my-eyes. Then I remembered to shut the door.

I made a beeline back to the poster. It was a big one, engulfed in a bright silver frame. One could definitely hide something behind it—a USB drive, a DVD, probably Lyla's entire movie collection.

No way I'd get that entire thing off the wall, much less back *on* the wall after I was done. I'd have to settle for peeking at each corner and praying Lyla possessed just as little arm strength as I did.

I started with the corner closest to me. Why take extra steps if you didn't need to? I tried to peek behind it but only succeeded in hitting my head against the wall. So I tried again, this time using my hand. Nothing there but the back of the frame. Undeterred, I walked to the other side and repeated the entire process, head bump and all.

Jackpot.

Something was taped to the back right corner. Although the word "taped" implies someone used one, maybe two, small pieces of Scotch tape. Lyla had tape-overdosed, bypassing Scotch and going straight for packing. And she hadn't stopped at just a couple of pieces. She'd used ten.

I know because I took every single piece off one-handed while trying to hold the frame with the other. It was like one of those sick jokes where you opened a box only to discover a smaller one inside. I kept taking off one piece just to discover another. And another. And another.

After much prayer and a minimum of almost-cursing, I had all the tape off. It was worth the scabs I'd probably have on my hands, because I found the flash drive.

I left the office, completely forgetting I'd been in there illegally, and ran smack-dab into Kitt and Sienna. "We thought maybe you'd gotten lost," Kitt said, then glanced inside Nina's office. "That's not the bathroom."

If that had been Sienna talking, it would have been the very definition of throwing shade. But Kitt sounded genuinely confused. I palmed the flash drive and lied as smoothly as a politician up for reelection. "I lost my earring back and thought maybe it was in there. It's not, though. But if anyone sees one, please let me know. We have to go. Bye."

The transition was so random and so abrupt that Kitt looked even more confused. I used the opportunity to grab Sienna's hand and take off toward the lobby. Unfortunately, Kitt caught up. "What about the interview? Sienna's all set up."

"Just email me!"

By then we were at the exit. Kitt stopped as if the door were the South Korea / North Korea border.

"See you tonight," Sienna said as I practically dragged her through the lobby.

"Tonight?" I said as we pushed the button for the elevator.

"I played the 'we solved Lyla's murder' card and convinced her to put us both on the list for the 18th Annual Silver Sphere Awards Official Gift Lounge Presented by the Brand New Toyota Prius!"

Great.

The camera was high, imitating the view if you were a bird, a plane, or just not able to afford floor seats. The footage was clear but not crystal. The camera seemed stuck in a poor corner somewhere, giving us an angle from stage right. Not that there was much to see. The stage didn't have any of the theatrics normally associated with big-budget concerts.

Though it was bare, it wasn't empty. Anonymous men sat behind their instrument counterparts. Drums. Bass. Keyboards. All accounted for and at the ready. The camera angle gave us a money shot of a guitar player's shiny bald head. Their outfits—jeans, T-shirts, sneakers—in combination with the lack of stage decoration or people in seats let me know it was a dress rehearsal of some kind. Of what, I wasn't quite sure. It could have been for a tour. An awards show. A charity performance. Or something else entirely.

I didn't recognize the musicians. Just like I didn't recognize the stage. I took it to mean this wasn't a band. These guys weren't the stars of this show. Just another accessory like makeup or glittered stage attire meant to make someone else look—and sound—good. I watched patiently as they tuned instruments and made unintelligible small talk.

After an eon, they began to play.

I knew J. Chris would appear before she actually did. Partly due to my mad investigation skills. Mainly because I recognized the song.

"Love Overdose" was one of those sweeping ballads you turn off every time you hear it on the radio yet still manage to know every single word.

It was her first and so far only hit. And it was a duet. Mack would join her after sixteen bars and a lovelorn chorus. But for the time being, J. Chris was alone.

She floated out from the side farthest from the camera, taking slow deliberate steps like she was walking down the aisle. She paused dead center, turned to the seats like they contained thousands of people, put one hand up dramatically like she was about to praise the entire Holy Trinity, and slowly but surely raised her microphone to her mouth. She didn't quite command the stage but she gave it her best shot. And it was all a ruse to mask that she wasn't singing live.

The voice's volume stayed steady no matter where J. Chris melodramatically moved her mic. A dead giveaway she was using a backing track. Someone else's at that.

She finally hit the chorus and Mack came out exactly on cue, an entrance nowhere near as drama-filled as his wife's. Not that I paid much attention. My eyes followed J. Chris's every move, looking for that one screwup that had cost Lyla her life.

J. Chris was clearly not a fan of sharing the stage, not even with the love of her life. Mack sounded as good as ever. As he crooned, J. Chris did everything short of straight up yelling "Look at me! Not him! Me! Me! Me!" She swayed. She placed her hand on Mack's various body parts. She even managed to covertly pull her shirt down ever so slightly—a move from the same "school of distraction" as Sienna.

Mack didn't mind the blatant theatrics, even if I did. He married her, after all. He knew what he'd signed up for. It also helped that his eyes were closed through most of the performance, which was his trademark. It was probably number one on the checklist of what not to do while performing in front of a captive audience of thousands. Right up there with stage diving and throwing anything into the crowd that you ever wanted to see again. Yet for him, it worked.

I kept staring at J. Chris but Mack made it hard. His stage presence was apparent even from a cheapo security camera forgotten in some high corner. By the time he got to his climax, I stopped fighting the urge to watch his every move.

Eyes closed. Hand caressing the mic like it was the love of his life. Sweat glistening off a brow that even managed to be sexy as heck. Even in a boring old rehearsal, he was amazing. I held my breath in anticipation of the goose bumps that would appear when he finally hit the highest of his five-octave range. I leaned closer as his voice soared. Higher. Higher. Higher. Just as he was about to hit the note, I held my breath.

And that's when Mack's backing track skipped.

# *Seventeen*

Sienna and I weren't the only ones shocked and appalled by the turn of events. J. Chris also wasn't a very happy camper. At all. Whereas I was too speechless to speak, Mack's wife did not share that particular problem.

"You said we fixed this. Why are we even using this stupid track anyway? Tommy was supposed to have that guy record new vocals. People are going to start noticing you sound exactly the same when you're supposed to be singing live."

Mack wasn't as concerned. The band also seemed unbothered. The guitar player tuned his instrument. The drummer yawned. The keyboardist checked his cell. "Tommy's trying to get him into the studio but he's holding out like he always does," Mack said.

"You've already paid him out the wazoo. He should sing the dictionary if you asked him to."

"He'll come around and it'll be fine. Tomorrow will be amazing."

"Yeah, right."

It went on like that for a few more minutes before the screen abruptly went black mid-argument. Sienna and I rewatched it a couple more times before turning it off for good. "Piper isn't a woman," Sienna said.

He sure wasn't. We'd assumed, mainly because of the name and "pretty" references. But I thought back over the blind. Lyla had never used "she." Or "he" for that matter. "That's obviously what Lyla wanted," I said. "She knew everyone would guess J. Chris. The clues still fit. Mack is just as much involved in the *$3,000* remake as his wife. And he has way more to lose. He's built his career on his voice. J. Chris treats it like a fun little hobby. Like if this doesn't work out, she'll just pick up sewing. She can withstand a scandal. He can't."

"So now what?" Sienna asked.

I wanted to transfer a copy of the video to my laptop and put another one on my iCloud. But I remembered it was copy protected. Hopefully Emme could do it. "I don't know. We definitely need to keep this in a safe place. At least until I can talk to Aubrey."

Sienna took the flash drive out of her laptop and put it in her cleavage, then did a shimmy to get it in there good. She glanced up in time to see my look. "No one's been anywhere near these parts in months. This is the safest place in LA."

"Give it here, please."

"Fine, but only if you agree to go to the Silver Sphere Gift Lounge with me. Cake and Bake is going to be there. Free crack pie!"

I was too busy calling Aubrey to respond. Truth was, I probably wouldn't have gone anyway. I avoided all things Hollywood like most actresses avoided gluten. Aubrey picked up with a "Hello, Ms. Anderson."

"It's Mack Christie," I said, all dramatic-like, then quickly updated him on the video. "He's the one lip-syncing!"

I listened for a reaction. Instead, I got silence. "You don't know who Mack Christie is, do you?"

"Apparently, he is a murderer."

Touché. "So what now?"

"We need to get the video to the police as soon as possible. Is it in a safe place?"

I glanced at Sienna's boobs. "Sure ... "

"I will pick it up and take it to the police," Aubrey said.

Sounded like a plan. It was only after we hung up that I remembered I needed to call the LAPD tip line first or risk losing the reward. Of course, calling the police meant another possible conversation with the Voice. Maybe it was her day off.

No such luck. I heard the snap, crackle, and pop of her gum before she said a thing. "Tip line."

"It's 1018."

"Haven't heard from you in a couple weeks. Thought maybe you moved to Alaska."

Same. "You know I'd still call to say hey. I may have a name in the Lyla Davis murder."

I waited for reaction. Nothing. "You know what I'm talking about?" I finally asked.

"We have hundreds of open murder cases." She said it like this was a good thing.

"The Silver Sphere Award publicist gunned down at an ATM," I said. "We talked about her last time I called ... "

Still nothing. Always the first one to lose a quiet contest, I spoke again. "The police caught the killer a few days ago. He killed himself. It was on the news."

There was a pause. "They caught the guy?"

"A few days ago. Yes."

"So that would make the case closed."

"Yes ... but it may be reopened. It should be reopened." Fingers crossed. "Look, we think we found the guy who hired him. Mack Christie. We have a video."

"The singer who goes everywhere in a tour bus?" She sounded doubtful. "He confessed to you on camera?"

"Not quite. Just pass the info on to the detective in charge. Tell him we'll be dropping off a video."

"Fine, but don't hold your breath. Chances are slim to none anyone is going to bring some rich white man celebrity in for questioning on a closed case unless you have a confession."

We hung up. I just hoped she wasn't right about the police considering it a waste of time. I needed pie. And not just any pie. Crack pie from Cake and Bake. And I needed it pronto.

"Sienna, what time does the gifting suite start?"

The Google Alert appeared at the corner of Beverly and Santa Monica. Sienna drove, which put me shotgun. The radio was on KIIS FM and we were both singing loudly to the latest Kandy Wrapper song when my phone buzzed.

Because I was a glutton for punishment, I'd set up an alert for any mentions of Tomari online a couple weeks after Omari and I officially started dating. All the first few days had shown me was that Omari and Toni's "relationship" was the stuff that dreams—and fan fiction—are made of. An entire site had immediately popped up dedicated to made-up stories of how they'd met, how they "made their relationship work," and how they did *other* things. I hadn't read any of it but Sienna informed me some wasn't even half bad. I took her word for it.

After I'd gotten five alerts in a row for a five-part story involving Tomari that inexplicably took place in the same galaxy as *Star Wars*, I edited my alert to include just news articles and downgraded to one daily digest. It had become a lot more manageable—though way less exciting.

Of late, Tomari news had been slim pickings since a stripper-turned-reality star had been spotted courtside at a Lakers game wearing a jersey that just so happened to belong to the team's latest star. Most of my Tomari daily digests now consisted of "rumored beau" mentions in articles about what Toni wore and posts about Omari's Silver Sphere nomination. Apparently there was a Vegas pool to see if he'd take her as his date. Knowing the answer, I was tempted to bet.

The story was from Gus the Gossip's site and it was hot-off-the-press—or rather the Internet equivalent, hot-off-hitting-the-send-button.

His headline was a doozy: *Search and Frisk-y: Hollywood Lovers Tomari Caught in Steamy Embrace in a Gus the Gossip Exclusive!!!!!*

Overdramatic much?

Not worried in the least, I clicked the link. Someone had probably caught Emme and Omari when we were all together at some point. It wouldn't be the first time a paparazzi sold misleading pics.

The photos were blurry but still clear enough to make out Omari. I'd recognize that dome anywhere. Just like I could recognize the back of Emme's head. That was definitely not Emme. Either there was a triplet I didn't know about or Omari was indeed with Toni.

I leaned in as the air rushed out of my body.

They looked ready to kiss.

# Eighteen

I blamed the angle for it looking like their lips were about to touch. Both leaning into each other, heads tilted at opposing angles, Omari's one visible hand placed comfortably around her black leather and lace mini-dress. Toni's mouth was open just a touch and the tip of Omari's tongue peaked out.

It looked like a movie poster.

Except it wasn't. There was no question who it was. Who they were. There was a question of why they were together and why my boyfriend had neglected to bring it up.

That's what concerned me. Not the actual kissing or at least the appearance of the act. I'd taken enough selfies and mirror shots to know angles could be more deceiving than a two-hour David Copperfield performance. They weren't kissing any more than they were about to pull a rabbit out of a hat or cut someone in half. But Omari should have mentioned the meeting. He knew people were always watching, always gossiping, always taking covert cell phone pics.

Call me old-fashioned, but you should tell your real girlfriend when you run into your imaginary girlfriend somewhere. It was common courtesy.

I immediately texted him the link, waited an obligatory two minutes to give him a chance to click on it, and called him. When he picked up on the second ring, I didn't give him a chance to say hello.

"You got the text?"

The tone of my voice made Sienna throw me a 99-mile-per-hour glance, but she knew better than to say anything. I'd forgotten she was even in the car.

"Someone caught a millisecond of a ten-second hug."

"I know. But you could have told me you ran into her."

"I did." He sounded so confident that for a second I thought maybe he had. But I was mildly obsessed with Tomari. I would have remembered.

"I don't think so," I finally said.

"Hey Day, I ran into Toni at an event the other night. I hugged her, said hi. She asked me how you were doing. She told me to tell you hey. So, hey. From Toni."

"This doesn't bother you at all? That people think you're dating someone you're not?"

"Why would it? It's not true. Just like you know it's not true. Addressing it will only bring more attention to a conversation that lasted one minute before her publicist dragged her away to talk to someone else and Nina tried to corner Will Smith so we could get a quick pic."

Ugh. Omari and his male logic that managed to be clueless and make perfect sense at the exact same time. I was tempted to say something but decided it wasn't worth an argument. It was probably what Nina wanted anyway.

Nina who had probably engineered the entire thing. I immediately flashed to her asking Gus about some exclusive. Was this what she was talking about?

Omari's voice slashed through my thoughts. "Look, my trainer is giving me the death stare. Can we discuss this later?"

"Fine."

We hung up but I kept talking about it. To her credit, Sienna listened obediently as I whined and moaned. It was the epitome of "first-world, hot-actor-boyfriend" problems. But still. Talking about things normally made me feel better. Yet by the time Sienna pulled up to the W hotel, my mood still hadn't improved. "I'm not feeling up to this. Maybe I should just go home."

"Maybe," she said. That settled it. We were going home. I put my seat belt back on, ready for her to pull back into the street. Instead, she opened her door.

"Maybe Dante can give you a ride," she said.

Ride? She was not coming with me. "You're just going to leave me? To be sad and alone?"

"You're gonna mope anyway. You can mope while sitting on the couch at home. You can mope while waiting in the car. Or you can mope while people hand you free stuff inside. Call it multitasking."

The girl had a point.

When we got to the Gifting Lounge, we found Kitt in the hall manning the list and ignoring the crowd of tourists and gawkers standing around not even pretending to look busy. That was what separated an LA resident from a visitor. We *all* noticed celebrities. Those of us who lived here just pretended we didn't. While tourists took pics, we performed head-to-toe evaluations that we could casually mention over drinks with friends.

Kitt waved us right over and for a brief minute I missed my fifteen minutes of fame. I'd peaked around eight minutes and fifteen seconds, when Chubby's had sprung for a Super Bowl commercial. That thirty-second spot got me VIP entrance into every club in LA for the rest of month. Of course, the next month I was back to waiting in line with the other mortals. Good times regardless.

"Hi ladies. So glad you could make it! Enjoy this complimentary beverage from Dom Perignon. Don't worry. It's gluten-free." She handed us a champagne glass, our first freebie of the evening, then immediately followed it with the second—a bag made from a material so rough I could use it to exfoliate. I downed my shot as Kitt went into her spiel.

"This is a one hundred percent biodegradable tote made from recycled soda cans discovered by homeless people living on the island of Manhattan. It gives them a sense of purpose as well as a source of income. The bag retails for $300 and one percent of the proceeds go to the Home Less Charity, which benefits celebrities no longer able to afford their homes in their Hollywood Hills neighborhoods. Please use them to hold any products that you wish to take home this evening."

I was impressed. Not so much about the Home Less Charity. More so that Kitt had recited all that without once looking at any notes. Sienna and I nodded appropriately. I noticed Sienna surreptitiously grab a second bag from the table. She clearly wasn't here to play any games. I couldn't judge her much. By that time, I was on free drink number two. Three if you count the one I took for the road.

Biodegradable, homeless-employing bags and probably not-biodegradable shot glasses at the ready, we stepped inside. It turned out I didn't need to permanently borrow the extra glass of champagne. There was plenty more where that came from. Servers walked around with trays of flutes for the taking. Good to know.

As one might expect from the 18th Annual Silver Sphere Awards Official Gift Lounge Presented by the Brand New Toyota Prius, the first thing we encountered was, in fact, a brand new Toyota Prius. Someone had parked one smack-dab at the entrance. I wasn't sure how it got there, especially considering we weren't on the first floor. But I guess when there's a will, there's a way.

The rest of the room was just as impressive. The W was the type of place that didn't have conference rooms or meeting rooms. It had event spaces. Of course, the W's event space looked just like a conference room. Only difference was that it had a permanent chandelier. It gave the entire proceedings the look of a really fancy trade show or—depending on your level of bougie—a blinged-out swap meet.

About twenty vendors had set up shop, or should I say booths. None had skimped on branding. A candle vendor seemed to think SSO gave out awards for glitziest setup. They'd gone all out with lots of shiny, happy objects and shiny, happy people. Another vendor created a two-foot-tall chocolate replica of the Silver Sphere Award. And a manicure station had been set up to highlight a line of edible eco-friendly lacquers.

I still hadn't rectified my aborted mani attempt so Sienna and I immediately signed up for a later appointment, then went "shopping." I finished glass number two as we headed back to the candle vendor, which had a complimentary tea station anchored on both ends by two Keurigs. Past experience showed me we had as much luck getting a man to Mars as I did of properly operating one of those machines, but the tea smelled so dang good that I decided to risk it.

I put my third glass of Dom down, then grabbed a cup and headed to the machine on the left side of the table. I was trying to stuff the K-Cup in the hole area when one of the vendors approached. "May I help you?"

I smiled. "Just trying to get some tea. It smells amazing. I can never figure out how these things work."

"That's because that's our diffuser. You're smelling our home goods scented pod line. That's our Pomegranate and Apricot White Tea scent."

I nodded appropriately. If she could act like having a K-Cup look-alike meant to smell like a tea meant to smell like a fruit was perfectly normal, then so could I. I was about to say something equally ridiculous when I heard a voice behind me.

"Is Omari here?"

I turned. There she was. The source of my relationship angst. Nina. I immediately wanted to thrust my phone in her face while screaming about the article. Instead, I played it cool. Since I wasn't getting any tea, I snagged a glass of champagne from a passing waiter. My other glass was too far away. I calmly took a long sip, then spoke. "He's with his trainer. I saw the Gus the Gossip article."

I was proud at how casual I sounded. It was almost as if I hadn't spent thirty minutes of my life I'd never get back hardcore obsessing about it. She looked at me blankly as I took another sip. If she wanted to play dumb, then okay. "About Omari and Toni. Making out."

"Oh, that. I don't know where Gus gets this stuff."

She had the nerve to look innocent. I downed the champagne, then spoke again. "You. He gets it from you."

Nina looked taken aback. Or at least attempted to. She really was too young for Botox but had yet to let that stop her from monthly injections. "What are you talking about?"

"I'm talking about a couple hours ago when you reminded Kitt to remind Gus to run some exclusive this afternoon. And Gus so happens to run an exclusive *this afternoon* about your client. Basically your only client. *My* boyfriend."

Nina continued to smile but there was a change in her voice. "I didn't give anything to Gus and if I did, it would be because it's why Omari pays me—to keep his name out there and help him get recognition and awards. Sweetie, jealousy looks about as good on you as that outfit."

And with that she walked away, leaving me to glare at her retreating back. She meant to intimidate me. It didn't work. At least not much. I wasn't becoming a jealous girlfriend. Right? Right? I knew I was. But still. I needed reassurance. Pronto.

I found it at a lingerie booth getting an onsite bra fitting. "I'm not a jealous girlfriend, right?" I said.

"Nope." Sienna's reply was so automatic that she sounded like a robot. What made it worse was she was holding her hands above her while a "lingerie expert" carefully lifted one of her boobs.

The expert stepped back and eyed Sienna's chest like a jeweler appraising a diamond. She spoke. "Normally I'd suggest one of our patented bras, but you still have a good three years left on your breast enhancement. You should go with something from our playful line."

And what that, she disappeared while I kept on. "I'm tempted to contact Gus. Let it leak I'm dating Omari. Beat Nina at her own game." Technically, I was the one speaking, but it was really the champagne talking.

I was feeling nice. So nice I got another glass when a server wandered by. As fun as the fantasy sounded, I'd never do it. Could never do it. Omari would kill me. Still, the thought was fun, even if it was just for a second.

"Great idea," Sienna said, still on best friend autopilot.

I doubted she was even listening. Not that I let that deter me. "And if I'm acting like a jealous girlfriend—"

"Which you're not," Robot Sienna interrupted.

"—then it's because Nina has made me like this. I mean, who plants stories like that? I just wish he realized how much of a big deal it is to me even if it isn't to him."

"Exactly," Sienna said. "Look, if this is bugging you—and it clearly is—you need to talk to him about it."

She could sense my hesitation because she spoke again. "You know I'm right."

"I don't wanna."

"What's the worst that could happen?"

"He tells me I sound jealous?"

"Maybe, but at this rate, keep holding this in and one day you're going to lose it. And they'll be interviewing me for your *Snapped* episode. Talk to the man. He's a not a mind reader. And he might actually understand."

The lingerie expert returned and handed her a bag stuffed full of bras. Sienna smiled her thanks and the vendor asked for a quick photo. It wasn't a fan selfie. She wanted a pic to use for their marketing efforts.

"Of course," Sienna said. "I can even take my shirt off."

There was a pause as the lingerie expert considered it. Finally, I broke in. "I don't think that's necessary. Fully clothed is fine."

They both nodded. Sienna posed for a few pics holding a variety of bras and then turned to me. "It's time for my edible mani. You gonna be okay?"

I nodded. That's when I realized I was drunk. Off three-ish glasses of champagne. Great. Apparently gluten didn't just prevent food from tasting like cardboard. It also helped me hold my alcohol. Too late now.

I still had fifteen minutes to kill before my own appointment so I attempted more free retail therapy. My aimless wandering led me to my second surprise of the afternoon: the Focals booth. What made it even better was that they were giving out not-yet-released next generation versions of Emme's birthday present. I immediately grabbed one, then looked around. The vendor was busy talking to someone I sort of recognized. I grabbed another. Might as well get one for myself, too.

Emme would be so happy—and actually surprised—when she opened two pairs on her birthday. She could brag to all her friends on that online game where they just sat around doing laundry. I was so happy—read, drunk—I skipped to my nail appointment.

The most noteworthy thing about my manicurist was her nails. Understandable. Free advertisement and all. They were a complicated stiletto design covered in shiny silver that made her look like the female version of Wolverine. For a brief moment I worried she might slip mid-mani and stab me with one.

I took a seat anyway. Even the risk of impending stitches was not enough to deter me from a free manicure, especially one I desperately needed. I'd soaked the remaining gel off myself but hadn't had time to put on polish. She took my left hand in both of hers and began to gently rub them as she spoke. "I'm Shine. What are we doing today?"

I imagined myself jabbing dagger nails like Shine's in Nina's face the next time she ran an "exclusive." The only thing that stopped me was they looked like a pain in the you-know-what to get off. "Just a regular manicure is fine."

"Great." Shine proceeded to get to work. Her hands were soft and in a weird way calming. Like she probably gave the most amazing massages. "You enjoying the suite so far?"

"I tried to make tea in a diffuser," I said, then smiled.

She acted like my response was the most normal thing she'd heard all day. Considering this was Hollywood, it just might have been. "Have you tried the sensory deprivation tank yet?" I threw her a look, signaling I hadn't. She took her cue to continue. "It's the latest thing.

Rock the Float sent over a few of their new take-home pods for guests to try out. You should sign up ASAP because the spots are going quick. I just saw Mack Christie heading up there."

I literally jumped at the sound of his name, almost causing poor Shine to clip off more than just a cuticle. Mack Christie was here getting his sensories deprived while poor Lyla was still dead? Not fair. And not cool. At all.

The Voice had basically told me we needed a confession from Mack. In my drunken stupor, I took it as a sign that we happened to be in the same place at the same time. The investigation gods obviously wanted me to talk to him. Stat.

I jumped up and snatched my hand away from poor Shine. "I have to run to the bathroom."

Then I went to find Mack. Of course, I also used the bathroom.

Finding the sensory deprivation tanks wasn't hard. There were helpful "human arrows" that consisted of actual humans holding arrow posters every fifty feet, directing me to another floor, where Rock the Float had taken over a trio of hotel rooms off in a corner of the hotel. They'd even slapped names on each door. *Tranquility. Serenity.* And *Check-In.*

I was surprised to not see any entourages or bodyguards hanging around in the hallway, but then I remembered this was the W. No way they let anyone loiter in the hallway and disturb paying guests. The assorted celeb hangers-on were all probably hanging in Check-In. I only had to step inside to discover I was correct. They'd removed the bed and replaced it with office equipment. One lone woman employee sat at a table in the middle of the room between a couch and table full of healthy snacks. Gag.

She wasn't alone but she was clearly the only one working. A handful of people milled about. Mack Christie's requisite entourage.

Though conversation never stopped, all turned to appraise me as soon as I came in. Within .01 seconds I was dismissed as "nobody important." They turned away in unison. I wasn't offended. At all. That was the official greeting in these parts. Call it the Hollywood Hello.

The plan was to wait it out so I ignored them, pretending to busy myself looking at a flyer someone had thoughtfully taped on the closet door explaining the At-Home Sensory Deprivation pod, a truly immersive experience allowing one to get in touch with one's innermost feelings by recreating life at its origin—the womb. Frankly, I was surprised they didn't refer to exiting the pod as a rebirth. Missed opportunity there. I checked the price tag. One could own their very own isolation tank for $3,000. Or one could just turn out the lights and get in one's bathtub for free.

The flyer also included instructions on what to do for your appointment. Apparently clothing was optional and you needed to key in 2222 to enter the guest room.

"Hi!" The Rock the Float woman came up next to me. "Are you our second 5:30 appointment? The pod is ready and waiting."

Ugh. She clearly was not going to let me just loiter. I shook my head and did an immediate—if somewhat awkward—about-face to leave. The good thing about being a lower than Z-list celebrity was everyone immediately forgot I was there. I intended to use it to my advantage. Instead of heading back toward the elevators, I turned toward Tranquility and Serenity. Mack Christie was in one of them. I just needed to figure out which one and get inside to talk to him.

It wasn't the smartest idea, but unfortunately I had a history of chasing after murderers. Why stop now? I tried Serenity first. The lock had both a key entry and a number pad. I typed in 2222.

It buzzed.

I stepped inside, immediately locking the door behind me and sliding the security bar for good measure. Then I took in my surroundings. There wasn't much. Like with the check-in room, they'd taken out the bed. But instead of ho-hum office furniture, they'd replaced it with what I could only assume was mankind's latest, greatest invention: The At-Home Sensory Deprivation pod. It looked like it could have shipped a baby Superman from his home on Krypton. It was round and shiny and definitely wouldn't fit in the décor of anyone's apartment I knew.

I waited, expecting Mack to pop out any second, curious to see who was depriving him of sensory deprivation. When he didn't, I marched over and knocked on the outer pod. Then I waited. Nothing. I knocked again, more insistent this time. Again, no answer. The thing needed a doorbell or something. I listened for movement inside, worried maybe I'd picked the wrong room. Maybe no one was in there. Or maybe, just maybe, sensory deprivation actually worked.

There was a button on the side of the pod. It wasn't labeled but I figured it for how one communicated with the outside world and they communicated with you. I pushed it and spoke. "I know your secret. I know what you did. You will pay."

I sounded pretty kick-butt, if I do say so myself. But again, I got nothing. Blurg.

Mack Christie wasn't in there. I'd picked the wrong room. I was heading back to the hall to check what was behind door number two when someone knocked on the room door. The voice was muffled yet I understood every word—even through my champagne haze. "Hotel security. Open up!"

Fudge.

I didn't answer. Big shocker there. They tried again. "Open the door."

No and thank you. Even if they typed in the code, I'd put the deadbolt and the security bar on. It gave me a false sense of confidence. I was alone. I wasn't hungry—for now. I would need to use the bathroom, but that was the thing with hotel rooms. They all came equipped with one.

Security wasn't getting in. At least not anytime soon. I had every intention of waiting it out ... until I heard the sound of what could only be the pod opening.

# Nineteen

I wasn't opening the room door. Jumping out the window was definitely out. My only option was to hide. Stat. But there wasn't a bed to crawl under and the pod was already occupied. I chose the closet.

I squeezed in and closed the door as best I could, sending up silent prayers that Mack hadn't heard a thing. Maybe he'd assume I left before security stopped by. Or that I was some super cool, kick-butt black girl detective who could scale a balcony—instead of a scared one who hid in a closet.

I shrank back as I heard Mack emerge from the pod. A few minutes later, I made out a flash of naked white flesh as it streaked past me to the front door. I expected to hear the hotel room door opening. Instead, I heard nothing. A second later, the mound of flesh was back and standing right in front of me. Only an inch of wood stood between me and a killer.

Nothing like standing in a peewee-sized closet hiding from both security and a lip-syncing country music criminal mastermind to sober a girl up. This was such a bad idea. I was literally caught between a rock (god) and a hard place. Where was Security? I'd rather be permanently banned from the W than dead.

I instinctively sank farther into the closet, as if giving myself an extra ten seconds to live would help. The closet door opened and I went on the attack. Eyes closed, I charged. I couldn't get up much speed in less than a foot, but it was better than nothing. My momentum pushed Mack back. He let out a sigh as he hit a wall.

I turned toward the exit and opened my eyes. The security bar was still on. I needed to change that. Pronto. I'd just gotten it disengaged when I felt hands around my waist, pulling me back. My clothed back came in direct contact with wet skin. "We meet again," a voice whispered in my ear.

A voice that sounded suspiciously like the one I'd heard in the *Man in Danger 3: Man in Serious Danger* red band trailer the last time I went to the movies. I looked back and made direct eye contact with Todd Arrington. A Todd Arrington wearing nothing but a towel. He spoke again. "We really need to stop running into each other like this."

Who was he telling?

The door to the hotel room opened and Todd and I were face to face with two security guards and the Rock the Float rep. I didn't know who was more surprised. Todd finally let me go. I tried to sidestep a guard to exit the room. No such luck. He had me before I could escape. His touch was nowhere near as gentle as Todd's had been. The guard spoke first. "Mr. Arrington, we're so sorry for the disturbance. Do you know this woman?"

"No," I said, before he had a chance to. I didn't care if I was incriminating myself. The last thing I needed was Todd telling people he knew me because I'd broken into his house and interrupted some innocent role play between him and a possible prostitute.

"Didn't think so. Would you like to press charges?"

Todd looked at me. "That won't be necessary."

The guard looked disappointed. This was clearly the highlight of his day. I briefly imagined him sharing the story with his wife over the mashed potatoes and chicken she served for dinner, overembellishing so that he broke into the room and took me down just as I almost attacked the famous movie star. "You sure?"

Todd nodded and the security guard pulled me out the door. I glanced back in time to see Todd give me a wave. "See you soon," he mouthed.

I sincerely hoped not. As we left, I saw the security cameras shoved every few feet in the ceiling—something I really should have noticed earlier. Blurg. We passed a cluster of people. And at the center? Mack Christie. Maybe it was the lingering effects of the alcohol but at that moment, I didn't care about a confession. I just wanted him to know. Know I was on to him. Know I wouldn't let him get away with it. Know he was going to go to prison. As we made eye contact, I smiled and said one word. "Anani."

There was no physical reaction, but the eye-to-eye combat ended as quickly as a low-rated canceled TV show. That was enough for me.

The guards made a big show of parading me through the Gifting Lounge instead of a more celeb-friendly private exit. People openly gawked as I was dragged by. I'd never been more embarrassed in my life—if you didn't count five minutes before when I'd broken into Todd Arrington's Sensory Deprivation Tank session, falsely accused him of murder, and hid in the world's most easily found hiding place. Even two-year-olds knew to check the closet first.

We were midway through the lounge when I realized my eco-friendly gift suite bag was still waiting along with Shine at Global Nails. My mind flashed on Emme's birthday gift. "Can I get my stuff please? I left a bag."

"You'll be all right," the guard said. "And so we're clear. You are not to set foot on these premises again. Ever."

I bit back a question about whether my photo would be posted at check-in like some Most Wanted poster. I honestly was afraid of the answer. We kept walking and were almost to the door when we passed Sienna. My bestie looked in my direction, then quickly looked away to grab another pair of retro sunglasses. I couldn't blame her. She obviously wasn't done shopping yet. I just hoped she picked up a few pairs of Focals so I could still give one to Emme.

I was deposited outside the front entrance, where I dutifully waited twenty minutes for Sienna to finally join me. The good news? She had, in fact, gotten my bag. When she'd gone to find me at the nail booth, Shine told her I'd gone to the bathroom thirty minutes prior and had not returned. Shine didn't think much of it—having attributed my absence to perhaps eating too much dairy.

Sienna readily agreed. She'd recently read that 75 percent of all black people were lactose intolerant, which caused her to immediately remove all forms of milk products from our condo. I was okay with it. As long as she didn't take away my gluten. It obviously kept me from getting drunk and making bad decisions involving would-be murderers.

If only it could help me solve Lyla's murder. The Voice had been rude, but she'd also been right. I needed more. There was no way anyone was letting me within throwing distance of Mack Christie, so *Confrontation Part 2: Electric Boogaloo* was out. It would have been nice to have the email from Viv mentioning the threat. But I didn't, thanks to drafts, which meant I needed something better. Viv herself.

When we got home, I opened my laptop. What I needed to write required more than just thumbs going to town on a small touchscreen. I titled the draft: "Anani is dead."

Overdramatic? Not at all. I laid it all out. How Lyla was Anani. How she was brutally murdered. How Junior killed himself. And, finally, how Mack Christie was the one behind it all.

*I'm going to stop him but I need your help. You need to come forward with what you know. If not for Lyla, then do it for yourself. Before you end up just like her. Your life is in danger. And the only way to protect yourself and put a stop to this is to come forward with what you know.*

*Please.*

Then I shut my laptop and waited.

There was no word from Viv the next morning, which meant I had two choices: refresh the inbox religiously or go visit my boyfriend.

I ended up doing both, tempting the traffic gods by checking Gmail on my phone at every stoplight. It may have been the first time ever I appreciated LA traffic. By the time I made it downtown, there was still nothing. I'd forgotten my parking lot key fob so I parked on 12th Street smack-dab outside Omari's building, then took the elevator up to his apartment. I found him eating breakfast. Shirtless.

"There she is," he said. It was as if he'd already forgotten about our conversation yesterday. Blurg.

As much as I wanted to forget myself, I couldn't. Sienna was right. I needed to talk to him about how I was feeling.

"What do I owe the pop-up visit?" he asked.

"We need to chat. But first, you need to put on a shirt."

He smiled. "Oh, it must be a serious convo if it requires clothing."

I said nothing, just waited as he grabbed a shirt from the dryer and put it on, all the while willing myself to not chicken out. When he finally sat back down, I launched right in. "It bugs me that the entire world thinks you're dating Toni."

It took him forty-three seconds to respond. I counted. "Okay ..." he said.

That was it. Just okay. Blurg. I waited him out and after another thirty-four seconds, he spoke again. "You know there's nothing I can do about that, Day."

"You can tell people it's not true."

"Is it really that important?"

I waited a beat, then finally said one word. "Yes."

"Fine," he said. "I'll call Nina."

I wasn't expecting him to cartwheel to get his phone or anything but I would have appreciated a little more enthusiasm. It was clear he still didn't see the big deal but was doing it because I wanted him too. I was going to have to be fine with that.

I said nothing as he selected a number and put it on speaker. Nina answered before the first ring even had a chance to finish: "You weren't there yesterday. Dayna was, though."

Fudge. I probably should have factored my minor little incident involving Todd Arrington and Mack Christie into my plan. Nina was going to snitch on me. It took every ounce of restraint not to grab the phone and throw it out the nearest window. Instead, I focused my energy on plastering an innocent smile on my face and brainstorming scenarios about why I'd been permanently banned from W hotel.

"I didn't get to talk to her much," Nina continued. "There was an incident involving a drunk groupie trying to have sex with Todd

Arrington. They found her in a hotel room with him. Of course, he was half naked. They escorted her out of the hotel before I could find out any more."

This was how things got misconstrued. In less than twenty-four hours, my drunkenly confronting Todd Arrington because I thought he was Mack Christie had morphed into a groupie drunkenly seducing Todd Arrington and getting him out of his artfully ripped jeans. Not saying the actual scenario was any better. But still. I'd take it.

"Sounds like that was for the best," Omari said and I nodded vigorously. "Listen, I want you to issue a statement that Toni and I aren't dating."

Crisis averted. I smiled. For the first time ever, I wanted to see Nina's face. Her jaw had to be on the floor. To her credit, she didn't scream out "No!!!!!!!!!!!!!!!!!!!!!!!!!!!!" though I was sure she thought it. When she finally spoke, her voice sounded calm. Too calm. "I thought we don't comment on your personal life."

"We don't comment on true stuff. This one's a lie."

"If this is in reference to that Gus article, I spoke to him about it," she said. "He assured me it won't happen again. Let's just hold off on any statements right now. If we don't say anything, it's bound to get lost in awards season coverage."

To his credit, he rolled his eyes. "Just issue the statement."

I was pleased. Nina, however, was still not ready to go down without a fight. She didn't care that the match was already over. "Look, can I be honest with you? Just for a sec. Normally I'd totally agree, but you know you're up for that part in the new Spike Lee movie. It's good to have your name out there."

"Issue. The. Statement."

There was a pause. She had to be debating what tack to try next. So far, she was zero for two. "Fine. Will do."

It sounded like Nina had given up, but I knew her better than that. It wasn't a concession. It was a retreat. She'd just lick her wounds and come back stronger than ever. I'd be ready.

He hung up.

"Thank you for breaking up Tomari."

I was being playful but he turned serious. "I know you think I don't care who people think I'm dating. It's not that. I don't want our relationship to become a cute nickname. Our dates to be likes on Instagram. Our vacations crowdsourced by people who think we should have gone to this place instead."

"I get that," I said, because I did. "You can take your shirt back off now."

I was about to say more when my phone beeped.

"Aubrey?" Omari asked.

"He doesn't text. It can wait," I said, but threw a quick glance at my phone anyway. What if it was Viv?

If I'd hoped Omari didn't notice my throwing lustful looks and not at him, I was disappointed. "Check it," he said.

"You sure?"

He gave me a quick peck and headed upstairs to the bedroom. I checked to see which app had sent the notification. Someone had indeed logged into the Viv3000 account. My heart beat faster—the technology equivalent of watching a horror movie. Except instead of what was waiting in the closet, I wanted to know what was waiting in drafts. Viv had to help me—without her I had nothing. Geppetto would be as free as Pinocchio immediately after he'd lost his strings.

I sat down and forced myself to log in. It took the inbox forever to load. And when it did, I immediately wished it had taken much longer.

It was empty. Viv had deleted the draft altogether.

I'd messed up again. Pushed too hard, again. Too fast. And I didn't know how to fix it. This was my one connection to Lyla's source. Much like that messy impulsive drunk sext you immediately regret sending to your ex, all connections to Viv was now in the ether, with no hope of getting them back.

Fudge.

Aubrey would know what to do. I hoped he wasn't as tired of my rookie mistakes as I was. It was a convo I wanted to have in person, which meant that I needed to head to Los Feliz.

I ran upstairs to give Omari a quick goodbye, then headed to my car. But when I put the key in the ignition and cranked the engine, nothing happened. I'd just paid to get the car fixed. This wasn't supposed to happen. I was this close to repeatedly banging my head against the steering wheel when I heard the knock. Apparently I'd left my window cracked.

"Want me to jump you?" The voice was male and as melodic as a black preacher forty-five minutes deep into his Sunday morning sermon.

I looked up. He didn't look like a preacher, more like the guy that caused you to go to church in the first place to repent or secretly ask God for a reason to repent. He was tall and a sturdy that couldn't be bought by spending six days at the gym with skin a warm, deep brown so flawless I suddenly understood writers' obsessions with describing black people as food and drink. The suit was as flawless as the skin tone, a perfectly tailored creation someone had to have created just for him. It was all-black everything, from the jacket and shirt down to the shoes.

"Thanks, but I don't need any help," I said.

He didn't bother to bend down. Of course, that didn't stop him from smiling at me, a lopsided grin that nevertheless lit up his entire face. "You sure? Because I'd love to jump you. You know, if you wanted me to."

I most certainly did not. "I don't take help from strangers. That's like rule number one in kindergarten."

"I'm Z. So one, we're not strangers. And two, I think the first rule is listen to your teacher." He motioned for me to open the door and that's when I noticed the cufflinks. They were purple squares, with as many boxes as a Bingo card. Strange.

I forced myself to look away from them as I spoke again. "I don't get help from people who don't even know my name."

"That another thing they taught you in kindergarten, Dayna?"

He said my name like we'd known each other for years. We hadn't.

Here's the thing about fame—fleeting or not. People know you. Or at least think they do. At the height of my Chubby's celebrity, immediately after the Super Bowl commercial and the *Today* show appearance, I'd get "Hey Dayna"-ed at least once a week. Omari already had it worse. When he was out, people called his name from across busy restaurants and even busier streets.

It was possible that this Z, who had appeared like a fairy godmother in my time of need, was a fan. Surprisingly, I still had a few of those. Only thing was, he didn't seem like the type to watch TV at all, much less commercials. And that made me more nervous.

Here was a stranger who knew my name. Who knew where my boyfriend lived. Who knew where I'd be and when. I was a woman—a black one at that—and I was alone on a street in downtown LA. If I went missing, I'd be lucky if the news even noticed. I'd have to hope someone tweeted my pic and it somehow went viral. That would be my only chance of escaping from the hole in Z's basement. I made a promise to myself I would *not* put the lotion in the basket. No matter how melodic his voice was.

I was contemplating it all when he spoke again. "Viv wants to talk to you."

Viv? Wanted to talk to me? He really should have started with that. I went from scared to excited. Wondered where he or she was. I looked around and still saw no one.

"Come get in the car," Z said.

To my credit, I did not in fact get in the car. At least not his car.

"I'll follow you in a Lyft."

And that's exactly what I did. My driver was named Jamal. He smiled at me as I got in. "You didn't put where we're going."

"I don't know." I pointed to the Mercedes that Z got into. "Just follow that car."

Jamal did as told. He didn't say anything at first, just kept glancing at me in his rearview mirror. Finally he spoke. "Did we go to high school together?"

There it was.

I decided for once to be honest. "The black chick in the Chubby's Chicken commercials? That was me."

"Yes! I loved that phrase of yours. *Don't think so, b—*"

I cut him off. "Please don't say it. You're gonna give me flashbacks."

He laughed. Ice broken, we followed Z as Jamal regaled me with stories about how much he loved his wife and two kids. Their pictures—and there were a lot of them—were adorable. In between oohing and aahing over Jamal's twins, I texted Sienna and Emme what was going on and then immediately enabled the Do Not Disturb function on my phone. I didn't need either of them telling me it was a bad idea. I already knew, which is why I'd made sure to bring my pepper spray.

We followed Z as he stayed on 12th Street and headed east. We were heading to the Fashion District, an area I'd practically lived at during my pre-fame days. Then we turned down a street I didn't realize existed. That didn't bode well. At all. Just where did this Viv live and why couldn't we have met at one of the coffee shops he or she loved so much? I was glad that Sienna, Emme, and I had enabled share your location on our phones.

Our final destination was a two-story warehouse that looked ready to crumble at any second. Someone had thoughtfully spray-painted *Die* in bright red letters at least three feet tall. The door looked like it would take a crowbar to open. I was pretty sure I'd seen it used in a horror flick once. One where the black chick died first.

I had one thought: *Don't think so, boo.*

I leaned forward so Jamal could hear every word that came out my mouth. "There's no way in hell we're stopping."

He kept going.

I had Jamal drop me off at the most public place I could think of—a complex called LA Live across the street from the Staples Center. There wasn't a game or a show at the Microsoft Theater so the place wasn't crowded. But it was busy enough for my purposes—staying alive. I wanted to talk to Viv. I just didn't want it to be my last words.

The way I saw it, if Viv really wanted to meet me, he or she would come to me. Of course, I hadn't told Z of the change of plans. In my defense, I didn't have his number. So I went to email, leaving a quick note in the Viv account drafts: *I'm at LA Live. You have a half hour.*

No response, but Z showed up within fifteen minutes. I wasn't surprised to see him again. I gave him a friendly wave as I palmed my pepper spray in my other hand. At first I thought he'd brought cinnamon pastries, but then I realized it was his cologne.

"Something tells me you don't trust me, Dayna," Z said.

"Don't know what would give you that idea."

And that was it for the small talk. I busied myself nervously checking Sienna's Instagram account while Z just stood there. It went on like that for five minutes.

"Is Viv coming or not?" I asked.

"Impatient, aren't we?" He glanced down. "We can always wait in my car. I know those shoes aren't comfortable."

They weren't, but that was the whole point. They were Pink Panthers, a hot pink stiletto that came with panther spots and a three-and-a-half-inch heel.

"Is that what you do?" I asked. "Drive Viv around?"

He shook his head but didn't say anything. I took it as a sign that I should continue to probe. "But you do work for Viv?"

"In a sense."

"Doing … "

He smiled then. "Problem solving."

This was LA, which meant only one thing. The problems he solved had nothing to do with math. "You're a fixer."

Fixers were the LA equivalent of a unicorn. You knew they existed but it was rare to see one in the wild. They were who big-time celebs called when they had a major problem like a baby on the way from someone who wasn't their wife, or being caught red-handed in a den of iniquity. In short, they *fixed* problems and made them go away.

I'd heard rumors about fixers for years but this was my first real sighting. Even with the circumstances, I was a little bit excited. Sienna would freak. Well, she would after she yelled at me for going somewhere with a stranger. Even though I didn't actually go inside.

"I'm not a fixer," Z said. "I'm a problem solver."

I didn't realize there was a difference. "And I'm a problem?"

He didn't respond. At first I thought he didn't have a snappy comeback. I was all set to be disappointed when he glanced at his cell. "Viv's here."

I quickly glanced around. All I saw were couples on dates and families heading to the movie theater. Was Viv a soccer dad who wore flip-flops? I hoped not.

Z noticed my pending disappointment. "Not here. Parking lot one. Top floor. Viv is staying for five minutes before leaving."

I had a choice. Go there or go home. A stranger had approached me on the street and convinced me to go with him to meet another stranger. My mom, Sienna, and Emme would be standing over my casket all arguing over who had last "told me so."

"What if I want to go home?"

"You don't. You may think you do. But you don't." He paused. Then, "And you can always use that pepper spray you've been holding on to for dear life."

True. All of it. But despite my tough talk earlier, I wanted to talk to Viv. It might be my only chance. It was a parking lot, not an abandoned warehouse. Somebody would be around in case things went left.

The parking lot was across Chick Hearn Way behind the Staples Center. I headed in that direction. It took me about ten feet to realize Z was still where I'd left him. "You're not coming?" I said, as if I'd known him years instead of minutes.

He shook his head. "I have no doubt you'll be fine without me."

"You gonna be here when I come back?"

Instead of answering he recited a string of digits. "Call if you need anything. Like another jump."

He walked away.

I watched him go, then crossed the street and was at the elevator before I knew it. It took forever to come. When it arrived, it was empty. I hit the button for the top floor. When the doors opened, the parking lot was practically deserted. A few cars, no people. One vehicle stood out, a shiny black Range Rover with pitch black windows taking up two handicapped spots. I couldn't see inside, which was the point. Besides, I didn't have to. I know who was in there.

Viv.

I stood in the elevator, not one for covert rendezvous. I hated when they happened in movies and wasn't really feeling them in real life. I didn't have to get out, just stay there until the doors closed. Head back downstairs. Head home and watch *The First 48* marathon that Sienna saved on the DVR. But I didn't. Z was right. A key to solving Lyla's murder was waiting for me behind the car door. I decided I was ready to play *Let's Make a Deal.* Mack Christie needed to be behind bars.

I stepped into the garage and walked straight toward the Range Rover about twenty feet away. Slowly at first, then picking up speed, figuring I might as well get it over with. I walked toward the car just as the engine turned on.

I was reminding myself for the kajillionth time I didn't have to do this when the back passenger window rolled down, bringing me face to face with Viv.

Or, should I say, Mack Christie himself.

# Twenty

It was my third encounter with Mack Christie. I wouldn't describe it as a charm. He didn't get out of the car. I stayed put too, hugging the wall like a sixth grader at his first coed party. We just stared at each other for almost a minute. I counted.

Finally, Mack must've realized I was just as wary of him as he was of me because he suddenly smiled, one of those megawatt numbers normally reserved for an arena stuffed full of fans paying over $100 just for the cheap seats. I half expected him to break out in song.

But the only singing I wanted Mack to do was like a canary. None of it made any sense. Z had made it clear he was taking me to see Viv3000. If Mack was Lyla's source, then he'd snitched on himself. I didn't get it. I'd read enough blind items to know Lyla hadn't exactly been kind to the Christies. Maybe he knew that she knew about his lip-syncing and pretended to be a source in order to out her before she outed him.

But what if that wasn't it? If he truly wanted the lip-syncing revealed, there were much easier ways to do it. Send a tweet. Post on Instagram. Do Facebook Live. Or just do an interview with Gus the Gossip or one of the national morning shows.

Much like Lucy, he had some 'splaining to do. I just didn't want him to do it too closely. We continued our standoff to see who would talk first. For the first time ever, I won.

"Don't worry," he said. "I sent my driver for a walk. No one else is here."

That's what I was scared of. "No tour bus today?"

He shook his head. "I hate that thing, but it's good for the brand. Makes me recognizable. Relatable. So they tell me."

"So everything about you is a lie."

"Not quite. I don't drive. That part is true. How do you want to do this?"

"You tell me. You brought me here."

"You asked me to. I got your message. The one accusing me of being a murderer."

He sounded more amused than offended, like this was all one big misunderstanding that could be cleared up over a plate of nachos and red Kool-Aid. Except I wasn't quite ready to drink. Not just yet. "How do I know you're not?"

A valid question. At least in my mind. He clearly didn't think so because he leaned back in his seat as if the weight of the world was pushing him down. "I wouldn't kill anyone."

"Right, because you're a moral, upstanding citizen who never lies."

"It didn't start off as a lie." I wasn't in the mood for the audio version of his autobiography. I got it anyway. "I can sing. Could sing. That first album? All me. Second one too. And I sang live on both world tours, which turned out to be the problem. I noticed the issue when recording album three. I wasn't sounding right. My manager, Ben, took me to a doctor who told me I have muscle tension dysphonia—a fancy way of saying I overused my vocal chords. Ironically, I should've been lip-syncing more back then. We tried therapy. Vocal rest. Everything. None of it worked. It was gone."

He paused and I found myself feeling sorry for him, at least until he opened his mouth again. "A couple of years ago, Ben says he has a guy who can do some stuff, make me sound like I used to. I get to the studio, record a few tracks. Few days later, someone leaks one of the songs to get folks excited my third album's finally coming out. It gets something like a million hits the first day. Critics rave it's my best work in years. Except when I hear it, I know it's not me. I never had that range. I called Ben out on it too. But we owed the studio one more album. Ben said it would be a quick fix. I promised myself just that one time. Then the album went triple platinum. The record company literally threw money at me to sign one more contract."

"You had to know it was bound to come out somehow," I said.

"I did and I thought about that every day. Just didn't expect it to come out like that. You have the video. You *saw* the beginning. It was supposed to be a closed rehearsal."

"You didn't notice the camera?"

"Sure. There were cameras around but there's always cameras around. I didn't expect them to be on. We had the snafu with the backing track but it was taken care of. The actual performance was fine. And then we get a message a few days later."

"From?"

"Gus."

"The Gossip?" I asked, more so because I was so shocked. I flashed on a sliver of a memory of Mack and his wife performing at last year's Silver Sphere Awards. It would certainly explain how and why Lyla had gotten her hands on the video so quickly. I walked over so we were finally face to face. "What did he want?"

"At first? To be 'helpful.'" Mack went as far as to make quotation marks with his hands. "His exact words. Right after how sorry he was and how he didn't know the camera was recording. And right before how he understood how potentially embarrassing it could be. He promised to make sure it was destroyed."

"The video is almost a year old," I said. "If Gus was going to release it, why wait so long? Why not do an exclusive on his blog right away?"

"Because I paid a lot of money for him not to."

He let that one hang, waiting for me to catch the meaning.

"He blackmailed you?" I asked.

As the nickname indicated, Gus made his living off gossip. But was this really how he got paid? Not from what he knew but from what he knew and didn't tell? And had Lyla with her Anani Miss blind item threatened to ruin it all?

"You think it's a coincidence we're hosting the Silver Sphere Awards this year?" Mack asked. "Another Gus suggestion on top of what we were giving him each month to keep quiet. Made me realize Gus Ortiz would bleed me until I was dry."

"So you contacted Anani? Or was it vice versa?"

"I contacted her. I've been living this lie for four years now. I'm sick of pretending. I wanted to retire but I knew Janet wasn't having that. Gus hated that Anani blog. Heard him say it himself. Felt like 'her type' made it tough for 'real journalists like him.' I don't think she even knew it was me. I certainly didn't know who she was when I emailed her, told her I had some info on Mack Christie. She suggested the Gmail account. When I told her about the video, I was surprised she was able to get her hands on it. I've never seen it myself. But I guess now it makes sense."

"Was she going to implicate Gus?"

"That was our agreement," Mack said. "She didn't like Gus any more than I did, though she never said why. She had me convinced Gus put the camera there on purpose. Like maybe he'd heard about the lip-syncing and just needed proof."

Of course, if Lyla outed Gus, she also outed herself out of a job. A job she'd just gotten when Nina left to open her own agency. A job Nina claimed Lyla desperately wanted when she'd been her assistant. Gus would have definitely gotten fired by the SSO board. Even if no one figured out Lyla was Anani, I doubted any SSO president who replaced Gus would have kept Lyla—or any of his staff—around.

"Gus had to have seen Anani's blind item," I said. "You talk to him about it?"

Mack nodded, taking the time to rub his hands through his $500 haircut. It was worth every penny, too, because every strand immediately fell back in place. "He was pissed but still playing Mr. Nice Guy. He didn't know I was Anani's source. Just kept apologizing that the video leaked. Promised he'd take care of it."

By *it*, did he mean the situation or Anani herself? "He ever mention a Javon Reid or Junior to you?"

Mack shook his head, then closed his eyes and sat still for so long I was tempted to check if he was still breathing. "I just wanted out," he finally said. "To see Gus get his comeuppance. I didn't want anyone to die."

But someone had. If Gus was involved, the police needed to know. It would help if Mack had proof to go along with his accusations. "How'd you pay him?" I asked.

"Always multiple money orders in small amounts so not to arouse suspicion. Always in Gus's name. Always sent directly to the SSO office each month."

Money orders were better than cash, but not as good as a personal check. "You keep any receipts?"

It was a long shot, but they would have Gus's name on them at least. Mack shrugged. "There might be some at home. I didn't plan to give them to our accountant or anything."

"Can you look? It'll help when you go to the police. Along with any correspondence you guys had. Texts. Emails. DMs. Anything."

He hesitated and I sighed. "You have no plans to go to the police with this?" I asked. "Even if there's a chance Gus killed Lyla to keep your secret? And his money?"

"I don't want Janet—or Gus, for that matter—to know I'm involved in revealing it."

That explained our covert meeting in a deserted parking lot. "We're beyond being able to keep any more secrets," I said.

"I figured you'd say that. I'll look for the receipts. See what else I have. I'm not the only person he's doing this to."

"You have names?"

"A few, but I'd rather keep them out of it if possible. I'll get you the stuff you need."

"Once you do, I'll call the tip line and get them to the police."

Sienna was on the couch when I finally made it home after getting someone to jump my battery. We spoke at the same time.

"I've got news," she said.

"You'll never guess where I was," I said.

We both abruptly shut up. It was the polite thing to do, after all—let the other person go first. Then we realized we both were letting the other go first. Which led to the second-most polite thing—follow the other person's wishes. We spoke at the same time. Again.

"So," she said.

The same time, I said, "Like I—"

Again, we went the polite route. "You go," I said.

"I did my interview with Gus in his Airstream today. You know I don't trust that Nina's actually going to issue any Tomari statement so I kinda, maybe, somehow let it slip you and Omari are a couple. Completely accidentally, of course."

She gave me an exaggerated wink.

I nodded. "About that. Gus may be Geppetto."

It was Sienna's turn to nod solemnly. "Well ... maybe he'll run an item about you and Omari before he's arrested."

That was my Sienna. Always glass half full.

"Let me get Emme on FaceTime and I'll update you guys on that and the case," I said.

I did just that. Both were pretty quiet—minus double-teaming me about going somewhere with a complete stranger. Apparently, I "kept doing things like this" and they wanted me to stop putting myself in "potentially dangerous" situations. They brought up past incidents where I may have chased a potential suspect down an abandoned street in stilettos, and sat outside another suspect's house and confronted him when he got home. Sienna was there for that one. A fact they both conveniently forgot.

I just nodded, maybe made a joke about how I'd come out alive, injury-free, and with a new murder suspect to boot. They pretended not to be impressed, but I knew better. After I wrapped up, we discussed next steps. Emme would start a background check on Gus and Sienna would call her gossip ring to see what they knew about Gus's extracurricular blackmail activities. If he was doing it to others, someone out there had to know.

We got off the phone with Emme. I left a message for Aubrey, then checked the SSO website. It was silver and white with lots of moving parts—all virtually screaming, "We spent a buttload on this website designer and we're getting our money's worth." I clicked on the *About Us* section. It didn't take long to find Gus's bio. One tap of the "page down" button and there he was smiling at me.

*Gustavo, better known to his millions of fans as Gus the Gossip, is one of the leading entertainment journalists in the nation. He's served as President of the Silver Sphere Organization for over a decade. In that time, he's transformed the annual Silver Sphere Awards from a small online superlative post to a can't-miss television spectacular that's one of the most respected awards shows in the US and the biggest party of the Awards Season!*

It made no mention of his possible penchant for blackmail. Shocker.

I went to his website to check out a few interviews featuring Gus and his increasingly A-list interview subjects driving around in his bright yellow classic Airstream, waxing poetic while also dealing with LA traffic and waving at fans who recognized the trailer. The interviews were streamed live and looked like low-budget affairs but I knew better. There were probably several crew members hiding in the back.

I was watching a replay of Gus's interview with A-lister Luke Cruz when Emme called.

"Come over," she said. "*Now.*"

# Twenty-One

Gus was broke.

Well, not broke broke. He wasn't going to be panhandling in Santa Monica anytime soon but he lived paycheck to paycheck like the rest of us. Emme showed me his financials. He had a mortgage, less than $2,000 in savings, and was apparently paying way too much for that Airstream he adored. Nothing about any of it screamed "I have a burgeoning blackmail empire."

"I don't get it." I peered over Emme's shoulder at her monitor. "Is he hiding money in offshore accounts like some mob boss in a John Grisham novel?"

"IDK and won't know either. Even I don't have the skills to find that stuff."

"Maybe it's going out as fast as it's going in." I turned to Sienna, who had just hung up the phone. She was sitting on Emme's couch, still working her contacts. "You hear anything about a drug addiction, gambling, something?"

"Nope." She got up. "Nothing about him blackmailing anyone either. I'll see you at home later."

She took off like she'd spotted Joseline surrounded by a bunch of paparazzi and wanted to get in the background of the pics. Weird but I didn't give it much thought. I was too concerned about Gus. If he blackmailed people, he was doing a really good job of covering his tracks. I needed to speak with Mack Christie again. I texted the number he'd given me.

*Have a follow-up question. Can chat in person if you want. Just no creepy warehouses.*

I spent the rest of the evening waiting for a response that never came. I didn't worry too much. Mack was a busy guy who was hosting the Silver Sphere Awards in a few days. He'd promised to get me the receipts and information I needed. He would. Then we could figure out the next steps to prove Gus was Geppetto.

Omari had a late call so I spent the night at home. I needed to drop my car off at the mechanic and yell at him for not fixing it, anyway. I woke up to Sienna standing over me like a horror movie villain. Of course, Jason and Mike Myers never brought their victims breakfast in bed. Sienna carried a tray of scrambled eggs, bacon, and the food *de resistance*—sweet potato pie French toast. She watched me tear into her breakfast.

It was only after I finished that I realized something had to be up. "What's wrong?" I asked. She'd run out of Emme's apartment the day before and now she was cooking my favorite foods.

Sienna feigned an innocent look.

"Nice try," I said. "You want me to be in a good mood. Why?"

"Maybe I know how hard you've been working on the case."

"Cases don't demand sweet potato pie French toast."

She avoided my gaze and grabbed my cell, which made me more nervous. After a minute, she handed it to me. I gave her a look, then gently took it from her hand.

The headline on Gus's site was in all caps. *WORLDWIDE EXCLUSIVE: THE LATEST ON TOMARI! ARE THEY DONE? READ ON TO FIND OUT.*

It was mostly a rehash of the same inaccurate info about their relationship. Gus had saved the new "worldwide exclusive" details for the end. *A rep for Grant issued a statement saying that Grant and Abrams have known each other for a long time and are "just friends."*

I dropped the phone on my bed. "How. Dare. She."

Sienna grabbed my hand. "It could be worse."

I ignored her. Instead opting to call Omari. I chose FaceTime even though I hadn't yet put on a stitch of makeup. A clear sign of how upset I was. He answered on the second ring, smiling as he did so.

"Nina issued the statement." I didn't mention she'd issued it to my current number one suspect. I could only deal with one crisis at a time, and personal life was it.

"I saw. Glad we were able to take care of it."

If his smile got any wider, I'd be able to tell if he had tonsillitis.

"She said you and Toni were just friends," I said.

"Because we *are* just friends."

"No, you're friends. You aren't 'just friends.'"

He looked confused. "There's a difference?"

I exchanged a look with Sienna. "Of course there is. When someone says they're 'just friends' it's Hollywood for 'we're boning every chance we get.' And last time I checked, you and Toni were doing nothing of the sort. Right?"

"Right," he said. Then, "You do remember this was your idea."

"I do."

"But now you're mad that she did what you wanted her to do?" It was clear he thought I was off my rocker.

And much like a rocker, I was moving but not getting anywhere. Just going back and forth. "I know it sounds ridiculous, but trust me on this. Nina made things worse."

"Right." That word again.

I gave up. So much for me being ready for Nina's next move. "We'll talk later."

When I ended the call, Sienna spoke. "We'll fix this. Don't worry."

She gave me a quick hug and left me with just my phone. Blurg. I forced myself to reason. This wasn't a matter of life or death, especially when I was dealing with actual life and death regarding Lyla.

I checked my cell notifications. Still nothing from Mack. Not a text. Not a voicemail. Not even a missed call. I began getting worried. It was the part of dating I always hated. Waiting, hoping, wondering if he was going to contact you and when. It wasn't much easier in a professional capacity. Taking a cue from that dating experience, I upped my game by actually calling him.

No answer. I left a message. Then I did something else I always did in the chess game known as dating in the twenty-first century—phoned a friend to overanalyze the situation.

Unfortunately, that friend was Aubrey.

"Hey," I said, then jumped into my excuse for contacting him. I couldn't very well admit I called to whine. "Just checking to see if you're all set for your PI license exam tomorrow."

"Well, Ms. Anderson, I—"

"Can I just tell you how rude Mack Christie is? I've been blowing his phone up, texting him nonstop. No response. Not even a 'K or an emoji. Why give out your number and tell me to contact you anytime if you aren't going to respond?"

"He could have simply not found the time to call you back." Aubrey was clearly not as good at this as Sienna, though he was on par with Emme. "Or he could be avoiding you because of something you may have done to annoy him."

"First, I'm not annoying." I waited for Aubrey to agree. When he didn't, I kept talking. "Second, I've done what I said I was going to do. I played my part. He needs to do the same. Not be—" My phone buzzed. I pulled it away from my ear to check it and did an immediate 180. "Oh, it's Mack. He says he's been busy, but he hasn't forgotten. Cool! Hold on a sec."

I texted him back with a "When?" and then added a smiley face. Because though I'd sent him four texts, made three calls, and left one voicemail, now that he'd written back, I didn't want him to think I was pushy or anything. Just like dating. To his credit, he did respond. "He's working on it," I told Aubrey. "Promises to check in tomorrow. You think we should still pursue other avenues just in case?"

I'd heard that all the time on *The First 48*. Glad I finally got a chance to use it.

"I do, Ms. Anderson. For Mr. Ortiz to be a viable suspect, we need to look at motive, means, and opportunity. You have a motive for Mr. Ortiz, but can you definitively prove he knew that Ms. Davis was this Anani Miss? Furthermore, how can we connect him to the hitman Mr. Reid?"

Both good questions, ones I didn't have answers for. "I'll see if I can prove Gus knew about Lyla. You wanna take the Junior connection? I'm sure his grandma loves you."

"I will head to her neighborhood and see if she recognizes Mr. Ortiz's photo."

After we hung up, I pulled up the Anani Miss email account and did a quick search for Gus's name. A good number of emails came up, but no threats from Gus. For kicks, I ran a search for Lyla's name, too. Nothing there either.

My best bet was probably to talk to Gus himself. I just needed to figure out a way to do it without going in guns blazing screaming bloody murderer. During my limited PI experience, I'd quickly learned most people don't respond well to that. At all. I needed a more undercover approach. I'd already googled Gus, but I figured it wouldn't hurt to do it again.

When I clicked on his site, the Tomari article was still front and center. I quickly scrolled to one of his interviews. It reminded me how I'd blown off Gus's interview request.

Maybe it was time to remedy that. Gus wanted something from me and I wanted something from him. I fired off an email to his official SSO addy saying that I had time to speak with him. Could he squeeze me in later today or even tomorrow morning?

The response wasn't immediate and it wasn't from Gus. Kitt called early afternoon when I was camped out at the mechanic waiting for my car. I didn't recognize the number, so of course I didn't pick up. Luckily, she did when I called back from home. I managed to multitask while wrapping Emme's birthday gift.

"Hey Day! Saw your email. Things are a bit hectic with the awards in a few days but Gus really wants to interview you as soon as possible."

"I could stop by this afternoon."

"We were thinking Thursday. That work?"

Not at all. "Sure thing."

I wasn't trying to wait two days but it looked like I had no choice. Of course, if I couldn't talk to Gus, I could always settle for the next best thing. I'd spoken with my former manager's assistant more than I spoke with him. Assistants always know just as much as their bosses, if not more. Maybe I could get Kitt to provide some insight into Gus's finances or at least his relationship with Lyla and the Christies.

"You free for lunch tomorrow, Kitt?"

"Yes! I love to eat."

A girl after my own heart. "Me too! Let's get together."

"I know the perfect place."

Emme's birthday party was the next day. I didn't hear from Mack like he'd promised, which led to round two of Operation: Blow Up His Phone. I was tempted to set up shop with the paparazzi and the stalkers in the bushes outside his house. It was probably like a summer BBQ out there all day and night.

Instead, I called Z. Don't know what surprised me more—that I remembered his number or that the thing went straight to voicemail. He didn't even have an automated message. I dialed. It beeped. I was not ready. At all.

"Hey. This is Dayna. Anderson. We met the other day. When you just showed up at my car. Still kind of creeped out by that, by the way. We went to the Fashion District. Well, not together. I was in a Lyft. Guy named Jamal. Really cute kids. You don't know that because you didn't see his pics. Trust me, they were adorable. Anyway, I'm trying to reach Mack. Figured you could help me. Okay. Bye."

I went into the living room to see if Sienna was ready for Emme's birthday party. It was at Vitality, which may have sounded like a Hollywood hotspot that made you stand in line for forty minutes even though there were only two people inside and then charged you $15 for a mixed drink to boot.

But Vitality wasn't a club at all. It was the hottest life simulation game going. It was my first online birthday party. Coincidentally, it was also the first birthday party I'd ever attended in sweatpants and no bra. I could definitely get used to that. The shindig started at 7 p.m., but Emme informed me we needed to sign on early to create our avatars. At precisely 6:45, Sienna and I sat next to each other on our bright red couch and put on the headsets Emme let us borrow.

Not to go all SAT prep, but headsets to Emme were shoes to Sienna—an utter weakness. Emme had over twenty pairs and chose which ones to use based on the day's agenda. Apparently, one worked best for gaming. Another for video chatting. And a completely different one for online karaoke. Who knew?

Once I'd adjusted my headset for maximum comfort, it was time to choose my avatar. It started off simple enough. It asked me my gender. I nailed the answer. Things got more complicated from there. There were fifteen options each for face, ear, and eye shapes, not to mention an entire color hex chart to choose your precise skin tone. I learned something new—I'm #af7041. Though I'm not psychic, I sensed I'd never need to use that information again in life.

I stumbled when it came time to pick my lips. The makers of Vitality clearly didn't know many people of color—or with lip injections. The mouth options were all so thin they were practically transparent. They didn't do much better when it came to noses. All looked like what you might see at a plastic surgeon's office, not like what I saw in the mirror. I chose the biggest size for both and hoped Emme could recognize me.

Having had a nose job, Sienna didn't have half as hard a time as I did choosing her likeness. She was already there when I "arrived" at the "bar" for Emme's twenty-fifth bday extravaganza. The place was packed. If I had half the social life in real life that Emme did online, I'd be exhausted. No wonder she sat in a chair all day. Besides Sienna and Emme, there was no one I recognized.

A DJ blasted music. Sienna danced atop a table while the other avatars watched in complete lust. Her avatar was gorgeous—just like in real life. I beelined to the coat rack. Vitality let you choose your clothes and I'd made up for what I could no longer afford in real life, opting to arrive in an expensive red wool jacket. Virtual reality was the only place in Cali cold enough to wear it.

As I waited in line for coat check someone came up next to me. He had white skin crowded with features that looked cobbled together by Dr. Frankenstein. It didn't help he had a black crew cut. His outfit barely matched. He didn't have a coat, but that didn't stop him from getting all in my personal space. Or should I say "avatar space." I ignored him, mainly because I couldn't figure out how to enable the chat function to politely ask him to back the heck up.

I grabbed a drink. A drink that was most definitely real. Sienna and I had stopped by the liquor store. Wasn't like I was driving or anything.

Virtual Day checked her jacket and made herself comfy on a wall. I surveyed the surroundings. As is my custom whenever I enter a new place, I searched for the bathroom. Then I realized I wouldn't need it. Score.

My mind kept wandering back to Lyla. Gus was still our most viable suspect but it wasn't looking good. So far, my only way to connect him to Anani and the blackmail was Mack. I'd set up my interview, but I doubted Gus would confess to murder on his own web show. No one is that desperate for ratings.

I hoped I could get him to admit he knew that Lyla and Anani were the same person but I wasn't holding my breath on that one. Not with my current track record. I much preferred concrete proof. There had to be a way to connect Gus with Anani. Unfortunately, Lyla had gone above and beyond to protect her identity with separate phones and restricted social media. The only thing that could possibly connect to Lyla was the Anani website. Had Gus found her through that? I knew from registering ASAP Investigations that you had to list a site owner for the domain. I was tempted to check when Frankenstein appeared next to me again.

He leaned casually against the wall, again way too close for even virtual comfort. What was up with this guy? I waited for him to say something. Didn't happen. Maybe he was like me and couldn't figure out how to chat. I didn't stick around to find out. I needed to talk to the birthday girl. I patiently joined the crowd around her, hoping I would figure out how to type before I got to the front.

I'd just realized the game had emojis when Frankenstein came up behind me. Again. I decided to play nice. I hit the smile emoji. Like clockwork, Virtual Day smiled at him.

A conversation popped above his head, followed by three dots. Being a texting aficionado, I knew exactly what to expect. He was forming a thought. There was a sound too similar to passing gas for my liking. Vitality really needed to work on that.

*Come here often?* popped up above his head.

I noticed Sienna across the way, her chat bubble overflowing with words. No fair. "How do I chat?" I asked out loud.

"Right click on your head and it'll pop up," Sienna said.

"I think this guy's hitting on me."

"Yes. He's kinda cute too."

"He's an avatar."

"Not all of us can be picky because we have boyfriends, Day."

On screen, he must have taken my silence for playing hard to get. *You are by far the prettiest Avatar I've seen.*

Thank God I didn't see a rolling-your-eyes emoji. I right clicked and selected chat. *Thank you but I have a boyfriend.*

His response was instantaneous. *You're not just friends?*

# Twenty-Two

It was Omari.

I hit the smile emoji button again, then typed, *Different look for you.*

*It's called "Hit the first option for everything because you're on lunch break." Trying to make it a thing.* Omari had a night shoot, so even though it was evening, they still called it lunch.

I nodded and made my avatar do the same. Then I kissed him.

"You guys are moving fast!" Sienna said.

"It's Omari."

"Oh. If you take him to the closet, we'll probably still be able to see you. FYI."

I don't know if it was the Avatar or alcohol, but my usual PDA hesitation went out the window. I grabbed his hand. *Sienna thinks I should take you to the closet.*

He responded: *I've never done it in a closet. Real or fake.*

"Aww. Closet sex is great," Sienna said. "Definitely try it."

Wait, what? "How do you know what we're talking about?"

"Because I can read. Your chat is public."

Oh right.

Fudge. I typed again. *Let's discuss in person.*

He said nothing. He did nothing too. It was like he was asleep standing up. After a minute, I finally realized he'd had to go back to work. I spent the next ten minutes standing next to him in case he came back. Emme approached me while I stood guard. A chat popped up above her head. *Thank you for the Focals! Everyone is jealous I got the new ones already.*

That had been the plan. I shrugged as if to say "No big deal" but it wasn't as effective on screen as in real life. She motioned to Omari, still shut down next to me. *Who is that?*

*Omari. I think he got called to set. Is he just gonna stay like that?*

In real life, I would've made sure he got to the car and then tucked him in. But here, I wasn't sure what to do.

*If he doesn't come back soon, he'll just disappear,* she wrote. *How's the case going?*

I hated to talk shop at a birthday party but she brought it up. My other option was discussing Phishing and Whaling. And the only reason I knew whaling didn't involve a sea creature was because I'd eavesdropped on the guys next to me. Not quite willing to—literally—chat about it, I called her on the phone. "How come no one ever figured out who Anani was? Wouldn't someone connect her to the domain?"

"You can pay to keep it private. Instead of having your addy, it would list a company."

No doubt that's what Lyla did. I closed the Vitality box to pull up a domain search site. Sure enough, Anani Miss's domain owner was listed as Private Parts, Inc., with an address in Claremont, California. It was local—if you considered a forty-five-minute drive east on the 10 to be local. I did another search and was surprised how easily I found the owner of Private Parts, Inc. Someone named Andy Stevens. "Have you heard of a domain registration company called Private Parts?" I asked Emme.

"Yep. Cheap but you pay for it. Technically they mask your personal data so no one can find your name or even personal info. But the joke is they'll give out your info to anyone who stops by and says hello."

Worked for me.

I'd been to Claremont exactly once—three in the morning at that. That trip had started off badly before ending with a key revelation in the Haley Joseph case. Fingers crossed I'd hit the investigation jackpot twice. Maybe Claremont was lucky for me. I made a mental note to buy a lotto ticket in town just in case.

Aubrey had his PI exam that morning, so I didn't even bother to ask him to ride with me. Factor in Sienna having an audition and Emme already reaching her monthly quota for leaving the house, and I was riding solo to the Private Parts office. Couldn't say I was happy about it. Mainly because I lacked what one might call a game plan.

So I asked the investigation gods for assistance. When none immediately came, I did the next best thing. Procrastinate. I called Mack. When he—shocker—didn't answer, I left a message, then texted him to tell him to check his voicemail. Then went on Instagram and fired off a DM telling him to check his text message telling him to check his voicemail. I was nothing if not thorough. All bases covered to my complete satisfaction, I had no choice but to figure out the best way to see if Gus had contacted Private Parts, Inc.

It wasn't like I was the police. I couldn't just storm into an office building demanding info. Of course, maybe that was a good thing. Granted, my knowledge of domain privacy sites was extremely limited, but there was one thing I was pretty sure about—they probably didn't want cops coming anywhere near their office. A $9.99 annual fee to mask a domain probably wasn't worth jail time or huge lawyer fees. I could use that to my advantage.

Especially since I didn't even want to know who owned the Anani Miss site. Already had that one pretty much figured out, thank you very much. I wanted to know if someone—specifically, Gus—had wanted to know who owned it. Hopefully he'd stopped by and didn't just call. I'd flash the photo that I'd screen-grabbed from his website. The Private Parts receptionist could nod yes and I'd be out of there—no police involved. And that would be all, folks.

I practically skipped to my car and got in. I cranked the engine. And—non-spoiler alert—the freaking thing didn't start. Again. Luckily, this wasn't my first rodeo. I knew exactly what to do.

I had my Lyft app open when Z walked up on my driver's side, giving me a sense of deja vu. This time I was determined to wait him out. And I would, granted I didn't have to go to the bathroom.

At least my doors were locked. Three months ago, that wouldn't have been the case. But Aubrey had an annoying habit of opening other people's car doors and taking a seat. To his credit, Z didn't try to get in. He didn't even bend down to look at me. He just stood there, giving me a front row view of another all-black ensemble. His cufflinks were once again purple, pale lavender jewels that could've doubled for studded earrings.

I forced myself to stop thinking about wearing his accessories and start thinking about what he wanted and why wasn't he in a rush to tell me. Last time he'd made an appearance, he'd taken me to see

Mack. Conveniently, Mack was the exact person I was now anxious to see. Was Z sent to fetch me?

I jumped out of my car so quick he barely had time to get out of the way. He retreated to my hood, leaning against it with an amused expression on his face. "Two minutes," he said. I just gave him a look. One he incorrectly took to mean *continue*. "That's how long you held out."

He walked toward his car, not bothering to look back. It was like he knew I'd follow him like a Twitter account. I did. It might have been foolish, but I rationalized it with the fact that he hadn't kidnapped me during our last go-round. Plus, I really wanted to talk to Mack Christie. I texted Sienna and Emme just to be safe. A few minutes later, our seat belts were fastened and we stared at each other. "So where are we going?" I asked.

"You're supposed to tell me."

Huh? I would've definitely remembered any discussions with Mack about meeting somewhere. Had I missed a voicemail or a text? "He didn't tell you?" I asked. Z just gave me a blank stare. "You're supposed to take me to see Mack. That's why you're here, right?"

The look on his face said he wasn't.

"I've been calling your boss nonstop and he's been ducking me."

"He's not my boss."

"Right. He's not your boss. You're not a fixer. And I'm not having much luck confirming the info he gave me. He promised he'd look for some things I need. Time's a ticking."

It seemed like news to him. He finally spoke. "I'll let him know."

He made no move for his phone. Guess he didn't mean right then. I was about to get out when Z spoke again. "So where are we going?"

I looked back at him. My brain screamed "Bad idea." So of course I did it anyway, reasoning I needed a ride to Claremont. I pulled up the address on my GPS app and we were on our way. He didn't even blink at how far inland we were going.

It turned out Z wasn't much of a talker. He didn't even ask me why we were heading to Private Parts. Fine by me. I was uploading photos to Sienna's Lady of the Red Vine Instagram account when Kitt texted me: *U still comming today, right?*

Another text immediately followed it. **Coming. Always spell that wrong.*

I'd almost forgotten I'd invited Kitt to lunch to get intel on Gus. I wrote back, *No prob. Knew what you meant. Where are we meeting?*

She responded: *Say Cheese on Wilshire. Coupla blocks up from Fairfax.*

I sent a brown thumbs-up emoji, then went back to uploading Instagram pics and trying to ignore Z. It would have been easier if it weren't for that cologne reminding me of cinnamon. This time I could also smell sandalwood and amber. It was intoxicating.

We'd just gotten off the 10 when his glove compartment rang. He leaned over me and took out a cell. I inhaled.

"Did you just smell me?" he asked.

Yes. "No," I lied, and would have gotten away with too except I sniffed him again. "I was just trying to guess the scent. Valentine's Day is coming up and I need some ideas for what to get my boyfriend." I looked at him smugly. That's right. I had a boyfriend. A super-hot, famous boyfriend.

Z didn't even blink. "You want your boyfriend to remind you of me?"

That went left quick. I couldn't even think of a witty response. Not that it would have mattered. He somehow managed to misinterpret anything I said. I settled on just rolling my eyes.

"I'll take that as a yes," he said.

I changed the subject. "Let's go over the plan for when we get there."

"Okay."

"The plan is, you stay in the car."

"How long did it take you to think of that one?"

Longer than I would have liked. "I'm just gonna run in, head up to their office for a sec, and come back down. Shouldn't take more than ten minutes."

"You're the boss."

My first hint things weren't going to go as planned was when Waze, the GPS app I used, assured us we'd reached our final destination. Considering we were smack-dab in the middle of a residential neighborhood, I wasn't quite buying it. The lawns were plentiful. The houses were all modest and one-story. Not even one person had slacked on taking down the Christmas lights. I half expected to see a straight white couple walking their dog along with their 2.5 kids.

But Waze insisted. I had to change up my game plan. The lack of an office probably also meant lack of a receptionist. This was clearly a solo operation, probably one Andy Stevens, owner extraordinaire, operated out of his childhood bedroom while his parents were at work. I wasn't above using that to my advantage. "Okay, well there's a slight change of plans." I got out of the car. Z got out with me. I turned to him. "The part of the plan where you stay in the car is still intact."

"Got it."

Good. I headed toward the door of the address. So did he. This would not do. At all. Andy Stevens, who'd probably never known the touch of a woman yet was very familiar with the touch of his own hand, might be way less forthcoming talking to Z and not my fake boobs.

"What happened to me being the boss?" I asked.

"I can't use the bathroom?"

I had no business turning someone away for having to use the facilities. Especially since I had to use them myself. "Fine, but make it quick and leave as soon as you're done."

We rang the bell and a woman answered in a track suit. She was the classic, busybody mother in the rom-com who constantly parent-pressures her daughter to finally get married. The one who called the lead actress from her Zumba class to tell her she'd met a nice man perfect for her. Her head bobbled back and forth between me and Z before settling on him. I jumped in, eager to let her know I was the one in charge.

"Hi, I'm looking for Andy Stevens. Is he home?"

She didn't look the least bit shocked. Made me wonder how many people came rolling up to talk to Andy. "Who's asking? And what is it about?"

I gave her my business card. She didn't even glance at it. "I'm Dayna Anderson of ASAP Investigations. And it's a private matter. Is Andy home?"

"Yes." That was all she said.

"Can I speak with him?"

"I need to know what this is about."

"It's for an investigation. Not sure you'd understand." I wasn't sure if she even knew her son ran a website. It sure as heck wouldn't get me brownie points if I snitched.

"Try me."

"It's about the Anani Miss blog."

She nodded, then spoke. "I'll tell you the same thing I tell everyone else who's asked about that blog. I don't reveal my clients. You'll have to come back with a warrant."

My clients? This was Andy. Oops. Z turned to me. "Going well so far."

I ignored that to play my ace in the hole. "I actually don't need to know who owns the blog. I'm more interested in the 'everyone else.' We have reason to believe"—not really, but it sounded good and I needed to redeem myself for the completely and absolutely understandable Andy confusion—"a person of interest in a murder may have inquired about the owner of the blog. I have a photo. You'd just need to say if he's been here."

"How serious are you about finding this person out?" Andy asked.

"Very ..."

"Okay, then I'll tell you the same thing I also tell everyone else. I need to get my roof replaced."

"That sucks," I said, because it did. "Maybe you can start a Go FundMe or something? That's how my cousin bought Beyoncé tickets."

"Yeah, well, I need something a bit more immediate," she said.

"I bet."

Z leaned into me. "She wants money."

We'd already covered that. "Yeah, I know. For her roof."

"For her to tell you who else has been looking for the blog owner."

Oh. Wasn't expecting that. At all. I reached into my bag to grab my wallet. A cursory check confirmed my cash reserves were currently four bucks, most of which was nickels and dimes. At least no pennies though. "I don't suppose you take Venmo or PayPal."

She didn't even warrant that with a response. Not that I was honestly expecting one. I turned to Z and tried my best to whisper. "Can we chat for a sec?"

He and I made a big show of moving off her porch.

"Let me guess," he said. "You don't have any money."

"If I'd known bribery was on the day's agenda, I would've stopped by the ATM."

He sighed and reached for his wallet. "How much?"

"I don't know, like, $50?"

"You're going to owe me." There was only a 50 percent chance he was talking about money but at that point, I was willing to risk it. Turning so his back was to Andy, he pulled out a stack of cash. He handed me a hundred-dollar bill and we walked back over to the front door.

I tried to hand her the money. She didn't even blink, much less motion to take it. The only thing that moved was her mouth. "Know how much a roof costs these days?"

I nodded, then looked at Z. "Can I get another hundred?"

"Make it two," Andy said.

"Two hundred," I said.

"I only have an extra fifty," Z said. "Take it or leave it."

Now was not the time to negotiate, especially when I knew he was lying. He'd pulled at least $300 from his wallet. Their standoff was just long enough for me to regret not just offering to run to the nearest Wells Fargo. After a moment, Andy held out her hand. "Fine."

"Not so fast," Z said. "You look at the pic first."

Another standoff. Z won that one as well. Andy impatiently motioned to my phone. I showed her Gus's pic. Her eyes barely took him in before she was talking again. "Never seen him before in my life."

Blurg. "Maybe you've talked to him on the phone. His name's Gus Ortiz."

She shook her head. I sighed. The only thing I had connecting Gus to Anani was a Country music star who not only was an admitted liar, but who also seemed horrible at checking text messages and social media. I needed Aubrey. I couldn't even call him because he was in the middle of his exam. I didn't know what to do, so I did what I always do. Asked if I could use the bathroom.

Andy must've felt sorry for me because she pointed me down the hall. I left her and Z to make small talk. Maybe they'd talk about the weather. Maybe they'd talk about the Clippers. Maybe they'd talk about how I suggested she start a GoFundMe campaign for her bribery scheme. So many options.

When I came back, they weren't discussing a thing. Both stood as if someone had pushed pause until I got back. I smiled at Andy. "It was nice meeting you. Good luck with your website domain business."

I walked past but Z stopped me. He motioned to Andy. "Tell her what you told me," Z said.

She did, though she didn't look too happy about it. "There've been quite a few people over the years looking for Anani. Most call, but a woman stopped by January 5th or 6th."

I did the math. That was a few days after the Piper blind. "She give you her name?"

Andy shook her head. "I didn't ask. She contributed to the roof fund and I let her peek at the files. She didn't seem surprised. It was as if she knew and just wanted confirmation."

Gus obviously wasn't a woman, but he did have an assistant who was. One that did everything for him. Did that extend to unwittingly helping him plan a murder?

Needing a pic of Kitt stat, I pulled the Silver Sphere Awards site up on my phone. Unfortunately, I couldn't find any pics. I also couldn't remember her last name. I googled Kitt and Silver Sphere Awards, stumbling across their Instagram account and a photo of her with Nina from the press conference. It was supposed to be candid, but I could tell it wasn't, mainly because Nina was smiling and her claws weren't showing.

I happily showed the pic to Andy. She grabbed it out of my hand and took a nice, long look. "That's definitely her."

I exhaled. It wasn't a direct link to Gus, but it was the next best thing. Kitt and I were still on for lunch. Maybe if I plied her with a few drinks, she'd inadvertently incriminate her boss.

Andy handed me the phone back. "That pink shirt she's wearing is horrible. She had a similar one on when she came here."

One problem. Kitt wasn't wearing a pink shirt.

Nina was.

# Twenty-Three

I'm not sure why I was so surprised. Yes, I'd declared Nina my lifelong sworn enemy. Sure I was certain she'd wanted to kill me as many times as I'd wanted to kill her, but I never took her for an actual murderer. Of course, Nina had taken pains to portray her relationship with Lyla as a good one, but then she was a publicist. It was her job to spin things like a wheel. This one obviously landed on the 'I taught Lyla everything I knew before passing her the Silver Sphere reins to start my own PR agency' section.

Something clearly wasn't adding up. After Z and I left Claremont, I quickly texted Emme to run a background check on Nina, including a peek into her finances. Of course, that wouldn't give me a peek at their relationship. And I knew Nina wouldn't volunteer what was really going on. Luckily I'd already made lunch plans with just the person who could: Kitt. I still planned to ask her about Gus. I'd just ask her about Nina too. If things went well, I'd have a clear motive for one of them so I'd know what steps to take next.

I'd never heard of the place where Kitt wanted to meet for lunch, Say Cheese. It was only after Z dropped me off at my car—which shockingly decided to play nice and start—and I made my way to Wilshire that I realized why. It was a food truck.

Every day, trucks hit different locations in the city, using Twitter and the like to let LA's hungry know exactly where they'd be during the lunch and dinner rush. It wasn't uncommon for five or six trucks to line up back to back on the same busy street. I got out of the Infiniti and spotted Kitt near the front of a long line five trucks down. That had to be Say Cheese. As I walked over, I couldn't help but scope out the menus. Sushi burritos. Lasagna cupcakes. Something called Wachos.

When I finally got to Say Cheese, Kitt was already near the front of the line. After I'd stopped hitting the LA club scene, I vowed never to stand in a long line again—unless of course it was for the bathroom. I hugged her and settled in next to her, ignoring the exaggerated sigh of the person behind me. Like he wouldn't have done the exact same thing if he had any friends. "Have you tried their grilled cheese before?" Kitt asked.

I shook my head. As much as I loved myself some food, Sienna and I had never been a huge fan of trucks. Her reasoning was she didn't chase food, much like she didn't chase men. I just preferred not to eat standing up.

"This is my favorite truck in all of LA. I eat here the days they're in Miracle Mile. Ronnie is a master of the mac and cheese sandwich."

I'd heard of her kind, people who followed their favorite truck all over Los Angeles proper like they were the Grateful Dead. Kitt was a food truck Dead Head. Would that make her a Food Dude? Or, since she loved this truck in particular, a Cheesy?

We took our sandwiches back to Kitt's car, a classic pink Volkswagen Bug complete with eyelashes glued on the headlights. Cute but probably a pain when it came to the Cali emissions test. We settled in. "You excited for the show?" she asked me.

Nope. "Yep. I've been to the People's Choice Awards but never something as big as this."

"We're still figuring out seating arrangements, but I'll messenger your tickets over as soon as we do."

I thanked her and bit into my taco grilled cheese sandwich. I must have audibly sighed because Kitt spoke through a mouthful of mac and cheese. "Good, right?"

It was, but as much as I enjoyed the sandwich, it was not why I'd come. I needed to shift the convo to suspect number one: Gus. "I see why you follow it all over the city. Gus doesn't mind you leaving the office twice a week?"

"He's barely there himself. As long as I'm available by phone, we're good. Besides, it's awards week. Only people in the office right now are the poor interns. Rehearsals start tomorrow and Gus is busy running around town getting last-minute interviews for his site."

"I barely visit his page. I kind of prefer Anani Miss," I said, knowing full well I was baiting her.

But Kitt just laughed. "Me too. Of course, I'd never tell him that."

"Please tell me they had beef? I kinda love the idea of people who report on other people's drama having their own."

"Not really. I don't think he paid her much attention. He didn't consider people like her on his level."

"He never mentioned her at all?" Mack had claimed Gus wasn't one of Anani's biggest fans.

"Only if she scooped him. Like that whole Omari Grant/Toni Abrams thing. He swears he had it first, but he wanted to check his sources before revealing it."

I thought back to his exclusive. "He certainly is on board now, even though they aren't together."

"Do we really care if they are?" Kitt asked.

Kinda, especially when he's your boyfriend.

She continued. "I mean, that's the whole point of blinds and gossip, right? Guessing is the fun part. Who cares if it's accurate?"

I used to agree with her. Instead of arguing, I changed the subject. "What else did she scoop him on? He also have the Piper blind first? He must know who it is."

"I asked, but he just got annoyed and didn't answer. Who do you think it could be?"

I figured I didn't have anything to lose by telling the truth. "Mack Christie."

Kitt dang near choked on her food. "No way!"

"It's not impossible, right?" I went through exactly how he fit Piper's description but didn't mention that I'd had a personal confirmation.

"You may be right," she said when I'd wrapped up.

"You must know him since he's been so involved with SSO these past couple of years. There haven't been any hints?"

"Not really. His people are always calling the office offering to have Mack and J. Chris do things. Gus finally relented and let them host this year after Chris Rock fell through. It was too late to get anyone else."

That was definitely not how Mack had portrayed it. Made me wonder if he was suddenly avoiding my calls because he had lied to me about his relationship with Gus. Also made me want to just call him again to ask. In the meantime, I figured I'd ask Kitt first. "Did they get along? Mack and Gus?"

She shrugged. "Gus felt like J. Chris was a piece of work but he never complained about Mack. Mack really wanted to win last year. Campaigned hard for it. Performed, even. They seemed disappointed when he didn't win but they came back to host this year, right? Couldn't have been that upset."

Or it could also have been blackmail. Kitt's response made me wonder who else besides Gus knew about the lip-syncing. I could see Gus keeping a tight lid on the actual lip-syncing—Kitt clearly didn't know, after all. But people talked. Folks at least had to know there'd been some type of situation, even if Gus had explained it away as technical difficulties. "How was their performance last year?" I asked. "I'd heard there were issues beforehand."

Kitt swallowed the last of her food. "Don't know. Didn't have time to watch rehearsals or the show. Honestly, I just kind of suspected Piper was his wife. Guess we'll find out soon enough."

That reminded me that no one knew Lyla and Anani were one and the same. No one except Nina. "True," I said. "Right after the awards, too. I know Nina's running you ragged."

"She's worse than ever. I was really looking forward to not working with her this year. I'm going on vacation as soon as the show is over and I cannot wait to get away from her." Kitt paused before speaking again. "God, that sounds so selfish. I'm working with Nina again because Lyla's dead and I'm complaining about it."

It was true. What was also true was she was helping find Lyla's killer. She just didn't know it. I had to keep her focused. "Lyla was probably well aware of how Nina could be," I said.

"We used to try to one-up each other on what Nina asked us to do. Lyla always had me beat. She was basically doing Nina's job while Nina got all the credit."

That didn't surprise me. "Nina acts like she taught Lyla everything, including how to tie her shoe."

"Typical Nina. I'm sure she told you she left Silver Sphere to fulfill her long-held dream to start her own boutique agency, right? More like she was fired."

Now that *did* surprise me. "Really? Why?"

"I don't know the details but I do know it had to do with Anani. Word on the street was that Nina was feeding Anani info. Nina denied it, but next thing I know, Nina's out and Lyla's taking her place. Don't even think they let her box up her stuff. Lyla just sent it to her."

I finally understood why Nina was so busy looking into Anani. I still had one more question. "Why would Nina come back?"

"Because she never wanted to leave."

Aubrey wanted to meet at Runyon Canyon, which was technically a park situated in the Santa Monica Mountains. Key word: *technically*. It was Hollywood's outdoor workout of choice. On a good day, you could find more celebs than on NBC's primetime lineup. Even on a bad day, you might catch a news anchor. If you entered from the southern end at the bottom of the hill on Fuller Ave, it wasn't uncommon to pass outdoor yoga classes before making your way up a hiking trail that ended way up on Mulholland Drive. At least that's what I'd heard. I've never made it that far. Hadn't even tried.

Aubrey knew me better than I realized because instead of suggesting we meet at the entrance, he chose a lookout point about a mile up that had an amazing view of Los Angeles proper.

I wasn't happy about the trek, which is why I'd gotten the ice cream on the way there. Call it the "Calories In, Calories Out" exercise method. I made sure to time things perfectly so I made it to the landing just as I finished my first scoop. I sat and pulled out my phone. There was a text from Emme.

She'd written "Nina" and attached two screenshots. The first was a bank statement with an available balance of $879.77. Ehh. I'd seen much worse. I had much worse. It wasn't a big deal. The $50,000 withdrawal, however, was. The next screenshot was of the check. Nina had made it out to cash.

Bingo.

I looked up in time to see Aubrey finally approach. "Could you have not left your ice cream in the car, Ms. Anderson?"

Of course not. It would have melted. "I have good news." Well, as good as news could be when it came to murder.

"So you got the ice cream because you were celebrating this news?"

Nope. "Yes."

Aubrey nodded but I suspected he didn't believe me. Before he could confirm my suspicion, I kept going. "Anyway, I found out Nina lost her job because of Anani. With Lyla dead, she gets revenge and her old job back. And get this. Nina took out $50,000 from her checking account. Depleted almost her entire savings. She could have used that money to pay Junior."

He stared at me for a good thirty seconds. "How do you know this, Ms. Anderson?"

Emme. "Nina. She mentioned it to Omari."

Sometimes it scared me how easily lies rolled off my tongue. Aubrey wouldn't approve of Emme's illegal searches, even if they were for the greater good. It helped, though, that I didn't consider it lying but rather necessary acting. Tomato, tomahto and all that.

"We just need to figure out how much Geppetto paid Junior," I said. "I bet it matches."

He gave me a look. "Who is Geppetto, Ms. Anderson?"

Oh. "I gave our killer a nickname."

To his credit, he didn't question it. "I have already spoken to Ms. Ruth about checking to see if her grandson hid any money from our Mr. Geppetto—"

I cut him off. "Geppetto. Not Mr. Geppetto."

There was a pause as he just stared me, like I was in the wrong for expecting him to get my nickname right. "As I was saying," he finally said, "I have already explained to Ms. Ruth that Junior might have hidden cash somewhere. As you may imagine, she has been more than willing to look."

"Guess she hasn't found anything."

He shrugged. "I doubt she would tell us if she did. She was too busy watching something called *The First 48* when I stopped by earlier."

I narrowed my eyes. A&E hadn't aired a new episode of *The First 48* since December. The only way to watch it was to catch the daily rerun at 11:00 a.m., which didn't make any sense. "How were you downtown at the licensing exam at 10:30 and at Junior's grandma's at 11:00? I thought the test took two hours."

"I did not make the test."

My eyes narrowed. "Traffic?" I asked, even though Aubrey didn't own a car.

"I decided not to go."

He must have lost his mind. "And when did you decide this?" He certainly hadn't informed me of this change of plans. And I was his partner. Kind of.

"I decided this morning. You were the one who was anxious for me to talk to Ms. Ruth."

"Yeah, but not at the same time as your test."

"I will take the exam—after we solve this case. We are making too much progress to worry about anything else."

Yeah, like going to jail ourselves for impersonating licensed investigators. I was about to say as much when I realized what was what.

He was scared he'd fail.

It was kind of sweet, when you thought about it. Aubrey had never told me his age but I'd had Emme look it up. Thirty-six. Not old by any means, but it meant he probably hadn't taken a standardized test going on twenty years. Couldn't blame him for feeling rusty. I got SAT prep flashbacks any time I had to do so much as fill out a tax form.

But as endearing as it was, it also wasn't helpful. We needed a license. I wouldn't last in jail. "You know, I came across a website offering license tutoring," I said. "I'm sure it's not that expensive."

"I have stayed up to date on procedures. I do not want to be behind when I am back with the sheriff's department." He said it so casually I thought maybe I'd misheard him.

"Back? You mean reinstated?"

He shook his head and I was immediately relieved. That lasted until he opened his mouth again. "Not quite, Ms. Anderson. I resigned from the department, so it is not a matter of being reinstated. However, I can apply for a new position. My lawyer thinks I have a good shot since there were no charges regarding my ... incident."

It was my turn to stare. This was the reason that Aubrey didn't have a license. It wasn't that he didn't have time. Or that he was nervous. Or that he needed a partner to help him out. He was biding his time and just never bothered to tell me.

I was pissed. "Were you going to let me know or just surprise me? 'Hello, Ms. Anderson, I have been reinstated as a deputy so you are on your own with becoming an investigator. I wish you luck in your future endeavors.'" My Aubrey impression was pathetic, but at the moment I didn't give one flying fudge.

"Ms. Anderson, do you not think you are overreacting a bit? I am not returning to the sheriff's department tomorrow."

"But it's going to happen, right? Even after how they treated you? Those people you want to be back with? Guess what? They made you the sacrificial lamb for that poor girl's disappearance. I've been in enough dysfunctional relationships to recognize one."

He showed no emotions. "Ms. Anderson ... "

But he was talking to my back. I was going for a grand exit. Of course, I was midway up a mountain trail, which made things a bit difficult. Normally I could just stomp to my car and drive off in a huff. Instead, I huffed and puffed for fifteen minutes, regretting eating that second scoop. What made things worse was that Aubrey continued his workout. He ran past me not once, but twice.

Neither of us spoke.

# Twenty-Four

I'd gotten the routine down pat. Text Mack. Call Mack. Stalk Mack's social media. My last phone call revealed a full voicemail. Good to know I wasn't the only one he was avoiding. If I'd been able to leave (yet another) message, I'd have told him I wasn't harassing him about Gus, I was harassing him about Nina. He knew them both. I wondered if Lyla had ever said anything about her, either as herself or as Anani.

When I wasn't blowing up every available method of contact I had for Mack, I was doing the same with Nina. She was a publicist. Translation: she had to answer her phone. What if I was *People* offering a cover story on Omari?

When I actually listened to her outgoing message instead of just hanging up, I learned that Nina was currently out of the office at the Silver Sphere Awards rehearsals. She would return my call at her earliest convenience—provided I clearly left my full name, phone number, and company.

I didn't. Instead, I got in Omari's car. I'd borrowed his Mercedes after dropping my Infiniti at the mechanic for the kajllionth time. If Nina was at rehearsals, Gus and Mack were probably there too. Both my suspects and a key, possibly unreliable, witness in one location? I was there.

I found a short-term spot in the parking structure behind the Shrine auditorium and headed to the nearest backstage entrance—careful to avoid the University of Southern California coeds riding bikes in short skirts and three-inch heels while simultaneously texting. I spied the production trailers serving as Ground Zero for the television crew and staff farther up, next to what would probably become the Red Carpet. I also spotted Gus's Big Bird-yellow Airstream and Mack's tour bus.

I knew they were there. I just needed to get in to see them. It wasn't like a studio where once you were in, you were free to roam. With shows, check-in was just the first stop. You needed a badge to get you anywhere, but especially backstage.

Like celebrity itself, awards show badges had different levels. A-list was the All Access pass. It could get you anywhere anytime. B-list was VIP. It still got you into the good spots. C-list was Working Staff. You could get most places backstage but you weren't rubbing shoulders with talent. D-list was reserved for the red carpet and press. You were lucky if security let you out of sight to go to the bathroom. And Z-list? Those were the seat-fillers, people who volunteered to sit in Todd Arrington's seat when he needed to run to the bathroom. The last thing a show producer wanted was for his or her audience to look empty during a telecast.

The badges were all color-coded so guards could immediately distinguish the haves from the have-nots with just a quick glance. They also each had a number and your name, in case you were tempted to make a copy for your friends. A big no-no.

Of course, any badge was better than what I had, which was nothing. Not that I let a little thing like that stop me. I reminded myself that if you act like you belong, most people think you do. And I did belong. I'd been personally invited to the show by Gus and Nina. Just not on this day.

I found the security checkpoint. The guard looked like he spent too much time at McDonald's and not enough time at his barber. He was pudgy, with a mop of curly dirty blond hair rising two inches from his scalp. He'd be immediately cast as the comedic lead against a super-hot chick who wouldn't give him the time of day in real life. I saw him flick his eyes down to my chest. For once he wasn't trying to peek at my boobs.

I played dumb. "Is this where I can pick up tickets?" Kitt promised she'd messenger them. Not that he needed to know that.

He smiled. "I don't believe ticket pickup has opened yet."

"Oh, I know." I didn't. "But I told Kitt I needed to get them early. She's in the production office. I'd be happy to just run in and pick them up."

I made a move to walk through the full-body scanner. He stopped me. No surprise there. "You're more than welcome to wait for someone to bring the tickets out to you."

"No problem." I pretended to fire off a text, then stood to the side.

Ten minutes later I was still out there. I'd learned the guards were Barry and Alissa. They were shocked at who'd gotten kicked off *Dancing With the Stars* that week. They both thought the '90s-era sitcom star was now a shoo-in to win it. Having watched the show myself, I begged to differ. I just couldn't, since I was eavesdropping and all.

Barry the Guard glanced over at me for what felt like the kajillionth time. Neither Nina nor Kitt had come to drop off my tickets. Shocker, since I hadn't contacted them. I pretended to be annoyed. "I have to be in Santa Monica in a half hour. Can't I just run in? I promise I'll grab my tickets and come right back out. I won't go rogue."

"I'd love to let you do that but I can't." He looked at me again. This time a bit more closely. "Did we go to high school together?"

There it was.

"Yes! I was just thinking the same thing. I'm Dayna. Barry, right?"

Thank you, mad eavesdropping skills. And thank you Chubby's for pimping me in twenty-three commercials in eight months.

"You look exactly the same," he said.

I bet. "You too."

"How's your mom doing?"

"Great." At least that wasn't a lie. I'd spoken with her the other day on her way back from Michael's. The New Year's planners were finally on sale and so cheap she'd picked up two. She promised to send me one. "She actually asks about you all the time."

"Really? I love your mom. I'd do anything for that lady."

"Like let her daughter in to get her ticket?" I made it seem like I was joking. Unless, of course, he let me.

"Yeah ... no."

It was worth a shot. "Gonna head out. It was nice seeing you again."

Barry nodded. I went back to the car, bypassing Mack's tour bus on the way. I resisted the urge to kick it. If Barry wasn't going to let me in, I'd simply wait for them to come out.

I found Z leaning against the driver's-side door of Omari's Mercedes. I wasn't surprised he knew I had the car. I figured I had two options. Talk to him or open the passenger's side and shimmy my way into the driver's seat. Neither was appealing.

He wore all black again, the purple relegated to his belt. I got within two feet of him before I stopped. I could smell the cinnamon. "Dude, what's with the purple?"

He reached for his belt. "You don't like it? Want me to take it off?"

"I'm good."

"Okay, but if you change your mind, let me know."

I most certainly would not. "I'm surprised to find you here," I said, instead.

"And I'm surprised not to find you waiting in the bushes."

I only used those to pee. "I didn't see any around and I forgot to bring my own."

I hit the automatic lock, hoping he'd get the hint. He didn't. Just stared at me some more. It took a full thirty-eight seconds for him to speak. I counted.

"You should be happy to see me," he finally said. "I have something you want."

"And what would that be?" I wasn't sure I wanted the answer.

"Money order receipts and something better."

"A confession?"

"Emails."

I was more confused than excited. "Why would anyone blackmail someone in writing?"

"'Criminal mastermind' is an oxymoron. Most of them are idiots. You want them or not?"

"Of course."

I stuck out my hand so he'd know I was serious. That's when I realized he wasn't holding anything and his pants were way too tight to have anything in his pocket. My eyes narrowed. "You don't have them."

"Not on me, but I'll get them to you... if you leave Mack alone. No more texts. No more calls. Definitely no more direct messages. Agreed?"

"I wouldn't have done all that if he'd given me this stuff when he promised."

"That's not an agreement."

I sighed. "Agreed."

I would take them to the cops as soon as he handed them to me. Aubrey would be pleased. The thought of Aubrey reminded me of his situation so I went for the abrupt subject change. "Got a hypothetical for you. Let's say a law enforcement officer becomes a scapegoat and is forced to resign. It's been a couple of years. How likely is the chance they'll be hired by a police or sheriff's department again?"

Z didn't even have to think it over. "Not good. They always suggest you resign because it looks better than being fired, but it's a trick. Your hypothetical friend should have stayed and gotten fired because he could have taken the case to arbitration. Most of the time the outside arbitrator will reinstate them. Any lawyer would tell them that."

"His didn't."

"Then he needs a new lawyer."

Great. Not only was Aubrey not getting back with the sheriff's department, he was paying someone to lie to him about it. That wouldn't do. At all. "Can you recommend one?"

"Hypothetically?" Z asked. I shrugged. "It won't be cheap."

In that moment, I realized it was selfish to want Aubrey to remain a private investigator, especially if that wasn't what *he* wanted. He'd grown on me, but I could find another PI to apprentice with. He or she wouldn't have a collection of orange reflector suits or refuse to call me anything but Ms. Anderson or think he or she was a walking GPS, but still. I wanted Aubrey happy. Maybe we could use the reward money to hire a decent lawyer.

I looked at Z. "We should have some money coming in." I hoped. Said money was coming from my two main suspects. Hopefully the non-killer would be appreciative enough to still pay us for catching the killer-killer.

Z finally got up from leaning on Omari's car. "How about I make some calls to some people I know. See if I can help Aubrey out."

I wasn't the least bit surprised that he knew exactly who we were talking about. It was his job to. "Okay," I said.

Ten minutes later, I was at the Tommy's on Beverly, enjoying a chili cheeseburger while wondering if Z would come through and how I'd explain it to Aubrey if he did. Aubrey wasn't a rule-breaker, even when it came to helping himself.

Not that I was even sure I could trust Z. Mack either, for that matter. It all felt a bit too convenient. Mack had gone from telling me too much to telling me not enough to telling me nothing to suddenly offering proof by proxy that Gus was indeed blackmailing him. It didn't make much sense.

My Spidey senses refused to believe these emails even existed. If Gus was some blackmailing mastermind like Mack had claimed, wouldn't he be too smart to put it in writing? My only thought was that if they did exist, then Gus wrote in some sort of code. If so, I wasn't sure how much that would help matters. And it was all a moot point if I couldn't even get my hands on them. I wasn't sure if it was yet another delay tactic.

On the flip side, if the emails did exist, then Mack wouldn't be the only one with copies. I needed to take the middle man out of the equation and find them myself. I knew exactly where: Gus' office.

If this was a heist movie, the Silver Sphere offices would be secured three floors underground in an airless chamber guarded by a feral unicorn with a Rambo-approved knife as a horn. The only way I'd be able to get in would be using an air vent, some dental floss, and an entire can of unicorn repellent I'd bought off eBay. But it wasn't.

I didn't even have to use the Batphone to beg someone to let me in. A group of interns happened to leave as I got there. They didn't question my presence. One even held the door for me and I breezed right in.

As Kitt had warned, the place was practically deserted. The interns were gone and the few employees not at rehearsals were taking full advantage of the deserted office to play Candy Crush and surf the web. No one paid me any mind. Maybe they were used to seeing me. I'd sure been there enough.

It turned out the hardest part of my not-so-covert mission was finding Gus's office. During my vast array of visits, I'd never had occasion to see it, so I did two laps of the entire floor before I found it lurking behind a closed door in a random corner. I pretended to knock, then breezed in and shut the door behind me, ignoring the phone ringing from the room's depths.

It was exactly what I imagined—an ode to Gus. The same life-size photos that littered the outside hallways were also in here. The only difference was that these photos all featured Gus. Some with past winners and nominees. Some with just Gus himself. Even one of him casually caressing a six-foot-tall award replica like they were friends with benefits.

The room looked more like a lounge than office, the desk even shoved into a corner as if an afterthought. Gus clearly spent more time on the large leather couch smack-dab in the middle of the room. I didn't blame him. It looked way more comfortable. But I didn't check to see if it was, instead opting to head to the computer on the desk. Before I turned it on, I said a quick prayer to the password gods to show me mercy on this kind day. I would have given an offering, but the only thing I had on me was a half-used EOS lip balm and I had a feeling the gods didn't have to worry about chapped lips.

I turned the computer on. It loaded and went straight to his desktop. Thank. You.

I took a glance at his desktop screen. Not a file in site. He even had managed to remove the recycle bin. How do you recycle a recycle bin? The desktop was cleaner than my mouth. And this was coming from a girl who didn't curse. Much.

I clicked on the mail icon on the taskbar. Outlook loaded within seconds. I expected an inbox littered with thousands of messages. I got that and then some. It wasn't just littered. There was enough email in there to fill a landfill. It looked like Gus hadn't deleted a message since 2006. And most if it was unread, at that.

The latest one was from something called the Cisco Unity Connection Messaging System and it came with an attachment. Apparently Silver Sphere used a phone system that sent an email when someone left you a message. Fancy.

I searched the inbox, typing *Mack Christie*. His name popped up in a lot of emails, just none discussing videos or blackmail or any of that. Blurg.

For kicks, I checked Gus's sent items folder. Empty. I felt like Goldilocks. One was too full. One was too empty. Except there wasn't one just right. It definitely wasn't in his trash, because that was empty too. It didn't make sense. At all.

Exactly what was going on here? It wasn't like I could ask Gus and find out. Only thing I could think was maybe it wasn't the regular email account he used after all. Was he actually doing business from a Hotmail account he'd had since the dawn of civilization? Deciding to find out, I opened his web browser and checked his history. That too came up blank.

Great. I'd broken in for nothing. This never happened to Tom Cruise.

Never a fan of wasting anyone's time, especially my own, I forced myself to think. What were the chances Gus and Mack just communicated over email? There had to be text messages, in-person meetings, phone calls. And if there weren't phone calls, there were probably voicemails.

And if Mack had left a voicemail, the Cisco Unified Messaging System would have thoughtfully logged it for Gus's benefit—and mine. I didn't even need to pull out my phone to find Mack's number. I'd called it so many times I knew it almost as well as my ABCs.

I did a search. No hits.

I looked up the number for his management company. Still nothing.

I forced myself to think some more. Motive. Means. Opportunity.

I had motive for Gus: Anani threatened to put an end to his cash flow and out him in the process. Opportunity was a bit of a moot point since someone had hired Junior.

That left means.

If I couldn't connect Gus to Mack, perhaps I could connect him to Junior. A gossip blogger who lives in the lowest of the Hollywood Hills—I'd checked—doesn't normally come across a guy in the South Bay. Factor in the onslaught of 24/7 LA traffic and it was physically impossible. And it wasn't like you could find a murderer on Craigslist like it was a free couch or a sublet. Not that I ever looked.

Regina had given me Junior's number, so I still had it in my contacts. At the time I'd thought she was being bitter. Now I knew better. I typed the number and searched. A message popped up. I clicked on the attached WAV file and let it play.

Junior's voice was surprisingly high-pitched. "Hey man, it's Junior. Got your message. Call me back."

It was left the night he killed himself.

# Twenty-Five

I called the tip line as soon as I got out of there. No one picked up so I left a message. I'd hoped they'd bring Gus in for questioning before our scheduled interview but it didn't happen. I'd learned the hard way that information flowed one way when it came to providing tips to the police. Usually you only found out if it went anywhere from Google News Alerts. Certainly not from the police. I'd given them information more than once only for it to disappear into a file and never be seen again.

I just hoped that wouldn't be the case with Gus. The cops might know something I didn't, like whether his conversations with Junior were about the merits of coffee versus tea. But I doubted it, which was why I planned to follow through on my interview the next day.

The plan was to pick up my car from the shop and head over to the Shrine for the interview. It felt like forever since I'd scheduled it with Kitt. In that time, Nina had edged Gus out for first place on my number one suspect board only for Gus to have a last-minute resurgence.

They both had motive. Nina had discovered Anani's true identity and mysteriously wiped out her savings. Gus had promised Mack he'd "take care of it," and it wasn't every day one got a phone call from a murderer-for-hire.

I was curious to talk to Gus, especially in the company of an entire film crew. Television might look like two people in a room—or in this case, in a banana-yellow Airstream. In reality, there were tons of people lurking behind the camera. Cameramen. Directors. Lighting guys. Production assistants. Makeup artists. Hair stylists. Producers. Gaffers, which was a fancy word for electrician. It took hundreds of man hours to produce something you watched in thirty minutes and tweeted how much it sucked in 280 characters.

I, for one, would appreciate all their hard work—and constant presence.

If all went well, Gus would end up behind bars, the case would be wrapped up, and I could finally concentrate on actually attending the Silver Sphere Awards instead of investigating the people behind it.

Hearing Sienna in the kitchen, I walked down the hall to meet her. "We all set for tomorrow?"

She'd gone all out, hiring Dante to drive us to the Shrine and a Glam Squad to get us awards-show ready. Normally I'd shrug it off, but of course Omari's mother was joining us. Though it wasn't our first meeting, it would be my first meeting with her as Omari's girlfriend. I wanted it to go well.

"Did Fab have any problem with the dresses … " I trailed off when I saw the sweet potato pie French toast. It was the second time in a week she'd made it. Not good. I'd never been so scared to see food before in my life. She tried a smile but I wasn't having it. "Just tell me."

"Sure you don't want to eat first?"

I gave her the look all black girls are born with. The ones our moms give us at the grocery store, any time church goes past 1:00 p.m., and when we have the nerve to ask for McDonald's when we know we don't have McDonald's money and that we have perfectly good food at home. The ones that convey a very clear, concise message: Do. Not. Play. With. Me.

It worked. "Gus wrote about you and Omari," she said. "Good news is that it was a blind item."

I waited. Good news implied there was also bad news. When she didn't say any more, I motioned for her to get on with it. Instead, she turned around. "I don't want to burn anything."

Things were worse than I thought. I ran back to the bloset for my phone and pulled up Gus's site. He dubbed his blind items "Inquiring Minds." Unlike Anani, Gus chose a "less is more" approach.

*Which supposedly-in-a-relationship network TV star is actually a chubby chaser? Inquiring minds want to know.*

Chubby chaser? No, this potential murderer did not. I glanced up to see Sienna peeking into the room. "Is he saying what I think he's saying?" I asked.

"Yep! That you were a spokesperson for Chubby's!"

Not what I'd thought, but for the sake of my self-esteem, I decided to go with it. Besides, I had bigger fish—or should I say chicken—to fry. The "chubby chaser" himself. He was not going to be happy. Denying a fake relationship was one thing. Making a real one fodder for one of Hollywood's biggest gossip columnists was another.

I immediately texted him. He was already on set. When I told him I wanted to stop by to "say hi," he promised to get me a drive-on. I threw on some clothes, then called Emme on speaker. Sienna tried to calm me down as the phone rang. "Not sure why you're freaking out. It's so vague, no one's going to even know who Gus is talking about."

Maybe she was right. She had to be right.

Emme picked up the phone. "This the chubby that's being chased?"

Emme's social interactions were relegated to debates on the best *Star Wars* characters. If she knew about the blind, it was making its way around the Internet. I threw Sienna a look.

"If *you* already know who the blind item is about, then yes, it's easy to get," Sienna said. "But no one does ... hence the reason we told Gus in the first place, remember?"

"We?"

"Okay, me, but it was your idea."

Couldn't argue that one. Of course, I'd been tipsy at the time, but that wouldn't hold up in a court of law, much less with my boyfriend. I belatedly realized Emme was still on the phone. "So Emme, update. Thinking Gus might have killed Lyla. I was in his office yesterday—"

She interrupted. "You confronted another would-be killer?"

"Of course not!" That wasn't scheduled until later. "He wasn't even in the building."

I gave her a brief update on the Gus / Mack situation and the Gus / Junior situation. "You think you can find out whether Gus has another email address?"

"TBH?" To be honest. "Probably not. That's your expertise, not mine."

"I guess I can ask him when I talk to him later."

It got silent, I could practically see "You effed up" being written above my head. I'd already forgotten I wasn't supposed to mention that little tidbit.

Emme finally spoke. "The only reason you haven't confronted a killer is because he couldn't schedule you in right away?"

"It's a live-streamed interview. He won't try to kill me in front of 200,000 fans sneaking to watch on their lunch break. Gotta go!"

Omari's home-away-from-home was a Star Waggons trailer outside Stage 5 on the Paramount lot. Not surprisingly, Hollywood has almost as many studio lots as awards shows. All feature the studio essentials: Golf carts. Trailers. And soundstages that tend to be big, bland, beigy numbers that are home to some of the biggest movies and television shows of all time. You can easily go from outer space to the depths of hell just by walking from one soundstage to the next.

*LAPD 90036* shot on stages 4 and 5, which were separated by a street and an array of actor and makeup trailers. Omari shared a two-room, forty-foot trailer with a castmate. It wasn't your average camper. In fact, it was the antithesis of roughing it. Dark hardwood floors. Super comfy gray sofa bed. Microwave and fridge in one corner. And, perhaps most important, a bathroom complete with shower. It came on wheels, to be easily transported when they shot on location.

I knocked and opened the door without being told to come in. Girlfriend perk. Omari was writing at his desk. He jumped when I entered. I was surprised he didn't also scream "I'm not doing anything wrong, Mom." It was kind of adorable.

I decided to mess with him as I walked over. "You writing me a love poem?" I peered over his shoulder. He tried to turn the paper over but I saw enough. "You're writing an acceptance speech!"

"Yeah, though I probably won't win. But you know how bad I am off the cuff. Figured it wouldn't hurt to have something written down. But like I said, I'm not going to win."

"At least it's an honor to be nominated."

He laughed. "I know you didn't drive all the way here to mess with me. Why'd you stop by?"

Oh that. I decided to just rip the Band-Aid off. "Gus knows about us."

There was a pause. He finally spoke. "Yeah ... "

It was all he said, which wasn't nearly enough. Needing more context clues before I was ready to explain further, I kept it simple. "Yeah."

"How'd he find out?"

"Someone must have told him." That someone being Sienna. "It definitely wasn't me."

It was just definitely my idea. I was taking that to the grave, though, along with that one night my junior year of college.

Omari's response was to hold out his hand. "Can I see?"

Since I already had it up, I quickly handed him my phone, then retreated to the other side of the trailer. Omari read, then had the nerve to start laughing. "Chubby chaser?"

"Glad you find that so amusing."

"Personally, I like that you're thicker. Reminds me of the girl I had a low-key crush on in high school."

It took me a second to realize he was talking about me. "You had a crush on me in high school?"

There was a knock on the door. A production assistant poked her head in. "They're ready for you on set."

"Thanks, Mary Ann." He stood up and addressed me again. "I dang near overdosed on Altoids when we first practiced that kiss in *Guys and Dolls*. I gotta go to set, but stay as long as you want."

I planned to—at least long enough to pee. He gave me a quick peck and was out the door. I, in turn, went to use the bathroom. I was washing my hands when I heard the door open again. Was Omari back? I was about to yell out something ridiculously inappropriate when I heard the voice. It would have been impossible not to. Nina had come in and was screeching so high I briefly wondered if I was part dog. That was the only way I should've been able to make out what she was saying.

"I swear, if you do not take me off speakerphone—" There was a pause and then Nina's screeching resumed. "I gave you my entire savings because you told me you'd take care of it. Something told me not to trust you."

Something told *me* to stay in the bathroom. My intention wasn't to eavesdrop but mama would take what mama could get.

"I risked everything because you offered to help me and help him, only for you to screw me over because you think I won't tell anyone. That's where you're wrong. I will go to the cops and I will go to the news. I have proof that I gave you that money."

At that point, my ear was pressed against the door and my mouth hung lower than my grandma's boobs. Was Nina discussing hiring Junior? With who?

"You can call it a donation if you want but I paid you. He better win that award tomorrow or I want my money back. All $50,000."

Wait, what? Nina paid for a Silver Sphere Award? They gave out two dozen awards. Technically, she could have been talking about any of them. But of those twenty-four categories, she only had one client nominated in any of them.

Omari.

I banged the bathroom door open. Nina's shocked expression probably mirrored my own. I didn't give her a chance to breathe, much less speak. "You paid the Silver Sphere Organization to make sure that Omari wins? You have to be kidding me."

My freaking out just made Nina calmer. When she spoke, her voice was finally back to a frequency humans could hear. "Gus, let me call you back." She hung up the phone. "You're eavesdropping on people now?"

"If you want to call using the bathroom eavesdropping, then yes. What did you do."

It was more demand than question. I expected her to look away. Instead, she stared me dead in the eye, her leer worse than that one guy's who you keep making accidental eye contact with at the bar. Except this time, I refused to even blink, much less look away first. "You paid Gus for Omari's Best Actor in Television nomination," I said.

"No. He got that on his own." She sounded offended.

"Oh, you're really going to get technical right now. He got the nomination on his own but you're paying for the win."

Nina sighed. "Silver Sphere is technically a nonprofit, which means you can donate to them. Sometimes Gus can be ... convinced someone should win if you donate enough."

"I thought the members all voted."

"They do. For whoever Gus tells them to. This isn't the Academy. There aren't thousands of industry experts mailing in ballots. This is 109 people sitting in a room tomorrow deciding the winner so they can go get lunch."

Geez. Mack said Gus was corrupt, but I figured blackmail was his side gig. I didn't realize his shadiness trickled into his presidential duties. I didn't say that, though. In fact, I didn't say anything at all. Just stared her down.

"Don't look at me like that," she said. "You're the one who wants him known for something other than Tomari. That's what I'm trying to do."

"Oh, so you did this for me?"

"Wins lead to bigger roles. Bigger paychecks. It's why people don't have a problem giving donations. Actors get an ego boost. Bragging rights. The SSO gets money. No one's complaining."

"Except you." I thought it over. "Fifty thousand isn't a lot."

She shrugged. "I got a deal, the money and helping out with Lyla dying and everything. They didn't have to hire anyone new. Of course, now he's screwing me over because he's got my money. He won't guarantee that Omari will win."

If she was looking for sympathy, she was looking in the wrong place. I only felt bad for one person in this scenario. "Does Omari know?"

She shook her head.

"He can't," I said. "Ever."

She nodded. It was probably the only thing we'd ever agreed on. It would destroy him. I tried focusing on the bright side. At least I knew why Nina had depleted her savings. I still had one lingering question. "How does Anani play into all of this?"

Nina looked confused. "She's just some blogger."

"Who was your assistant, who got you fired. I know about your little trip to Private Parts. Someone hired Junior Reid to kill Lyla."

This time her confusion looked real. Too real. "That's ridiculous. It was a robbery gone wrong."

"Nope. Someone hired him, someone who knew her true identity and had enough cash to pay for the hit."

"And you thought it was me?"

"You drove to Claremont and you took all that money out of your account. I'm surprised *you* don't think it's you."

"I was upset Anani played a part in getting me fired. But I wasn't going to kill her, just give her a dose of her own medicine. Reveal who she was so she'd be dead in Hollywood. Not in real life."

"Did Gus feel the same way?"

"Why would Gus want to kill Anani?"

"Because he's blackmailing Mack Christie over lip-syncing."

She started shaking her head before I'd even finished the sentence. "Doesn't sound like him."

"The guy who takes 'donations' in exchange for wins and then lies about it doesn't sound like a guy who'd blackmail someone for millions of dollars? All righty then."

She shook her head again. "Blackmail isn't Gus. It's too threatening. He wants to be these people's friends. Donations are optional. Usually chump change for a movie studio. More like a scratch your back, you scratch my bank account situation. Everyone wins."

"Lyla didn't."

We didn't say much more after that. We didn't have to.

I had an appointment to get to, with someone I was pretty convinced was a murderer at that. As much as Nina annoyed me, I didn't think she was Geppetto. That left Gus. I'd been nervous for interviews before, but not like this. I thought about it the entire way to the Shrine. I took Arlington down to the 10 and caught it heading east. There was traffic, of course, but I made good use of the time. I wanted proof about Gus, but I didn't want it to involve my boyfriend. It didn't matter what type of spin Nina tried to put on it—Gus wasn't all that he seemed. There was just too much stacked against him. The donations. Mack so desperate to get out of dealing with him that he was ready to ruin his entire career. And the biggest thing of all, that message from Junior. Junior knew who he was calling back and it sounded like they'd spoken before. He was calling for a reason.

I ran everything in a loop as I merged onto the 110 South and got off on Adams Boulevard less than a mile later. There were too many questions, too many things not adding up. And I was over trying to do the math. I wanted the final answer and this was probably the only way I'd get it.

I parked in a metered space on Figueroa, then ran over to greet the only person who even understood all the parts of the equation. Gus.

His Airstream was parked on the same street. He must have seen me walking up because he opened the door to greet me. He seemed happy to see me, even if I couldn't say the same.

"I've been excited to talk to you," he said as I climbed in.

"Me too."

Gus motioned to a scruffy guy born to play a stoner in a comedy. "This is Orlander. He'll be in the back taking care of sound and the cameras."

"That's it?" I could feel my heart rate start to rise. I was expecting people. This wasn't people. This was one guy.

Fudge.

"You okay?" Gus asked.

"Yeah, I'm just anxious—about the interview. Can you give me a second?"

He went to talk with Orlander, who sat in back behind an open curtain checking camera angles and using headphones to make sure the sound was okay.

I wanted to get back in my car. Instead, I gave myself a pep talk. Sure, this wasn't part of the plan, but I'd just have to adjust. I'd done it before. I could do it again. I just needed to be smart about it. Keep the pepper spray in one hand, my cell phone in the other with 911 already keyed in. Plus, I made sure I was aware of the nearest exits.

I finally went over to Gus and his lone cameraman, but only after grabbing my pepper spray from my bag.

"We take a less-is-more approach with these interviews," Gus said.

That was an understatement. Gus's setup was as bare bones as you could get. He interviewed people while driving around LA. I spied three cameras mounted on the windshield—one on the passenger-side corner to get closeups of me, one on the driver's side to do the same for Gus, and a third in the middle for a classic two-shot.

"Let's get you mic'd and settled up front," Gus said. "We go live in ten minutes."

We got me set up and I made myself comfortable—or as comfortable as I could be considering the circumstances—in the front passenger seat. It was only after I sat down that I saw the cops in my side-view mirror.

I only noticed them pulling up right behind us because of their ride. It *wasn't* a patrol car, but one of those stereotypical brown four doors a decade too old to be driven by anyone but an officer of the law. At first, I was excited. I wouldn't have to call 911 after all in case things went awry. Then I thought it over. Why would the cops be hanging out behind Gus's Airstream?

It could be a coincidence, or it could be worse. Much worse. I'd always wanted to see cops act on my tips. But as with a restraining order, I expected to remain 100 to 200 feet away at all times. Not in the seat next to the guy I'd snitched on. I wanted Gus to go down. Not take me with him.

Blurg.

The good news was that they parked but didn't get out. Maybe Gus wouldn't notice them, especially since he was busy running his mouth about the interview setup. "The stream's only thirty minutes so please keep your answers short. I'll tap my steering wheel if you need to wrap up."

Orlander called out from the back. "We're all set for the run-through."

Gus started his engine. "We need to drive around the block to make sure everything's all set before we start. Just keep talking so Orlander can check levels."

"Okay. You still get nervous about the awards?"

He pulled out of his spot. The cops did the same. Lovely.

"Not really. It's a well-oiled machine at this point." He turned right on Jefferson. They were right behind us. He glanced in his side-view mirror. "Is that car following us? They look like cops."

"Maybe they're trying to get to the highway?" It was in the opposite direction, but still.

"I'll let them pass." He pulled into the right lane. Of course they didn't pass, just pulled over too. After a moment, both cars pulled into metered spots. "I just renewed my registration. We weren't speeding," Gus said, then continued to tick off the reasons the police shouldn't be following him. I stayed quiet.

They didn't get out. Just sat in their car. We did the same, Gus freaking out more and more with each passing second. "Why would the cops want to stop me?"

I shook my head and thanked God for my two years of acting classes at Speiser Sturges. At the time it felt pricey, but it was definitely paying off at that moment. "I'm sure it's fine," I said, then called out, "It's fine, right, Orlander?"

"You're screwed," he responded.

Thanks. Gus grabbed his phone and hit the first number on his favorites. Being Hollywood, it was his publicist.

"There you are," Nina said through the speakerphone. "I've been blowing your phone up—"

He cut her off. "The police are following me."

"Which is why I've been blowing your phone up."

"What's going on?"

"Dayna." For a second, I thought she wanted to talk to me, but then she kept on. "She's an idiot—"

At that moment, I agreed with her. Still, I quickly jumped in. "Hey Nina! It's me. Dayna, the idiot. Just wanted to let you know you're on speaker. You know, in case you say something you might regret." Or more likely, I'd regret.

"Great! Tell Gus how you think he's a murderer."

Like that.

I glanced at Gus, who gave me the side-eye of death, which was expected considering the news. "Why would I think he was a murderer?"

"Because you couldn't pin Lyla's murder on me so now you're harassing poor Gus."

Glancing at Gus, I shook my head and mouthed, "Ignore her."

He didn't. "What do you mean? She's here for an interview."

"That's how she tricked you? With me, she hid in the bathroom so she could eavesdrop."

"I wasn't hiding! I had to pee." I just happened to eavesdrop at the same time.

I tried to figure out the best method of escape. The good news was we weren't moving and the cops *were* right behind us, even if they weren't doing anything but sitting there. The bad news? I didn't have a door. I'd have to crawl over some random hump between the seats to get out the exit in the back.

"Dayna seems to think Lyla's killer didn't act alone," Nina said. "That you hired him."

I hoped Orlander was getting this all on camera so it could play at my murder trial. I tried to diffuse the situation. "I don't necessarily think it's you, Gus. I'm just exploring all options."

"Why am I even an option?" He had the steering wheel in a death grip. "Why would I kill Lyla? She was the best publicist we had. No offense, Nina."

Nina sighed. "First, Lyla was the best because I taught her to be. Second, Dayna doesn't think you killed Lyla. She thinks you killed Anani Miss. They were the same person."

"No, they weren't," Gus said. "Someone told me Anani was really some woman who worked at Fox."

"That 'someone' was probably Lyla," Nina said. "She told me the same thing."

I could see him working it out in his head. He finally spoke. "This looks bad for me."

Really bad, but I sure wasn't going to say that. So I said nothing at all. Instead, I glanced at the mirror. The cops were still there. What were they waiting for?

"I never spoke to Junior," Gus said. "He kept leaving messages, said his grandma was a huge fan, but he didn't say why he needed to talk. When I figured out he was connected to Lyla's death, I called him back. Hoping to get some info to help the police. But we never talked. Just played phone tag. I swear."

I didn't believe him. "I believe you," I said. He looked encouraged. "I'm sure you have a good explanation for the blackmail, too."

Judging by his abrupt change of expression, it was the wrong thing to say. Nina piped in from the phone. "I forgot to mention she thinks you blackmailed Mack Christie."

If ever I wanted a dropped call, this was it. I spoke. "Mack Christie claims, even though he's been super-duper hesitant to provide any actual proof whatsoever, that you secretly recorded his closed rehearsal for the show last year and have been blackmailing him. *He* thinks you might have killed Lyla to keep his money coming in and protect yourself."

Yes, I was throwing Mack under the bus, but that's what he got for not calling me back. Gus was now gripping the steering wheel so hard his brown knuckles were turning white. "And the police believe this?"

Considering they were behind us, I would say yes. "Like I said, Mack's been super sketchy about it. He claims he has emails from you."

Gus laughed. "I don't email. We always talked on the phone and even then it was only to help him. I told him I'd take care of the video. And I did. I know the donations don't make me look good, but there is a line." Clearly, a very very thin one. "We would never resort to blackmail. But of course, if a rich, handsome, award-winning celebrity says so, it must be true. I don't know why he's lying but he is. Now they're going to arrest me because of it. I can't go to jail."

He was definitely going to jail. "You're not going to jail. Just explain it to them just like you explained everything to me. You'll be fine. It's not like you can run from the police."

I laughed then.

"Of course not," he said. Then he turned on his engine and pulled out.

Not good. At all.

LA has been known for its car chases since the time OJ got into that Bronco. It wasn't uncommon for them to even be aired live. I'd watched more than a few myself. Just never thought I'd be in one. It was not on the bucket list. About the only good thing was at least we were traveling with a bathroom. Important, considering there was a 99.99999 percent chance I'd pee my pants.

I glanced in the side mirror again. The cops were so close I could make out the detective's wrinkles. Blurg. I forced myself to look on the bright side. At least it wasn't a high-speed car chase. In fact, it wasn't really a car chase at all. Those involved sirens.

Maybe this would all be okay.

Then I heard the noise. I glanced back to see the car's police lights going as well.

And that's when Gus hit it.

# *Twenty-Six*

It fortunately was the brakes. Luckily, I was wearing my seat belt because he slammed on them hard. Never mind we were in the middle of the road. The cops swerved to the right to avoid a collision. I made a mental note that if I ever was in another potential police chase, I'd request the driver pull into a parking lot in a safe and sound manner.

Nina immediately hung up to call a lawyer. We stayed in the car. They didn't get out either but we definitely heard them. A male voice on their speaker told us to step out of the vehicle with our hands up. I raised mine immediately even though they couldn't see, then waited as Orlander and Gus got out before me. It was the first time I was happy no one insisted ladies first.

By the time I got out, Gus was already in handcuffs and on his way to the back of the detective's car. He stayed there while they questioned me and Orlander, then told us we were free to go. They made it clear that Gus wasn't under arrest. He was simply a "person of interest" being taken in for some "routine questioning."

I walked the block back to Omari's car, my feet joining my brain in being thankful it wasn't a long chase. Z leaned against the car, a manila envelope in his hand. I was so annoyed I didn't even bother looking both ways before crossing the street. He wore his patented amused expression and all-black suit. I stopped a few feet away but still could smell the cinnamon. "You following me or you just happen to be in the area?"

"I have something for you."

I glanced at the envelope. It had to be the emails, which were a moot point now. I took them anyway. "Thanks but I already figured everything out—without these. The police just took Gus in to question him about it."

It felt good to rub it in his face. Really, really good.

He nodded. "Great job. You saved the day."

But there was something in his tone. I narrowed my eyes and held the envelope up. "You gave these to the police already, didn't you?"

"Of course. I would never want to obstruct an investigation."

"So you just told me about them to get me off Mack's back. You were planning on giving them to the cops first the entire time. Then hand them over to me with a 'I have something for you.'"

Pissed, I motioned for him to get out of my way. He spoke as he did so. "I wasn't talking about the emails."

I didn't care. I was over it. As I pushed past him, he gently grabbed my hand and pressed a piece of paper into it.

"What is this?" I asked.

"My apology," he said. "If Aubrey is serious about getting back with the sheriff's department, all he needs to do is call the number written on there."

If this was some melodramatic reality show, I'd have torn that scrap of paper into a million pieces. But it wasn't. So instead I just asked a question. "Who does it belong to?"

But Z was already walking away. "One way to find out."

He knew he had me. That he could screw me over and think if he gave me something else I wanted then everything would be fine between us. He was wrong. He would not be forgiven.

Of course that didn't mean I wouldn't pass the number on to Aubrey. I wanted to get to his house the next morning by eight. I made it by nine.

I'd been up half the night checking for updates on Gus. His being brought in had, unsurprisingly, made the news. Someone even managed to get cell phone footage of him being driven away. The video played on a loop on almost every major blog, social media account, and news site—all with different variations of the same headline: *Awards Show President Questioned for Own Publicist's Murder.*

The articles weren't nearly as juicy as the headlines. They knew less than I did. None mentioned Mack. Or Anani. Or the blind item. Being short on details, the article writers had embellished with recycled info about the Silver Sphere Awards history, Lyla's death, and Gus's bio. After refreshing Buzzfeed for the twentieth time only to find the same old information, it was finally enough to put me to sleep.

I woke up to the same news—no news—and then decided to get dressed and go see Aubrey. He was on his sliver of a porch with his feet kicked back, eyes closed, and cooler at the ready beside him, like he didn't have a care in the world.

I knew better.

I got about two steps before he spoke. "Ms. Anderson." I was beginning to wonder if I had a certain scent. Or, more likely, I was his only visitor. "I have been trying to reach you."

I was aware. I had the six missed calls on my iPhone to prove it.

"The news is reporting the police questioned Mr. Ortiz," he said.

I nodded even though he couldn't see it. "There's emails proving he blackmailed Mack Christie. And I found out Junior left a message on his voicemail. Motive. Means. Opportunity. Check. Check. Check."

That made him open his eyes. "Congratulations, Ms. Anderson. You are already an amazing investigator and you will only become better. You just have to ignore the mistakes because even the best of us make them. The key is not giving up but instead trying to correct it."

I was all for the warm and fuzzy moment. "I know. You've taught me that. You've taught me a lot these past few months. Most important thing? Bring a jar on stakeouts."

He laughed. I was shocked. Before that moment, I didn't even know Aubrey's lips were physically able to stretch like that. I took the paper Z gave me out of my purse. "I have something for you."

"And what may that be?"

"My apology." It had sounded way cooler when Z said it. I placed it next to him. "That number should help you get back with the department."

He stared at it. "How—"

"It's probably best if you don't ask any questions. Just call the number." I got up. Aubrey was too busy staring at the paper to look at me. "Let me know if you need a reference."

Sienna and I were on my bed giving ourselves sheet mask face treatments. The liquidy white paper covered our entire face save for our eyes, nose, and lips. We looked like the World's Cutest Horror Movie Villains. Since the Glam Squad and Omari's mom weren't due for a bit, I was updating Sienna on the past twenty-four hours. It wasn't something you could cover in a TL;DR version so it took a while. I was at the part where I'd just burst out of the bathroom in Omari's trailer. "The kicker? She used the money to pay for Omari's award."

"I'm completely and utterly shocked."

I couldn't make out her expression through the mask but there was something in her voice. Sienna, God bless her, was not the world's best actress. What she lacked in actual skill, she more than made up for in enthusiasm. And this one wasn't even enthusiastic.

"You knew ... " I said.

"Of course not."

"Sienna Michelle Hayes ... "

"Fine. Fab told me people paid for their wins when we first thought Gus killed Lyla. I didn't want to say anything because I didn't think Omari was gonna win. I knew you'd both be devastated. Of course, if I'd known the awards just went to the highest bidder we could have started a GoFundMe months ago."

"You're not helping," I said.

"Not now, it's too late. But definitely something to think about next year."

I was about to answer when my phone rang. I checked the ID. Nina. I wasn't really in the mood to talk with her but I answered anyway, putting my phone on speaker. Last thing I needed was sheet mask gunk on my cell. It definitely didn't need coenzymes and peptides. "Hey Nina! I can't talk long. Sienna and I are getting ready for tonight."

"Yeah, that's why I'm calling. You're both no longer invited."

Sienna ripped the sheet mask off as I sat up. "What? Why not?" I asked.

"Well, let's see. You thought I killed Lyla."

I needed to save this before Sienna never spoke to me again. "Yes, and I feel really bad about that. In fact, I'm sending you an Edible Arrangement."

"Like you sent Gus to jail?"

You'd think she'd be appreciative that I'd helped find Lyla's killer—again—but no.

"I've been dealing with calls all day," she continued. "Instead of discussing tonight's show, the news keeps replaying Gus in that police car. No one cares he was released."

Released? Hadn't heard that. Probably because I was too busy face masking and body scrubbing to check the news. Great. "They didn't charge him with anything?"

"Of course not. He didn't kill anyone. Just like he didn't blackmail anyone. I just wish they'd let him out before the members voted. I had to take over."

By that point, Sienna was pacing. I would do anything to get her to those awards, even beg. "I get why you don't want me there, but at least let Sienna go. She didn't accuse anyone of anything."

"Yeah, she just forced Kitt to get you both into the 18th Annual Silver Sphere Awards Official Gift Lounge Presented by the Brand New Toyota Prius so you could run rampant and attack Todd Arrington. Yeah, I know it was you. Gus doesn't want you there. I don't either. But we do hope you both watch the show tonight and share your thoughts on social media. Bye now."

With that, she hung up. I looked over at my best friend. "Sienna, I'm sorry."

As a response, she walked out of the room. A few minutes later I heard the front door slam. She'd left.

Fudge.

She still wasn't home an hour later, so when our intercom buzzed I hoped it was her—even though I knew she had a key. It was her condo, after all. But it was Omari's mom at the door. Great.

I buzzed her in while wondering how I could artfully explain that I'd been uninvited to the awards we were all getting ready for. I wanted to make a good impression. This was definitely not it. I was weighing my options when she swept into the condo and embraced me.

Miss Erica wasn't just a cool mom. She was a hot mom, the suburban neighbor in the movies the nerdy leads all secretly lust after. And she looked just like she had when we were in high school. "How you doing, sweetie?"

By then I'd settled on my excuse: Classic Sick. It had served me well throughout childhood. I hoped for the same this go-round. "Not that great. I've been nauseous all day."

She smiled—definitely a weird reaction. "Sweetie, you're pregnant!"

I may have jumped back in horror. "No! Never."

She looked me up and down. "You sure? You look kind of bloated."

True, but from food, not babies! Last thing I needed was that idea going back to Augusta with Miss Erica. Mama would freak. The only way she'd be even remotely happy was if she thought it meant Jesus was making his return to this good Earth. "I can't be pregnant."

I meant birth control, but she thought I was discussing something else. "Are you worried about the whole out-of-wedlock thing? Because I'll make Omari marry you."

"No!" I screamed a bit too loud. "I mean, I want Omari to marry me, just not because I'm pregnant." Her face lit up. "Which I'm not."

In what had become my custom, I was making things worse. I was two seconds away from showing Miss Erica my period-tracking app when Sienna burst through the door accompanied by Fab and another woman holding a makeup bag.

"Hi guys! Time to get ready for the show. Don't want to be late." Sienna was in way too good of a mood for someone who'd just been banned from the Biggest Party of the Year.

I waited until Miss Erica was getting glammed up before I pulled Sienna to the side. "What's going on?"

She handed me a laminated All Access pass. It looked just like the ones I'd seen at the Shrine. At least on one side. The other side was blank. I glanced up to find Sienna cheesing up a storm. "Some intern posted a pic of it on her Instagram," she said. "Even hashtagged it."

"I don't want to know any of this."

She kept going. "I got them printed out and laminated at Staples. Only cost five bucks. I'm so giving them a good review on Yelp—"

"I'm going for plausible deniability here. You're making it really hard."

"Oh sorry! I won't tell you about the coupon then. You're coming, right?"

"No."

"What! Why not? You scared of Nina? I got that covered. I've watched over 123 hours of *E! Live From the Red Carpet* specials. Trust me when I say the red carpet gets ridiculous about an hour before the show. That when the really big celebs finally show up and the D-listers drag their feet because they want to talk to as many news outlets as possible. Security will be so distracted, they'll barely glance at our passes."

"Yeah, still no. They take trespassing seriously at these things. You're going to get arrested. You can go if you want. I'll watch from home and wait for your collect call from jail."

"Fine. Let me know if you change your mind."

Not happening. I went back to the bloset to stew. The only thing going well these past twenty-four hours was my skin being extremely moisturized. Gus's release meant I was flush out of suspects and I had no clue why the police let him go. He'd admitted he was in contact with Junior. Of course, he didn't cop to the blackmail or emails.

Emails I hadn't bothered to look at. I'd dropped the envelope from Z on my dresser without as much as a second glance. I decided to finally check them out.

I read the first one. Despite what Gus had claimed, it was an email he sent to Mack from his SSO account. I glanced at a few more. Gus was out of jail, though, so there had to be something here. I kept looking. It took me an hour to figure it out.

The message itself was short: *You said the money order should be comming by 5 today. It has not arrived.*

I reread it, then checked others. "Comming" wasn't a one-time typo. Gus wrote it in more than one email. He clearly didn't know how to spell it. And he wasn't the only one.

I scrolled through my text messages until I found what I wanted. A text from Kitt. The one where she misspelled "coming" and even admitted she did it all the time.

Bingo.

I'd spent two months temping as the second assistant for a CEO. About the only good thing about the job was that it was always someone's birthday. Yay free cake. I'd also learned that most assistants have way too much access to their boss's life. Social security numbers. Credit cards. Email. Outlook even lets you add another email inbox on your account. I could check my boss's email and, more important, send an email from him.

Convenient when you were pretending to be your boss to blackmail the biggest country singer in the US. Of course, even if Kitt was in fact the blackmailer, she wasn't in jail. Not yet. Did the cops not know? She clearly was blackmailing Mack, but did she kill Lyla?

I needed to have a conversation with her. Stat. My first thought was to be ready and waiting when she showed up at work on Monday. But then I remembered something she'd mentioned during our lunch.

She was going on vacation as soon as the show was over. At the time, I hadn't given it much thought. But now, it seemed convenient.

If I wanted to talk to her, I'd have to do it tonight. The good news was that at least I knew where to find her.

I left a quick message with the tip line and ran to the living room where Sienna and Miss Erica were getting ready for the awards.

"Is there still time to do my makeup before we go?"

# Twenty-Seven

There are different types of traffic. Some you find anywhere, like backups related to construction, accidents, and weather. And some you can only find in LA, like awards show traffic. Sienna and I were in the back of a Lincoln in the drop-off line for the Silver Sphere red carpet. We inched along as I wished for a new superpower—the ability to jump to the front of any line. It would also do me well at Disneyland.

I had to hand it to Sienna. We both looked great. Her Glam Squad had given me the full second-season-of-a-reality-show-makeover complete with clip-on hair extensions and enough nose and cheek contouring to make a Kardashian weep with joy. Clothing-wise, Sienna had opted for a low-cut Jessica Rabbit inspired number and I'd gone for an off-the-shoulder purple classic silhouette that flaunted way less boob and way more booty. We both wore our hair down. The hair stylist had opted for a stick-straight look for Sienna and flowy beach waves for me. I was impressed. So was Sienna.

She was busying herself taking selfies when I got a text from Omari—a pic of him and his mom decked out in their awards show best. I loved it. I quickly texted back. *You both look great!! Good luck tonight.*

Then I thought about Nina trying to pay for Omari's win and it backfiring. I texted one more thing: *It's okay if you don't win. It's just a fancy doorstop anyway.*

He responded instantly. *I'll keep that in mind. See you there.*

Considering he'd probably be with Nina, I sure hoped not. I sent a few heart emojis, then turned to Sienna. "Okay, so you know the plan."

"Yep. Find Kitt. Learn why she was pretending to be Gus to blackmail Mack Christie. Confirm if she did or didn't have Lyla killed. Don't get arrested or hospitalized."

That was indeed the plan. I just hoped it would be as simple as she made it sound. We discussed a few more details just as Dante finally pulled the car to the front of the line. He'd been so quiet I'd forgotten he was there. "You ladies look great," he said as a guard opened the Lincoln's back door. "I'll pick you up after the show."

"We might leave before it's over."

"I'll stick around then."

We thanked him and got out. I took in a lungful of air and tried to convince myself everything would go fine. I'd flash our bootlegged pass, breeze through the red carpet, find Kitt, and be back in bed by the time they gave out the "Best Picture" award. Easy, breezy. Or not.

Our first stop was security. Everyone had to walk through a full-body airport-worthy scanner before being individually wanded by a guard. They were not playing games. Sienna was right. It was indeed a mess. I recognized tons of people, including the security guard from the other day. He held a Garrett security scanner wand. I just hoped he wouldn't recognize me. And if he did, he'd at least forget I was supposed to have a ticket, not a badge.

We made our way closer and closer until we were next. I stepped through the scanner and took it all in. It looked even busier on the "other side." Sienna, of course, was barely wanded. The guard attempted to look at her pass but didn't make it past her cleavage. I only hoped to be so lucky. He watched Sienna go and turned to me. "Hey! You tell your mom I said hi?"

"Yes," I said as he skimmed right past the cleavage and barely took in my pass. So far, so good. "She's glad you're doing so well."

He moved the wand up the side of my body. I continued. "She said she always knew you would."

He stopped to smile at me and his arm knocked my badge askew in the process. It swung side to side like a pendulum, the blank backside making an appearance with each circuit. If he glanced back down, he would know it was fake. I'd been free and clear, but of course I'd had to keep talking. If I'd just shut up, I would have been halfway down the red carpet by now.

I immediately wanted to amend my superpower wishlist for the kajillionth time. Mind control jetted right to the top. *Please don't look down. Please don't look down. Please don't look down.*

His eyes started to slowly move down in what felt like slow motion. I needed to do something. My initial instinct—turn and run for my life—would not do. At all.

"I always had a crush on you," I blurted out.

His eyes immediately went back to mine and he smiled. "I know." He stepped to the side and waved me in. "Enjoy the show. Glad you finally got your pass."

And I was glad a man's heathy ego finally worked to my benefit.

I stepped past the guard and took it all in. Awards shows are prime-time viewing for the entire country, meaning they usually air live. Great if you're in New York or Georgia. But the East Coast's eight p.m. is the West Coast's five. Come awards season, you had a lot of people in tuxes and full-out ball gowns, all set for a night out on the town—at 3:30 in the afternoon.

The red carpet itself was a beautiful chaos. I likened it to the world's nicest obstacle course. Up first were the photographers. Dozens screaming your name at the top of their lungs, demanding you look "this way" and "over here" while you stood in front of the Step-and-Repeat, a photo backdrop featuring event and sponsor logos. The nickname also served as directions. *Step* on an assigned X and try not to look as scared as you felt in front of a kajillion flashbulbs. Move a few feet down and *repeat* the entire process.

Once you survived that, you still had to deal with hundreds—and hundreds of feet—of journalists, bloggers, and news crews, all while avoiding tripping, stepping on someone else's dress, and getting caught mid-grimace in the back of another person's shot.

Sienna was already in line for the Step-and-Repeat. Brave girl. A publicist manned the entrance with a small whiteboard and marker she used to write celebs' names before they stepped in front of photographers. I bypassed it and went straight to the main part of the carpet.

My goal was simple. Don't stop. Don't make eye contact. Don't run into Nina.

It almost worked.

She was midway down the carpet with Miss Erica and Omari, watching him get interviewed by a news crew. Mother and publicist stood a few feet away so they wouldn't be in the shot. I stopped, trying to figure out the best course of action. The area was a madhouse. As long as she didn't glance back, I could walk behind them unnoticed and be on my merry little way.

I was about five feet away when I heard the voice. "Sweetie, you made it after all!"

Erica waved at me like she was Miss USA. I waved back, all the while staying on the move. But then both Nina and Omari glanced over to see who was causing Miss Erica to act a fool. Omari immediately turned back to the interview. Nina? Not so much.

Her eyes narrowed and she mouthed one word. "You ... "

Omari never stopped talking. I, on the other hand, froze. The only way to get inside was to walk directly by Nina. But that was not happening. At all. She spoke into a walkie attached to her dress. "Security, we have a trespasser."

Clearly not wanting to wait for backup, she then started toward me. That's when Omari reached out and put his arm around her. He pulled her in so she was in the camera shot. "And I couldn't do any of it without my publicist, Nina Flynn. She's amazing."

Nina ripped her eyes away from me and automatically smiled for the camera. "He's being modest."

"I'm not. I wouldn't have this nomination without you." As Omari spoke, he used the arm around Nina to motion for me to go.

An hour later and I'd only seen Kitt once. It was on a lobby monitor at that, one blasting the show for those desperate for a smoke, a bathroom, or a drink but who didn't want to risk missing their category. Sienna and I hovered in a corner since we no longer had seats inside the auditorium.

The show started right on time, opening with a wide shot of Mack Christie's ubiquitous tour bus. The one he admitted to me was only for show. The next cut was inside it, a close shot of a Silver Sphere Award that zoomed out to include Mack and J. Chris "getting ready." After some playful back-and-forth banter about how excited they were to host, they broke out in song to prove it.

The camera followed them as they left their bus conveniently parked right outside a backstage door and then sang and danced their way inside, passing backstage crew as they did so. I spotted Kitt right before they went onstage.

Tasking Sienna to keep an eye out if Kitt made it to the lobby, I ran backstage. I was so intent on finding Kitt I barely paid the security guy standing guard much mind, flashing him my faux pass and hurrying by.

Backstage was akin to Oz. Pull back the curtain and it's just a bunch of white guys standing around pretending to be more important than they are. Lots of women too. Some in suits. Some in dresses. Some in shorts and sturdy boots. Almost all rocking walkie talkies and headsets. No one questioned what anyone was doing back there. Worked for me.

By the time I found the hallway where Kitt had been on camera, she was long gone. I wandered aimlessly for a good sixty minutes before finally stopping a young woman wearing a headset. "Have you seen the SSO assistant, Kitt?"

She barely acknowledged me, shaking her head while simultaneously talking into her walkie. "Anyone have eyes on Mack Christie? He needs to be back onstage in ten."

So much for that. I kept on the hunt, finally giving up on the idea I'd ever find her inside and headed out a stray door. I found a couple of people sneaking a cigarette and lots of parked cars, but that was about it.

I glanced around and spied Mack's tour bus off to the left, still parked a few feet from another entrance but no longer awash in lights, cameras, or action.

There was a car parked behind it with gold hubcaps and window etchings that looked familiar. It took me a second to place it, but I finally figured it out. It was the same car I'd seen when I went to talk to Regina at her job. I didn't know who it belonged to then, but now I wondered if it belonged to Mack. I *casually* walked over and peered inside, but the windows were too dark to see anything. The non-vanity license plate also didn't give any clues to the owner.

I was about to head back inside the Shrine when I heard something smash against the back window of Mack's tour bus. Of course, the mirror finish on those windows made it impossible to see inside.

Me being me, I decided to check anyway, especially since no one else seemed to notice. A lone security guard was a few hundred feet up. He paid me no mind as I walked to the bus's door on the other side—he was too busy flirting with USC coeds. I wasn't sure if that was a good thing. Reaching for the door handle, I was surprised when it turned. I guessed Mack and J. Chris hadn't had time to lock up after their song and dance number earlier. I inched the door open just enough to slip inside. I waited a beat, but no one noticed my arrival.

The décor was ultimate man cave. Lots of dark leather. Lots of shiny surfaces. And lots of beer. The Silver Sphere Award they'd used in their opening number was still on a table next to me. A ginormous flatscreen hung on the lone interior wall, tuned in to the show going on a mere hundred feet away. J. Chris was onstage. Mack wasn't with her.

For a second, I didn't think he was on the tour bus either. Then I heard voices coming from what had to be the bedroom in the back.

"I'm sorry. I wasn't expecting any of this. I'll give you money. Anything you want. Just don't shoot me."

That was definitely Kitt.

"It's too late. You're not giving me much choice."

And that was Mack.

Fudge.

I had a choice to make. Eavesdrop or find help. For once, I decided not to be stupid. I would just find someone way better equipped to handle the situation. When I peered out the window, I spied the guard still stuck in position. The coeds at least were gone.

"Please. I'll do whatever you want," Kitt said.

I turned to leave, catching a glimpse of the TV as I did. J. Chris was onstage and Mack was coming out to join her. But that didn't make any sense. If he was onstage, he couldn't be on the bus.

His voice, however, definitely was.

At that moment, I realized exactly where I'd gone wrong. My investigation had focused on Anani, then on Mack, then on the Silver Sphere Organization. What it hadn't focused on was the guy who was providing the literal soundtrack to Mack's career. He'd been just as invisible to me as he was to the rest of the world. He could have been anyone. I'd never given it much thought.

But he was clearly around and not happy at the recent turn of events. I was sure Mack had paid him a pretty penny to shut up and sing. And the blind item had threatened to end that.

I reminded myself it was a problem for the police, or at least a security guard. I was getting out of Dodge.

But when I turned to leave, I bumped into the Silver Sphere Award on the table next to me. The crash rang out at what felt like a thousand decibels. The voices immediately shut up.

The door opened just as I instinctively bent down to pick the award back up. I should've been hauling butt out of there. Talk about a really bad time for good manners.

I straightened up, gripping it, just as Dante stepped out.

His hands were behind his back and Kitt peered out from behind him. Like I said, the guy providing Mack's vocals could have been anyone. In actuality, he was a driver. One who looked ready to kill me. I didn't even have time to process the revelation. Instead I went into survival mode. For me, that didn't mean fighting. It meant trying to talk myself out of the situation.

"Dante!" I said. "What are you doing here?" I walked past him into the bedroom, leaving the door cracked behind me, and pointed at Kitt. "You need to get away from her. She hired Junior to kill Lyla. Let's get out of here."

Dante had no reaction. Kitt, on the other hand…

"He's the one who killed Lyla," she screamed. "He's going to kill me!"

I knew that. I just wanted her to shut up about it so I could prevent it from happening. I tried to grab his arm with my one free hand. The other still held the award. He wouldn't budge. "We need to go and find a security guard."

That's when he pulled the gun from behind his back. "Shut the door, put the award down, and give me your purse. You're not gonna need it or your phone."

I did just that, placing the award on the bed while Dante threw my bag into the front room. There went any chance to call for help. I needed to figure out another way out of there. Pronto. I apprised the situation. The room wasn't big enough to avoid a bullet. It was lined with windows but they were windows you couldn't open. There were drawers built into the walls on both sides of the door and above the bed, which also was bookended by two small nightstands. I zeroed in on the one on the complete opposite side of the room. It held a photo of Mack and J. Chris. Next to it were a few random odds and ends, including a pair of Focals.

I immediately came up with a plan, though it was a shaky one. In an ideal world, the glasses would already be set up to stream to one of Mack or J. Chris's social media accounts. One of their fans would see Dante trying to kill us and call the police. It wasn't the best plan I'd ever had, but it was all I had. And it could work. I just needed to turn the thing on and keep Dante distracted until help arrived.

"Can I sit?" I asked him. He was leaning against the window in the small space between the bed and the built-in drawers. "My heels are killing me."

"Fine," he said.

I walked toward the other side of the bed—and the Focals.

"No, next to Kitt."

Blurg. She was at the bottom of the bed, nowhere near the glasses on the nightstand. I took a seat next to her. If I could lay down, I could reach them. But I doubted Dante would believe me if I said I needed a nap. With "record and distract" not an immediate option, I went with just distract.

"You don't have to do this," I said.

He just gave me a look, all traces of the affable driver dead and gone. "Yeah, I already heard the spiel from Kitt. She started all of this. If she hadn't tried to blackmail Mack, he wouldn't have contacted Anani, and she wouldn't have run that blind item."

At the mention of her name, Kitt started bawling. I tried to ignore her. Dante? Not so much. "You need to shut the hell up!" he said.

In her defense, she tried. But she just couldn't do it. The silence lasted for less than a second. Her next round of sobbing started off low, then slowly gained momentum as if tumbling downhill. I tried to keep him focused on me.

"It's not her fault. It's Mack's. He's the one who took advantage of you in the first place. Who used your talent for his own gain. Because you have an amazing voice." It was stalling tactic 101, keep the guy talking. But it was also true. Dante had a beautiful voice.

By now, Kitt sounded like a thunderstorm. Dante banged the gun against the window. Kitt and I both instinctively jumped back as he screamed. "You think that's all it takes to make it? A pretty voice?"

The good news was that I was in reaching distance of the glasses.

"No," he went on. "It takes looks. It takes luck. It takes having the balls to get onstage in front of thousands of people and sing."

I "knocked" the Focals off the bed, then reached down to pick them up. He didn't notice. He was still too busy yelling.

"I sounded like Mack Christie. I just didn't have his luck or his confidence. I definitely didn't have his looks. I was stuck doing cover band shows at bars for $100 a night. You're acting like he was just making money off me. I was making money off him. Until you all ruined it. And what the hell are you doing with those?"

He used the gun to motion to the glasses in my hand. "Cleaning up my mess," I said as I pushed the record button and put them back on the nightstand. When I spoke again, it was a bit louder so the glass's built in mic could catch what I was saying. "You're about to kill me in the back of Mack Christie's tour bus, Dante. Sorry if I'm acting a bit nervous."

That calmed him down a bit. "You know I actually liked you," he said.

"Yeah? I actually liked you too."

"Even went and spoke to Junior's girlfriend for you so you could get that reward money."

He paused then, as if expecting him to thank me. I was too momentarily shocked to say anything. He was the one Regina was talking to in the parking lot that day? Before I could fully digest it, he continued talking.

"Hoped it would be the end of it, but you had to keep going."

"Yes, and I'm regretting it. Trust me on that. Can you just answer one question, since it doesn't matter?"

He motioned with the gun, a stark reminder of its presence. "Fine."

"You didn't know Anani was Lyla?"

"I did. I've known for at least a year. Just didn't care much until I had to. She mentioned it on a phone call when I was taking her somewhere. When you're a driver, people pay you no mind. You overhear their drama, their lovey-dovey sex talk, their business dealings. You did it yourself on the way here. How do you think I found out about Kitt?"

Kitt moaned but managed to keep quiet. I talked over her. "What about Junior? How'd you meet him?"

"My dealer."

His phone beeped just then, the notification ironically a Mack Christie song. He pulled it out of his pocket but didn't give it a glance. He was too busy looking at me. "He only wanted $10,000 for the job. Idiot."

The phone immediately beeped again. He finally glanced at it. "I was so happy when he killed himself. Saved me the hassle. He ... "

Dante trailed off, too busy reading whatever was on his phone. It didn't take a mind reader to realize what was going on. He jerked his head all around the room. "There's a camera in here. My boy says it's streaming on J. Chris's Instagram."

I felt immediate relief but it was short-lived. Dante spoke again, addressing anyone who was watching. "I swear if anyone comes in here, I will kill them both." Then he turned to us. "Help me find that camera."

I pretended to look for it as Kitt checked the dresser. Dante did more pacing than looking. He became more and more unhinged with each step until he finally screamed, "Where is it?"

That's when he went bananas. He started with the drawers, pulling them out one by one, throwing clothes on the bed, practically covering the Silver Sphere Award. Kitt and I just stood there. We exchanged a look. And I knew we were both thinking the same exact thing.

There was no doubt that he was going to kill us.

I needed to do something. Pronto.

But what?

He was mere feet from the bedroom door. There was no way I could get past him. Maybe Kitt and I could work together to take him down, but we weren't exactly in a position to have a planning session without Dante hearing the entire thing.

I looked around, getting frantic myself. I didn't want to die.

Dante abandoned the drawers and went after the blinds, trying to rip each one down. His back was turned and I just went for it, grabbing the Silver Sphere Award from under a T-shirt and using all my might to smack Dante in the head. He dropped the gun as I pulled the bedroom door open and ran, yelling, "Come on, Kitt!"

I thought I'd at least stunned him. I was dead wrong. I heard someone behind me, but it wasn't Kitt. Dante tackled me before I could even get past the kitchen. We both went down. I managed to scramble a few feet away but he grabbed my leg.

I tried to *Single White Female* him with a heel to the eye. It worked better in the movie. Dante just deflected, knocking my foot away so it crashed into a cabinet. I tried to kick him again. And that's when I heard the gunshot.

Dante and I looked up to see Kitt standing a few feet away, holding the gun with way more confidence than I would have expected.

"Go, Dayna," she said. "Get help."

She didn't have to tell me twice. I scrambled up and got to the front door without even looking back. I opened it to find a blur of faces. I ran for my life until a cop caught me and pulled me toward him. We stayed like that for I don't know how long. "They're still in there," I managed to get out between breaths.

"We know," he said. "You're safe now."

At least I think he did. I could barely hear him over my heart beating. He kept repeating it, which was a good thing because I needed the reminder.

I still didn't feel it. Not yet. I still felt exposed, especially when I finally glanced around and noticed all the cops and the cameras and the camera phones. Everyone stared at me and all I wanted to do was curl into a ball and cry.

I willed them to look away. And then suddenly they did.

I glanced back to see why. The cops were dragging a cuffed Dante out. Kitt was a few steps behind, her arm around a female officer as they walked side by side out of the bus. Dante smiled at the commotion, as if finally happy to be in the spotlight. It made me sick.

The only thing that made me look away was Omari's voice. "Dayna!"

I glanced over in time to see him and Sienna pushing through the crowd to get to me. The cop moved aside to give them access. They each took a side, Sienna cradling my head in her arms while Omari leaned down to kiss me. And that's when I finally felt at peace.

He leaned back and looked at me, as if searching to make sure I was still intact.

"Don't worry," I said. "I'm alive."

"Touché."

I noticed something in his hand. A Silver Sphere Award. "You won?"

He nodded. "My mom's even more excited than I am. For some reason she keeps mentioning that I'm going to make an amazing father."

I fainted.

# *Epilogue*

Dante was convicted of murdering Lyla.

Kitt was arrested for blackmail, but she was released after Mack and J. Chris refused to press charges. Still, she was fired from SSO and blackballed from ever working in this town again. For some, a fate worse than jail time.

Mack's secret came out during Dante's trial. Even his manager couldn't keep that under wraps. Instead, he sent Mack on a sympathy tour. A stint in rehab for exhaustion. An interview with the *Today* show and *Dateline*. Mack also signed a deal to write his memoirs and VH1 was currently casting for his authorized biopic.

J. Chris ultimately decided to stand by her man in his time of need. After Mack finished his rehab stint, they finally shot *$3000*. It was a flop.

Regina surfaced in Miami. I only know this because she started posting selfies again once Dante was arrested. I still haven't spoken to her.

It turned out cameras had been rolling when Omari kissed me. The video went viral. Stories about Tomari were replaced with how people loved Omari even more for his "regular-sized" girlfriend. It wasn't enough to warrant a nickname.

Sienna decided to create one for us. So far, nothing she'd come up with stuck. I was more than okay with that.

The mechanic finally figured out what was wrong with my car, which was a good thing. I still couldn't afford a new one since we never received the SSO reward money. No surprise there.

I took a month off to recover. Sienna, Omari, and even Emme took turns bringing me Tommy's chiliburgers. It definitely helped me feel better.

I was figuring out my next move when the envelope came in the mail. The return address was Aubrey's house in Silver Lake. We hadn't spoken since I'd given him that phone number. I was curious what he was sending me.

I tore the envelope open. Inside was a certificate letting Aubrey S. Adams-Parker know that ASAP Investigations was officially licensed by the state of California. I wouldn't have to throw away those business cards after all.

Z stopped popping up at my car. I didn't see or hear from him for three months.

Then one day, he was there like he'd never left, still smelling like cinnamon, still rocking just enough purple, still feeling like a pain in the you-know-what. He smiled when I approached him. "I need your help."

## Acknowledgments

The acknowledgements in my first book were two pages long, so I'm going to force myself to keep it short and just thank my family. So thank you to:

My Fuse family, especially Michelle Richter;

My Midnight Ink family, especially Terri, Sandy, and Jake;

My Pitch Wars family;

My iHeart family;

My Chicks on the Case family;

And, of course, my family-family, especially my parents, siblings, and aunties.

Your unwavering love means everything to me. I'm so lucky to have such an amazing support system in my life.

Finally, this book literally would not exist without the feedback, encouragement, and time of Stephanie Dodson, Mocumba Dimsey, Linda Halder, Marla Cooper, Ellen Byron, Cynthia Kuhn, Laura Heffernan, Roselle Lim, and Sonia Hartl. Thank you for giving me your amazing notes and reassuring me that the early drafts weren't as bad as I thought—though I'm sure they were!

Photo by Carucha L. Meuse

## About the Author

Kellye Garrett writes the Detective by Day mysteries about a semi-famous, mega-broke black actress-turned-private-investigator. The first, *Hollywood Homicide*, won the Agatha, Lefty, and Independent Publisher "IPPY" awards for best first novel. It was also nominated for Anthony and Barry awards. In addition to writing, Kellye serves on the national board for Sisters in Crime and is the Managing Director of Pitch Wars.

Prior to focusing on books, Kellye spent eight years working in Hollywood, including a stint writing for *Cold Case*. People were always surprised to learn what she did for a living—probably because she seemed way too happy to be brainstorming ways to murder people. Having moved back to her native New Jersey, she now spends her mornings commuting to Manhattan for her job at a leading media company—while still happily brainstorming ways to commit murder.

You can learn more at KellyeGarrett.com.